# "It's the end of the trail."

Matt couldn't keep the anger out of his tone. "In case you hadn't noticed, you were almost killed."

Anger colored Jamie's cheeks and there was a dangerous glint in her eye. "Why would somebody go to all this trouble to stop me from looking for Tony?"

"Face it, Jamie, you know nothing about him, not even his real name." Matt knew his tough-guy routine wasn't going to work, but he was too frustrated to stop. "You heard what I said."

She tossed back her windblown hair in a defiant gesture. "I'm going to find him—with or without you."

Matt grabbed her by the arms and held them tightly. "What is it with you and this Tony? Is it worth your life to find him?"

Jamie looked him in the eye. "You don't understand. He's—"

"A good kisser," Matt finished for her. "I know. But I'm tired of hearing that. Good kissers can be gotten on any damn corner in Texas." And with that he did the one thing he never should have done.

He kissed her.

## ABOUT THE AUTHOR

M.J. Rodgers is the winner of a *Romantic Times* Career Achievement Award for Romantic Mysteries, twice winner of their Best Intrigue Award and is also winner of B. Dalton Bookseller's top-selling Intrigue Award. She lives with her family in Seabeck, Washington.

## Books by M.J. Rodgers

# M.J. Rodgers
## ONE TOUGH TEXAN

## *Harlequin Books*

TORONTO • NEW YORK • LONDON
AMSTERDAM • PARIS • SYDNEY • HAMBURG
STOCKHOLM • ATHENS • TOKYO • MILAN
MADRID • WARSAW • BUDAPEST • AUCKLAND

THIS STORY IS FOR ANN RICHARDS, ONE OF
THE BEST AND TOUGHEST TEXANS TO COME
ALONG THIS CENTURY.

GO GET 'EM, GAL.

ISBN 0-373-22423-0

ONE TOUGH TEXAN

Copyright © 1997 by Mary Johnson

This edition published by arrangement with Harlequin Books S.A.

® and TM are trademarks of the publisher. Trademarks indicated with
® are registered in the United States Patent and Trademark Office, the
Canadian Trade Marks Office and in other countries.

Printed in U.S.A.

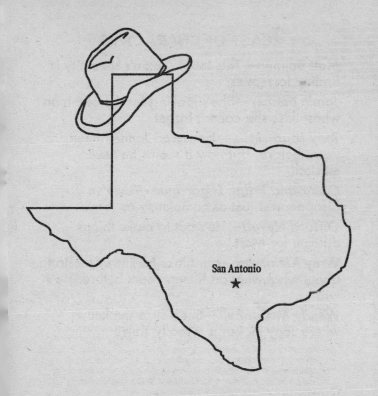

San Antonio

★

# TEXAS

# CAST OF CHARACTERS

*Matt Bonner*—This tough Texan's specialty is finding lost loves.

*Jamie Bonner*—She's looking for the one man whose kiss she cannot forget.

*Tony Lagarrigue*—He kissed Jamie fifteen years before, but now it seems he never existed.

*Oscar and Erline Lagarrigue*—They've disappeared just as completely as Tony.

*Clifford Nevelt*—He's out to make things difficult for Matt.

*Wrey Kleinman*—He thinks he knows the truth about what went on fifteen years before. He's wrong.

*Wendy McConnell*—She's sure she knows where Tony is. But is it really Tony?

# *Prologue*

Jamie climbed onto her bed at the back of the trailer. She braced herself against the wall as she cranked open the small, high window. Its rusted hinges screeched in protest.

She froze, her whole body tense as she waited to see if they had noticed the noise.

The boxing match blasted out from the TV in the next room. The man who watched it cursed loudly at one of the contestants who wasn't beating the brains out of the other fast enough. The woman beside the man laughed drunkenly. The thin door that separated the man and the woman from Jamie remained closed.

She let out a soundless sigh of relief.

The welfare money was always long gone by this time of the month. Had Jamie not found the nearly full bottle of whiskey hidden behind an easel in the utility closet at her high school, she never would have been able to manage tonight.

Jamie didn't feel guilty about taking the whiskey. She knew it had to be the old janitor who had stashed it in that utility closet. Way she figured it, she'd done him a favor.

Whiskey just made folks even more crazy mean than they already were. When those two up front in the trailer tied one on, they beat up on each other and anybody else around. Jamie didn't plan on being around tonight.

Keeping the whiskey bottle out of sight all week hadn't

been easy. But Jamie had managed. She had learned to manage a lot of things in her life in order to survive.

When she'd opened a kitchen cupboard just before dinner and pretended to find the whiskey there, the man and woman had nearly trampled her beneath their feet, so eager were they to get to it.

For once, she hoped they would get blind drunk. In a few hours they would either pass out in the front of the trailer or come staggering back to sleep it off. She didn't want them noticing her small bed in the corner was stuffed with nothing but the lumpy, old pillow and her precious stash of books.

Because if they noticed she was gone...

Jamie willed herself to go cold and numb inside so she wouldn't feel the fear. Tony Lagarrigue had asked her to the dance tonight. And for the first time in her life, she was going to let herself believe in miracles.

She hoisted herself onto the window's edge. The screen that once kept out the insects was long gone. She was still in her slip as she eased herself through the small opening. It was getting to be a tight fit for her fifteen-year-old hips. She knew that pretty soon she wouldn't be able to make it through.

It was another one of those scary thoughts that she pushed to that dark, cold place in the numb part of her soul. She was determined not to let her fears rob her of tonight.

She landed soundlessly, as her bare feet hit the dust outside the trailer. A foul curse blared out of the open front window. Jamie stiffened, until she realized the man was only yelling at the TV again. She let out a deep, relieved breath.

The still night air stunk of the feedlot next door. The bitter, pungent odors of alcohol and cigarettes that had eaten their way into the walls of the tiny trailer weren't any better.

She knew if it hadn't been for her books, she would have been driven mad long ago. Or worse yet, she would have been driven to be like them. She shuddered at the thought.

She reached for the dress dangling from clothespins on the makeshift line that extended from the back of the trailer to a tree. It was the only dress she owned—a hand-me-down from the woman inside the trailer.

The yellow daisies were faded. The rough, unlined material scratched her skin. The waist was way too big. But it was clean. She had washed it in the creek that afternoon when she had washed herself. She hurriedly put it on.

She sent a furtive look back to the trailer before she reached behind the tree for the shoes. The cheap and gaudy two-inch heels with the gold sequins on their pointed toes belonged to the woman. Jamie had found them stashed away in a box. They were the only pair of shoes that the woman hadn't beaten up real bad.

If Jamie got caught wearing them, she knew that woman would beat her up real bad.

It had been a big risk taking them. But for this night Jamie knew she would take almost any risk.

She brushed the dust off the bottoms of her feet and slipped on the shoes. They were a little large, but none of her shoes had ever fit. She walked a few steps, gaining greater confidence as she found her balance. She remembered escaping through the trailer window as a young child. Many a cold night she'd kept herself warm by dancing on her toes, pretending to be Cinderella at the ball.

Tonight she didn't have to pretend. Tonight it was going to happen.

She ran her fingers through her butchered hair and sighed.

There was nothing she could do about her hair. The woman in the trailer had been hacking it off regularly ever since she could remember. It wasn't even long enough to put a comb to.

One day she would get away from that woman. And that man. And away from clothes that rubbed her skin raw and shoes that never fit—and the need to go all cold and numb inside so as not to feel the fear and the pain.

But that day was still an eternity away.

Thank God tonight was here, now.

Jamie quickly slipped off the shoes and held them carefully

as she scrambled barefoot up the steep knoll that separated the old, run-down trailer in the ditch from the main road into town. When she reached the top, she stopped to peer into the twilight.

He was waiting at the edge of the road in the gathering dusk, just as he had said he would be.

Her eyes traveled over his dress shirt and dark slacks. His black hair was combed back, neat and shiny in the faint light.

Tony Lagarrigue was the handsomest boy in town, the handsomest boy in the world. And tonight he was *her* date. Her heart pumped with pride.

He called her name and held out his hand. She hurriedly brushed off the bottoms of her feet and slipped on the shoes. Then, slowly, carefully she stepped toward him, balancing adeptly on her toes.

She stopped in front of him, holding her breath as he surveyed her from the top of her butchered hair to the tip of those cheap sequined shoes.

"You look very pretty tonight, Jamie Lee."

Pretty. He thought her pretty. The air escaping her lungs was so full of gratitude that it left her feeling weak.

Tony pulled something out of his pocket. Jamie's eyes circled wide when she saw that he held a large gold locket on a heavy chain.

"This is for you," he said.

She couldn't believe it. She couldn't let herself believe it.

He leaned toward her, circling the chain around her neck. She felt the warmth of his breath on her cheek and a tickle at the back of her neck as his fingers fiddled with the clasp. Her stomach fluttered. For a few precious seconds even the smells of the feedlot were forgotten as she inhaled his rich cologne.

She heard a faint click. The weight of the locket came to rest on her breastbone.

Tony leaned back. "Do you like it?"

She held the locket in her palm and stared down at it. Tears stung the back of her eyes, but she would not cry. She never cried. Crying was a sign of weakness, and the weak were preyed upon. That lesson she had learned early and well.

She gulped down the lump in her throat and resolutely kept the tears at bay.

"It's beautiful, Tony."

He slipped a finger beneath her chin and coaxed her into looking up at him. He was smiling. It wasn't one of the smirking or pitying smiles she'd seen too many times before. It was an approving smile.

Her heart swelled.

She had never been this close to a boy before. Tony was so elegant. His olive skin was so smooth. His teeth were so white. His breath smelled like mint. His eyes were large and dark with mystery. Something was going to happen.

Slowly, he leaned down to kiss her.

Jamie had thought a lot about kissing Tony since that wondrous day the week before, when he had asked her to the dance. And now it was happening. It was really happening.

Tony's lips were smooth and firm as he pressed them against hers. They felt forbidden and wonderful. Her cheeks grew warm. Some delicious secret seemed to be opening up inside her.

She didn't know what it was. All she knew was that for the first time in her life, she felt...feminine. And that she would always remember this moment—this kiss.

Tony leaned back and smiled at her. "We'd better go. We're already late."

They walked hand in hand down the dusty road toward the school auditorium a mile away. It could have been five miles and Jamie wouldn't have cared.

She thought about taking off the shoes so they wouldn't get scuffed. But the extra height made her feel so much more adult. She needed to feel like an adult tonight. Adults had control over their lives. They weren't the reflection of anyone else.

When they reached the auditorium, Jamie halted at the bot-

tom of the steps. The lights and music and happy voices from
inside spilled down toward them.

Jamie looked up at the colorful crepe-paper decorations
strung across the entry. Etta Oates and the school's other popular girls had spent the previous day putting them up. Jamie
had seen them laughing and exchanging confidences on her
way home from the library.

All those other girls dressed so beautifully. They were all
so accomplished in flirting and putting on makeup and all
those other secret and sophisticated adolescent female arts that
eluded Jamie so completely.

Her heart sank. She knew what was going to happen when
she went inside. Etta Oates was going to point her out to the
other girls and make fun of Jamie's dress and shoes. Then,
the smirking and pitying smiles would follow.

"You ready, Jamie Lee?"

Jamie looked over at Tony. He smiled and squeezed her
hand.

Her heart lifted. Let Etta and the others snicker and shame
her. Every one of them would be wishing they were in her
shoes, gaudy or not. For tonight, Tony Lagarrigue was her
date.

"I'm ready," she said.

They started up the stairs together, hand in hand, toward
the lights, toward the music, toward what promised to be the
most wonderful evening of Jamie's life.

And then the shotgun blast deafened the music and shattered the night.

# Chapter One

*Fifteen years later*

Matt Bonner stretched his long legs out in front of him and rested his boots on the edge of his desk. The spring sun streamed through the huge picture window behind him to beat down on his neck.

That sun felt real good after the long weekend of rolling rainstorms that had ambushed San Antonio. He sprawled back in his big leather chair, soaking up those sweet, old rays.

"Bonner, are you listening to me?" Clifford Nevelt asked. As always, his boss's voice sounded way too arrogant coming through the telephone receiver stuck against Matt's ear.

"Hanging on every word," Matt said, in his best respectful, controlled Texas tone, knowing the sarcasm would be winging way over the head of the man on the other end of the line.

"Good, because I need you to get me last month's reports right away," Nevelt said. "It's time for me to put in my request for funding for the 'Finder of Lost Loves' show. We have to keep that valuable, necessary watchdog going."

Matt's tone stayed easy. "Sir, that 'valuable' watchdog is about as 'necessary' as tail feathers on my chicken-fried steak."

"Look, Bonner, I don't want to have this conversation again. The fact is that since *I* instituted that show last year and revised your clientele, we haven't had one incident of trouble.''

"We haven't had one incident of trouble down here since the revamping of the department five years ago. That TV show is a waste of good time and money.''

Nevelt sucked in breath like a vacuum. Matt could just picture his sour lips pursing and pink cheeks puffing. He was the worst kind of pencil pusher—the ignorant, closed-mind kind.

"I didn't ask for your opinion, Bonner. I asked for that paperwork.''

"Yes, sir. Since we're on that subject of paperwork, how's my request for transfer going?''

"It's not going anywhere.''

Matt's hand gripped the receiver. "Don't think I heard that one right, sir. You want to run it by me again?''

"I'm not letting you transfer out. You are doing important work. Think of all the people you help, who come to your P.I. firm and whom you put on the 'Finder of Lost Loves' program.''

Matt kept his cool. Barely. "With all due respect, sir, we both know anyone with an IQ as big as his boot size could emcee that TV show.''

"Market analysts tell me that your presence is a major contributor to the extraordinary TV ratings for the cable show. A major network is even interested in doing a syndication. You're staying. Now, fax those reports to me.''

Dial tone blared in Matt's ear. He dropped the telephone receiver onto its base with disgust.

Network syndication. This was supposed to be a quiet, unobtrusive operation!

Matt's jaw clenched. Inject Nevelt's intellect into a spider and it would start spinning earwax instead of a web.

Matt rose and stood in front of his huge picture window, digging his hands into the pockets of his jeans. The city glittered clean and fresh and bright beneath the morning sun. He wasn't appreciating it.

How had Nevelt found out about the network's interest?
Matt had sworn his staff to secrecy. Had one of them talked?
Damn, couldn't he even trust his own team?

He wanted that transfer. No, he *had* to have that transfer.
If he didn't get some real work real soon—

The intercom on Matt's desk buzzed. He leaned over to
punch the button. "Yes, Charlene?"

"You got a visitor."

Matt immediately took note of Charlene's phraseology. If
it had been a client, she would have given the person's name.
A pesky sales type was a solicitor. But Charlene had used
none of those labels. Nope, she had said, visitor.

And in Charlene's vocabulary, visitor meant family, friend
or foe.

"Which is it?" Matt asked, knowing Charlene loved this
game and that the only way out of it was to indulge her.

"She's a surprise. And she's listening in on this here conversation, so you might as well invite her on in, being as
she's knows you're in there and all."

Matt shook his head. He'd told Charlene that he'd wring
her neck the next time she pulled something like this on him.
And damn it, he didn't care if she was his favorite aunt—as
well as his secretary. She was going to get her neck wrung.

"Bring her on in, Charlene," Matt said, flipping off the
intercom as he turned to face the door.

Charlene bustled through a moment later, her arms gyrating
around her five-nine wrestler's body as if she were a baton
twirler leading a band. When Matt saw the petite, graceful
woman in the silk suit and high heels who glided in beside
her, he suddenly found he couldn't move a muscle.

Charlene caught the unguarded expression in the instant it
flashed over his face. Her resulting smug look said she knew
she was in no danger of being strangled this morning. She
marched out the door, closing it behind her.

"Been a long time, Matt," Jamie said, stepping forward.

Jamie's slightly husky voice felt like pure raw silk against
Matt's ears. Her long, butter-colored hair churned down her

shoulders in soft, thick waves. Her eyes were the precise shade of the spring bluebonnets blooming over the Texas hills.

Matt's insides ached like a big, old scar at the beginning of a brand-new rain.

He gave no verbal response to her greeting. He couldn't. He simply nodded and motioned her into a chair.

He remained standing, purposely refocusing his eyes on the papers strewn across his desk. But the shock of her being here had his mind drifting back to that day five years before, when he'd come home to San Antonio after a four-year stint in military intelligence. He'd been pleasantly bone weary from traveling around the world dabbling in a daring deed or two. He was looking forward to kicking back and being a plain, old cowboy again for a few weeks before accepting his new job.

And then, suddenly, there was Jamie, standing by the railing on his mama's and daddy's ranch.

Matt had stopped dead in his tracks and stared. For how long he had no idea. The moment was fixed—would always be fixed—in an endless space of time.

She was wearing a light cream silk dress that bared her slim shoulders and billowed up her thighs in the hot afternoon breeze. Her smiling face was lifted to the sun like a worshipping flower.

Matt's eyes followed hungrily as the sunlight rained hot kisses across the milky skin of her face and throat and churned through her long, butter-colored hair.

She turned directly to him, just as though she had been waiting for him. The instant their eyes locked, Matt knew with a certainty and a clarity he had never experienced before or since that this was the woman—the only woman—for him.

And then his brother, Cade, stepped onto the porch and introduced Jamie as his fiancée. That was the day Matt had learned the true meaning behind the words "brotherly love."

"So, how you been, Matt?"

Jamie's question snapped Matt's mind into the present.

He had himself back in control. He treated her to that polite, formal mask that he'd been wearing ever since Cade's introduction had made anything else between them impossible.

"Something I can do for you, Jamie?"

An amused smile twisted her lips. "There you go. Right to business. One day you're going to smile at me or ask me how I've been, Matt Bonner, and it'll probably shock me right off my chair."

His reserved manner always seemed to amuse her. She had never understood how hard it was for him to keep his distance.

From that first day, she'd tried to kid him out of his formality, get him to loosen up, let down his guard. She should count her blessings that she hadn't succeeded.

"I assumed this wasn't a social call," Matt said evenly. "And that your time was valuable."

She looked as bedeviled and disappointed as always, when her teasing with him didn't get the response she'd hoped to elicit.

"I know your time is valuable, Matt. I suppose I should've called first and not just dropped in like this. Truth is, I need you to locate someone for me."

"I'm not a regular private investigator. I deal exclusively in finding lost loves. Mothers looking for children they had to give up for adoption years before. Children looking for the mothers who gave them up. Childhood sweethearts who've lost track of each other. Brothers and sisters who were separated as children and scattered to the winds. These are the folks I try to bring back together."

"I realize that, Matt. Liz talks about you and your cases all the time."

Matt should have known his sister would. Every time he had dinner at his folks' ranch, Liz went on and on about Jamie and what she was doing. Liz's friendship with Jamie was as strong as ever, despite the fact that Jamie and Cade had untied the knot.

"It's knowing of your firm's specialty that brought me here," Jamie said.

Matt's curiosity had him asking the next question before he thought it through. "You're looking for a lost love?"

"He's someone I met a long time ago. Before Cade."

Matt circled his desk and sat down. Just great. She was looking for a man. The last thing he wanted to hear about was one of her old lovers. And the last thing he wanted to do was to go out and find him. If she was determined to look up this guy, then she was just going to have to do it without him.

"I'll give you the names of a couple of local P.I.'s who can help you," Matt said.

A thick, uncomfortable quiet followed his words. He didn't look at her. He rummaged through the Rolodex, searching for the names of those other P.I.'s.

"I don't understand," she said at the end of that quiet. "This is just the kind of case you handle. Why are you sending me to somebody else?"

"We're in a crunch here at the present."

"Charlene said this was your light season."

"It's still right busy."

"Matt, are you angry at me?"

Her question brought his eyes briefly to her face. "Why would you think I was angry?"

"Even Cade still gives me a smile and a hug."

Matt didn't even want to think about what that smile and hug must be costing Cade. He knew what it would be costing him if he had lost Jamie.

"I am not angry at you, Jamie."

"Then, what is it about me that you seriously don't like?"

Matt reached into his right desk drawer. He drew out a pad of paper and set it on the desk. He jotted down the names of the P.I.'s. When he looked up at her, he was careful to keep a polite, distant look on his face.

"There is nothing about you I don't like," he said simply,

formally and only too truthfully. He held out the paper. She didn't take it.

"Then why won't you help me?"

"Because, I couldn't face my brother if I were instrumental in getting you together with some other man."

Her eyes darkened with puzzlement. "Why would that matter to Cade?"

Lord, she said that with such innocence! There had always been a lamentable streak of emotional naïveté about Jamie, which continued to floor—and at times infuriate—Matt.

"How would you feel if I introduced Cade to your best friend and the two of them started dating?" Matt asked.

Jamie laughed and her eyes sparkled with the amusement. "Not a good analogy, Matt. Liz is my best friend."

He could feel the joy of her laughter bubbling inside him. He always could. It was just another one of the reasons he had avoided her company over the past five years.

"You know what I mean," he said, recognizing the old retaliatory gruffness that had begun to take over his tone.

"Matt, I hope Cade falls madly in love with someone who makes him real happy."

"You'll feel differently if and when something like that actually happens."

"No, I won't. I love Cade, but just as a friend."

"Folks who have been married and then divorced can never be just friends."

The corners of her mouth lifted in amusement. "Is that a fact? And this wise and worldly proclamation is coming from a man who's still single at the ripe old age of thirty-five, right?"

Her amusement at this observation rubbed a particularly sensitive spot. He delivered his next words with a growl.

"Are your memories of this other lover what caused the breakup of your marriage to my brother?"

He regretted his retaliation as soon as he saw the immediate dimming of that merry light in her eyes. She said nothing for a moment, then a small sigh of regret escaped her lips.

"I talked to Liz, your folks and Cade when I called out to the ranch this morning. Cade was the one who first suggested I stop by the office to get your help. I told him I'd have to pay you. He laughed and said that was all right because you were probably going to be mercenary enough to take my money. So you see, Cade's okay with this."

*Like hell he is,* Matt thought. *Cade has his pride, Jamie. He couldn't tell you how he really felt. You don't know what it's like to love, if you think it can be just switched off like that.*

Matt had fully intended to use Cade as the reason for not taking her case. He could see now that wasn't going to be possible. Cade's pride and her obtuseness were both working against him.

Only thing he could do was find this lover of hers and get this business over with quickly. He put aside the paper with the names of the other P.I.'s and poised his pen over a blank sheet.

"Who is he?"

"Tony Lagarrigue. L-A-G-A-R-R-I-G-U-E."

Matt wrote it down. "Middle name or initial?"

"I don't know."

"Age?"

"Same as me. Thirty."

"Birth date?"

"I don't know."

"Last known address?"

"Sweetspring, Texas."

"Your hometown?"

"I'm surprised you remembered."

She'd be even more surprised to know he couldn't forget one single damn detail about her. And why he couldn't.

"When did you last see Tony Lagarrigue?"

"When he left Sweetspring."

"And how long ago was that?"

"Fifteen years."

Matt put down his pen. "Are you saying you haven't seen him in fifteen years?"

"Yes."

Matt hadn't expected this relationship to have been one that ended so young. Surely, no one took a fifteen-year-old infatuation seriously? At least not fifteen years later. Maybe he had been reading more into this than what was there.

"Why do you want to find this Tony after all this time?"

Jamie paused to finger a cheap gold-colored locket hanging around her neck. Matt was surprised to see her wearing it. Her jewelry was normally exquisite and genuine, like the lady.

"I'm curious about what's become of him," she said.

"How long did you know him?"

"A few weeks."

"What happened during that time to make Tony so memorable?"

Jamie frowned and looked down at her hands. Matt recognized the gesture and hesitation for the stall it was. He'd never known Jamie to have to think about her answers before. After a moment she raised her eyes to his. There was almost a haunted look to them—something he'd never seen before, either.

"Tony's family moved to Sweetspring when I was fifteen. We got to know each other. He took me to my first school dance. Then his family moved away. They left so fast, I didn't even have a chance to say goodbye. I've always wondered what happened to Tony. Where he went. What he's doing now."

"This fifteen-year-old Tony apparently made quite an impression on you."

She smiled. "He did."

Matt hated the guy already.

"Who were his folks?"

"His mama's name was Erline. She was a homemaker."

"And his daddy?"

"Oscar. He sold insurance."

"What else can you tell me about them?"

"Not a whole lot. Tony took me by the house and introduced me one day when he walked me home. Their names were on the mailbox. I only saw them the one time. They were real nice folks."

"I don't suppose you have a picture of Tony?"

"Not a real good one," Jamie said, slipping her hand into her purse and bringing out a small white envelope. She handed it to him.

Matt wondered how many thirty-year-old women still had a picture of their fifteen-year-old heartthrob in their purse. Damn this adolescent Don Juan who could leave her with such lasting memories!

Matt knew he was thinking like a jealous fool. Well, hell, he was a jealous fool.

Matt dug into the envelope and pulled out a full-length vertical shot of a kid in dress shirt and pants. The picture had obviously been torn in several pieces and taped back together. It was an unposed indoor shot taken under artificial light by a Polaroid camera. Tony was looking slightly off to the left but his features were in focus.

"He was fifteen, then," Jamie said.

Matt studied the photo. Tony Lagarrigue had dark hair, dark eyes, blemish-free skin, clean features, straight teeth. Matt knew it was too much to hope for that this guy was now bald and fat.

"I'll need to keep this for now," he said.

"Okay."

"You realize it's likely Tony's married and bouncing a kid or two on his knee?" he said.

"More than likely," she agreed, calmly.

"And yet you still want me to find him?"

"I don't want to cause him any trouble, Matt. I just want to see him again and talk to him."

"To reminisce about old times? Or to see if that fifteen-year-old flame is still burning?"

"Do you always grill your clients this way?"

She had asked the question calmly, without a trace of rancor or reproach, despite the fact that she had been entitled to both. His comment had been way out of line.

Matt took a deep breath and silently cursed himself.

He moved his chair until he was facing the computer monitor that occupied the far edge of his desk.

Matt had positioned his screen so that someone sitting in front of his desk—as Jamie was—couldn't see the system he was accessing and how he was accessing it. A moment later the reply flashed in front of him.

"There are two Anthony Lagarrigues holding state drivers' licenses. One is twenty and the other is sixty-two. Obviously, neither is your Tony."

"You have computer access to drivers' license files?" Jamie asked, obviously surprised.

"I'm a private investigator," Matt said cryptically and then quickly moved on. "Let's try Oscar and Erline."

Matt entered the request.

"No Oscar or Erline," he said. "I'm going to check something else."

He keyed in a special access code that got him onto another computer system.

"There are two Anthony Lagarrigues with Texas telephone numbers," he said after a moment. "But from their addresses it's obvious they're the same two we found in the drivers' license search. There's no listing for an Oscar or Erline Lagarrigue. He won't be easy to find if he's moved out of state."

"But you'll find him."

Matt heard the complete confidence riding her tone. He looked up to see the warm smile she was sending him. The sunlight from the window slipped into the blue of her eyes and turned her skin to cream, her hair to gold dust.

God, he ached to touch her! But he couldn't. Not ever. For there was still Cade. There would always be Cade.

Matt knew it made no difference that Cade and Jamie had split. Had the situation been reversed and Matt had been the one who lost Jamie, Cade wouldn't dream of taking a step toward her, no matter what he felt. A brother did not move in on his brother's wife. Or ex-wife. There could be no worse betrayal.

"How much will you need as a retainer?" she asked.

"My regular fee is a hundred dollars a day plus expenses," Matt heard an annoyingly gruff voice say and realized that it was his own. He had no idea why he had even quoted that amount. His regular fee was a heck of a lot more than that.

His behavior was becoming as erratic as his pulse.

"I'll write you out a check," Jamie said reaching into her purse again. "How much in advance?"

He had no intention of taking money from her. A man didn't take money from a woman who stirred the kind of emotions this one had always stirred inside him. He looked away from her to the papers on his desk and pretended interest in one.

"When I start on the case, I'll let you know," he said.

"*When* you start on the case?"

"I have other matters that need attention. It'll be a few days."

"I was hoping you could get started right away."

"You haven't seen this guy in fifteen years. Surely you can wait a few more days?"

"No, I...I don't want to wait. I've taken this week and next as vacation. I don't have much time to find him."

There was an uncharacteristic tone in Jamie's voice that returned Matt's eyes to her face. He watched her shift in her chair. She stared down at the half-written check.

And that was when Matt saw what he realized he should have seen from the first, would have seen from the first if his damn emotions hadn't been getting in the way. Jamie didn't just want to see this guy. She *had* to see him.

Matt leaned across the desk toward her. "What is it? Why can't you wait?"

Her eyes rose to his as she fingered that large, ugly locket again. "I don't think you'd understand, Matt."

"My IQ hasn't dropped so low that Charlene's taken to watering me every morning."

"I didn't mean intellectually. I meant emotionally. Tony was the first boy who ever kissed me. It was a...real special kiss. I've never forgotten it. And lately I've thought a lot about him."

"All this urgency because this Tony was a good kisser?"

Matt knew his tone was way too gruff again. He couldn't seem to help it. He was mad at this guy for kissing her. And he was mad at Jamie for liking it so much. And he was mostly mad at himself for caring about any of it.

"Matt, just find Tony for me. As quickly as you can. Please."

She dropped her eyes again as her fingers fiddled with the edges of the check.

Damn. He wished she hadn't said please. He exhaled his anger with a resigned sigh. This was real important to her. And because it was, he knew he would do what she asked. Whatever she asked. No matter what it cost him. God help him.

"Make the check out for a hundred," he said, his tone even gruffer this time. "I'll put you on the show tonight. With luck, you'll be kissing your Tony again by week's end."

*And I'll be wishing I'd just put a bullet to my brain.*

"I thought your show was a local cable one. How will putting me on help to find Tony if he's moved out of state?"

"Someone in our broadcast area might recognize the Lagarrigues' names and give us a lead as to where they've gone."

"I see."

"Plus, the show's being picked up by other cable affiliates throughout the south and west now. Tonight the affiliates west of the Pecos will broadcast the show. Tuesday night's show can be picked up as far east and south as Florida. If we don't get any calls after tonight, we'll try again tomorrow."

She finished writing the check and held it up to him. "Much obliged, Matt."

He said nothing, didn't even look at her, just took the check. He was surprised to note she was still using her married name. Matt had assumed that independent streak of Jamie's would have had her reclaiming her maiden name right after the divorce.

"Something wrong with the check?"

Matt realized he'd been staring at it a mite too long. He slipped it into his pocket and latched on to a less revealing topic. "You're living in one of those townhomes on Klondike."

"Just moved in. I'm a biogeologist now, attached to a research team over at the university. We spent this winter studying the effects of climatic changes at the coast's national wildlife refuge."

She didn't have to tell him. Thanks to Liz, Matt already knew all about Jamie's job and her new townhome.

"Are you relieved to learn the check won't bounce?" she asked.

Since he had no intention of cashing it, that hardly mattered to him. However, as she was wearing an amused smile, he knew her question wasn't a serious one.

"I'll need you to be at the studio by nine tonight," he said.

"You can fit me on the show so soon? I thought you'd have your programming planned for weeks in advance."

He did, but he had no intention of telling her what kind of grief he was going to be putting Randy, his assistant producer, through by getting her on.

"Cable's a lot more flexible than national programming," he said instead, as though that should explain it. "We'll end the program with your story. 'Sweetspring, Texas gal gets her first kiss. Now fifteen years later she's searching for the man whose lips have spoiled her for any other.'"

A small frown appeared on her brow. "I'd appreciate it if you didn't mention Sweetspring."

"Why? It would help viewers to know he was there fifteen years ago."

"Please, Matt, just leave it out. His name and the name of

his folks should be sufficient to identify Tony. Will I have to learn any lines to say in front of the camera?''

"No, I'll do all the talking. We'll run your face next to Tony's two pictures—''

"*Two* pictures?''

"I have a computer program that will age him fifteen years, so that folks can recognize how he'll look today.''

"You mean something like what the police use?''

"Exactly like what the police use. Hold on there a minute, and I'll show you.''

Matt fed Tony Lagarrigue's photo into the computer scanner on the top of his desk. Tony's likeness appeared on the computer's monitor.

Matt manipulated the keys until Tony's face filled the screen. He entered Tony's age at fifteen. Then, he hit a few additional keys, instructing the software to show how Tony's face would have aged in the intervening fifteen years.

Tony's boyish cheeks and chin disappeared. His face took on a broader look, his nose larger, his eyes deeper set, his forehead narrower, his hair closer to his head.

As far as Matt was concerned, he still looked too damn good. Matt was so engrossed with the changes taking place on the screen that he didn't immediately notice Jamie now stood beside him.

She leaned over his shoulder to get a better look. Her soft, fragrant hair brushed his cheek.

Before he knew what hit him, the warm, honeyed scent of her had already seeped through his senses and brought every male cell in his body to sizzling attention.

Matt pushed back from the desk and propelled himself to his feet. He retreated until the windows would let him go no farther.

The blood was pumping in his ears. The perspiration was leaking out his pores. His muscles were so tense they hurt.

For the next few seconds all he could concentrate on was trying to rein in his runaway reactions and hoping like hell that Jamie hadn't noticed his odd behavior.

He needn't have worried. Jamie didn't even look at him. Her attention was captured by the computer-aged face of her long-lost love that filled the monitor.

"So that's what Tony looks like now," she mused, mostly to herself. "I wonder what he'll think when he sees me?"

# Chapter Two

"Who you looking for?" the little girl asked Jamie as they sat together in the TV studio waiting room.

The little girl wearing the name tag of Sarita looked about ten to Jamie. Her brown hair was tied back with a pink ribbon that matched the color of her dress. Her legs dangled off the chair, her feet making circles in the air. Her question to a stranger possessed that kind of self-assurance that only well-loved children could project.

"I'm looking for a boy who kissed me," Jamie answered.

Sarita scrunched up her nose. The idea of kissing a boy was apparently not something Sarita had on her agenda for any time soon.

"Who are you looking for?" Jamie asked.

"Another mama. Mine died."

Jamie rested her hand briefly on the little girl's shoulder. "I'm sorry, Sarita."

Sarita said nothing for a moment, just pointed her toes and made some extra large air circles with her shoes. "My mama was a real good mama. But she wasn't my first mama. My first mama had to give me up."

"Why?"

"I was just a little baby. She was kinda young. She didn't have any money. She was sad to give me away. My second mama and daddy were glad because they got to adopt me.

Only my second mama is dead now. So I got to find my first one.''

A story of love and loss and a lot of pain—all relayed in the concise, precise vocabulary of a child.

Rather than simplifying the great emotional upheaval inherent in such a story, Sarita's brief statements brought their images even more clearly to Jamie's heart.

"How does your daddy feel about your wanting to find your first mama?" Jamie asked.

"He's not too happy. But he wants to make me feel better about my mama dying."

"He must be feeling kind of bad, too."

Sarita's large brown eyes turned directly to Jamie. "He cries. I never saw my daddy cry before mama died. I don't want him to cry any more."

Jamie started to suspect that wasn't all Sarita wanted for her daddy.

"Sarita, when you find your first mama, are you hoping that maybe she and your daddy will...get together?"

Sarita stared hard at the toes of her shoes.

"My daddy's real good-looking. And he's nice. It could happen." Sarita looked up again at Jamie. "Couldn't it?"

There was such hope on her face. But the odds of that long shot were pretty astronomical. Jamie wished with all her heart that she could give Sarita the assurance she wanted so badly. But lying to a child was not something Jamie could bring herself to do. Nor could she dash the hopes of any little girl. When she was a little girl, sometimes hope was all she had.

Jamie leaned over and gave Sarita a hug, letting that be her response. When the little girl's arms came around her and returned that hug, a lump stuck in the middle of Jamie's throat.

"It's time, Sarita," Matt's gravelly drawl said.

Jamie released Sarita, looking up in surprise to find Matt standing before them. He moved real quiet and quick for a man the size of a mountain.

Matt's gaze was focused on Sarita. His rough features had softened into one of those rare, appealing half smiles of his. He held out his hand to the little girl. Jamie was amazed to see Sarita scoot off the chair and take his hand without hesitation. She had never pictured Matt charming a child before.

At the door, Sarita paused to turn around. Jamie and she exchanged waves. Then Sarita and Matt were gone.

Jamie redirected her attention to the TV monitor mounted on the wall in the waiting room. A taped commercial for a sale at a local store was just finishing. A moment later Matt was introducing Sarita and telling his TV audience about her quest to find her birth mama. Jamie studied his face.

Matt didn't have Cade's fine-chiseled features and ready smile. His craggy countenance was far too rough-hewn and rugged looking. His gravelly drawl was downright riveting.

But it was the strength in his face and the intensity in his eyes that seemed to leap right out at her. On the TV screen it was evident enough. In person, Matt Bonner made Jamie's nerves positively dance up a storm.

She'd never forget the first day they met. She'd been standing on his mama's porch out at the ranch, soaking up some rays, when suddenly his huge six-feet-six shadow had simply blocked out the sun.

She'd turned to see shoulders as broad as the Texas plains, dark blond hair, thick like mottled eagle feathers, skin creased and weathered like a clay furnace. And steel-gray eyes, assessing her from beneath the brim of a low-riding Stetson.

Cade had talked a lot about his big brother, Matt. But nothing he said had prepared Jamie for the impact of the man himself.

In those few seconds before Cade stepped forward to introduce them, Jamie hadn't even dared to draw in a breath.

And in that regard, things hadn't changed a whole lot in the past five years. The fact that he was executive producer of this show and geared his P.I. practice to finding lost loves never ceased to amaze her. Such pursuits seemed so tame for him.

Matt Bonner struck her as the kind of man born to be on the back of a bucking bronco or wrestling a bull to the ground with his bare hands.

And yet, she had just witnessed him charming a little girl with his smile. The incongruity of the two impressions filled Jamie with a familiar confusion. Not for the first time she wondered who, exactly, was Matt Bonner? If there was a key to him, he kept it well hidden.

She knew all about keeping things hidden. She'd been doing it all her life. Secrets were sometimes absolutely necessary to survival.

But there were some things that needed to be told. She fingered the heavy, old locket that she had polished and now wore constantly around her neck.

She had to find Tony Lagarrigue. He'd left more behind in Sweetspring than he ever knew.

So much had happened that fateful night he took her to the dance. How might her life have changed if Tony hadn't moved away so soon afterward? Would he have stood beside her in those dark days that followed? Was Tony's absence behind this empty feeling she carried inside her, as though something vital was missing from her life?

She wasn't going to let this question be something she wondered about anymore. If Tony was meant to be part of her future, she was going to find him and find out. Now.

The door to the waiting room opened. A technician stuck his head inside.

"Ms. Bonner, you're up next," he said.

Butterflies batted the lining of Jamie's stomach as she followed the technician out onto the stage.

While the camera refocused on Matt and he repeated the station's telephone number for viewers to call with information, Sarita left the stage to join a tall, smiling man with chestnut hair and sad eyes. Her daddy.

He looked real nice to Jamie. It must feel good to help folks like him and Sarita. But she'd hate to be the one to have to disappoint them. She wondered how Matt handled that part.

The studio lights blinded Jamie. The technician quickly powdered the shiny spots beneath her eyes before scooting away.

Jamie had watched Matt's show several times. It was informal. She knew Matt was going to do all of the talking for her segment.

Nonetheless, the butterfly in her stomach now had the wingspan of a red-tailed hawk.

She concentrated on her surroundings. The studio was quite small and simple with two stuffed conversation chairs facing each other, a couple of microphones dangling overhead and a dark blue curtain behind.

It had looked a lot larger and more plush on TV. But then everything about life had a tendency to look a lot larger and more plush on TV.

Except when her eyes settled on Matt Bonner. That man was like Texas itself. You had to see him in person in order to fully understand what big meant.

Jamie's eyes wandered to the three cameras trained on the stage. That seemed like a lot for a cable show.

She could make out a control booth in the back. Quite a few people appeared to be involved in this production. There was a professionalism about it that she hadn't expected.

Matt introduced her spot. She stared into the camera as she had been instructed and listened to Matt talking about the teenage girl who had been swept off her feet by the boy who had taken her to her first dance in a small Texas town.

Jamie knew that her image along with that of Tony's young face and his aged face would accompany Matt's words.

It was all over in sixty seconds.

Jamie rose to shake Matt's hand and thank him. But she wasn't quick enough. He was already off the stage, clapping the crew members on the back and giving them a hearty "well done."

Jamie watched him, reminded of all the times she had walked into a room out at the ranch only to see Matt quickly leaving it.

In the whole of the three years she and Cade had been married, Matt had remained aloof and distant and had avoided every overture she'd made to be friends.

She should have gotten the message by now that it wasn't going to happen. So why did she keep hoping it would change?

Jamie retraced her steps to the waiting room to collect her handbag. She was beginning to wonder if she had done the right thing by going on the show. If one of her fellow researchers at the university found out, she'd be in for a hard time. She could take the inevitable ribbing, but she didn't want to have to deflect their questions about Tony. There were some things that were just too personal to discuss.

"There's a call for you."

Jamie whirled around at the sound of Matt's voice. Once again she hadn't heard him come into the room.

"No one knows I'm here," Jamie said.

"The caller's responding to the broadcast."

"Oh, of course," Jamie said, feeling as dense as a hitching post. "I didn't think we'd get a reaction so soon. Is it someone who knows about Tony?"

"The caller won't say. But he asked for you by your maiden name."

Jamie's stomach fluttered. "My maiden name?"

"Since we only identified you by your first name on the show, it could be someone who knows you from your days in Sweetspring."

"Did you said it was a he?"

"Either a man or a woman trying to disguise her voice."

"Where can I take the call?"

"Pick up that phone over there and punch five. The switchboard will transfer it."

Jamie rushed over to the phone sitting on the table and tried to control the flapping in her stomach.

Could it be him? After all this time? She snatched up the receiver and punched in the five with a shaky finger. She waited through a couple of clicks, her heart picking up extra beats with each one.

"Hello," she said.

The other end of the telephone line was quiet for a moment before a voice asked, "Is this Jamie Lee?"

There was something about that deep, breathy voice that brought Jamie's spine ramrod straight.

"Yes, yes! Who is this?"

"Tony Lagarrigue doesn't want to see you, Jamie Lee. And he doesn't appreciate your broadcasting his name and face all over the television waves."

"Do you know Tony? Can you tell me where to find him?"

"You don't appear to be getting the message. So let me spell it out. Back off. You just forget you ever heard of Tony Lagarrigue."

"Who are you?"

"Someone who is in a position to affect your future health and welfare. You'd better think twice before you go placing them in jeopardy. Again."

Dial tone blared in Jamie's ear.

Matt watched all the excited animation that Jamie had been displaying visibly drain from her profile. She dropped the receiver as though it were burning her hand.

Matt's stomach churned as he started toward her. "Who was it?"

Jamie did a slow half turn and met his advance. "It wasn't Tony."

"Who was it?" he repeated, taking another step toward her.

"It wasn't anyone who knew Tony," she said, sidestepping

him, heading for her handbag. As soon as she collected it, she started toward the door.

Matt beat her to it. He extended his arm to bar her way.

"Who was it?" he demanded for a third time, his voice gruff with frustration and anger. "I'm warning you, Jamie, you're not getting past me until I know."

She raised her head and looked him straight in the eyes. "It was a crank call. And now let me warn you, Matt Bonner. I have a mean right, and you're going to be feeling it on that chin of yours real soon if you don't stand back and let me pass."

Matt was amazed at the strength of her angry retort, coming so soon in the aftermath of what had obviously been a shock or a fright. Ribbons of color flashed in her cheeks.

He stayed where he was for a moment, caught between the conflicting feelings of admiration at her fast recovery, frustration at her answer and amusement at her threat.

Then he realized she was close enough for him to smell the warm, honeyed sweetness of her hair and skin. And that was too close.

He dropped his arm and stepped back. Jamie rushed past without a backward glance.

Matt watched her go. A tiny, sane voice urged him to just let her leave and be done with it.

But he wasn't listening to it. He was listening to another voice—not so sane but far louder. He made his way to the switchboard and loomed over the operator. His name was Perry. He'd been with Matt from the opening of the show. He was a pro.

"What was the originating number on the Jamie Bonner call?" he demanded.

"The number didn't appear on the monitor, Matt. It had line blocking on it."

"You didn't override?"

Perry looked at Matt with startled eyes. "We've got one of those cases?"

"We're going to treat it like one. Record every damn number and every conversation that comes in for her from now on."

"Yes, sir," Perry said.

Matt whirled around and headed for his small studio office. He slammed the door behind him.

He'd snatched up the phone and had mashed out the number before he'd even sat down.

"It's me, Liz."

"It's nearly eleven, Matt. Why are you calling so late?"

"I need to talk to Cade."

"Cade flew to Tulsa this afternoon. He'll be gone for at least a week."

"What's he doing there?"

"A veterinary convention. Whole bunch of new methods on how to treat old diseases and save the hopeless. He's in hog heaven. You sound angry. What's wrong?"

"You heard Jamie's looking for some guy she knew when she was fifteen?"

"Yeah. Tony something. Cade and I told her she should see you. How's the search going?"

"I put her on the show tonight, and she got a bad call."

"What do you mean?"

"Whoever was on the other end of the telephone line said something to frighten her."

"Who did she say it was?"

"She said it was just a crank caller. I don't buy it."

"Why would Jamie lie?"

"How would a crank caller have known her maiden name? Liz, what do you know about Jamie's background?"

"Not a whole lot. Jamie's never been much of one to talk about the past, as you know."

"No, I don't know."

"Oh, yeah. I keep forgetting you left the ranch just about the time Cade and Jamie got hitched."

"Just about."

"One day you were talking about how great it was to be back home and the next you couldn't move out fast enough. Sometimes you can be a puzzle, big brother."

"And sometimes you can stray far away from the subject, little sister. Now, come on. You must know something."

"About what?"

"You and Jamie are best friends. What do you talk about when you get together?"

"Our jobs, friends, clothes, weight, chocolate, PMS, men, sex—just the usual stuff on a single woman's mind. Why?"

"I'm trying to get a fix on things. You roomed together in college. Who were the guys she dated?"

"I don't remember any names. No one steady, though. She didn't go out much. When she wasn't working, she had her nose in a book."

"What do you know about her background?"

"You mean the time before we roomed together in college?"

"Yes."

"Not a whole lot. She was orphaned real young. Foster family raised her. She moved to San Antonio right after high school to get a job and go to college. That's about it."

"What did she tell you about the foster family?"

"Not a blessed thing. Never even saw a picture of them."

"That seems odd, doesn't it?"

"I got the distinct impression that they weren't her favorite folks in the world. I know she worked her way through college without any help from them or anybody. And she's proud of it."

"You never met this foster family?"

"Never saw Jamie get so much as a card from them. They didn't even attend her and Cade's wedding, remember?"

"What about friends from Sweetspring?"

"She never mentioned any."

"When Cade calls the house, ask him to get in touch with me."

"In the meantime, I'd better warn you."

"Warn me?"

"Don't go trying to run roughshod over Jamie with that infamous Matt Bonner, tough Texan routine. It won't work."

Matt smiled as he remembered Jamie's threat to sock him in the jaw if he didn't move aside. She was pretty gutsy for a gal who had to stretch up a storm to measure five foot five.

"The warning's come a little late, Liz. Look, I have to know who called her. There's more to Jamie's desire to find this Tony Lagarrigue than just a curiosity about a fifteen-year-old heartthrob. Will you talk to her for me?"

"Sorry, no can do. If Jamie wants you to know something, she'll have to tell you herself. I'm not going to use my friendship with her to pass on confidences. Jamie was my anchor when that love affair with Hank ended up in heartbreak. She asked no questions, just gave me lots of support and love. I respect her right to privacy as she respects mine."

"She's going to have to tell me what's going on, if she expects me to help her."

"Why do you have to know, Matt?"

"What do you mean why? I'm trying to do a job here."

"Jamie just wants you to find this guy. She isn't looking for your approval of her reasons."

"But I'm looking for the lowlife who called her at the studio tonight," Matt said, adroitly changing the direction of the conversation. "Whoever it was frightened Jamie."

"Jamie doesn't frighten easily. I doubt a phone call could do it. You must have read it wrong."

"I know what I saw."

"I doubt most folks ever see the real Jamie. That pretty face and petite size of hers is mighty misleading. She's been taking care of herself for a long time. Whoever it was on the other end of that telephone call, I'll bet she can handle 'em."

"And what if you lose that bet, Liz? What if she's in trouble and afraid to say?"

"You're getting pretty riled up over a crank call. This doesn't sound like the cool, dispassionate Matt I know."

No, Matt supposed it didn't. But he was never himself when he was around Jamie.

He took a deep breath and quietly exhaled. He should have known he couldn't handle her case with his normal detached composure. Not that this was something he could ever admit to his sister.

"I'm trying to do my job, Liz. And my instincts tell me Jamie's keeping something back that could be damn important."

"Matt—"

"Liz, I don't like clients who won't be forthright with me. If I can't pry the truth out of her, I'm going to have to cut her loose."

"You don't mean that! Jamie's kin. She's counting on you. You're not going to let her down, are you?"

No, he wasn't. But he knew when to hang tough in an argument to get what he wanted.

"Unless Jamie tells me what she knows, I'm going to have no choice. An investigator is only as good as the information he gets. Remember, I'm trying to help here."

Liz sighed in his ear. "Oh, all right. I'll give her a call and see what I can do."

"Ask her to come by the studio tomorrow night at eight-thirty so we can talk. We'll do another segment on her and her Tony."

"You want to see if this creep calls her again, don't you?"

"You're not a bad private investigator for an accountant, Liz."

"Yeah, well, you've become the proverbial bull in a china shop when it comes to women, Matt. Jamie is a sweetie. She'll do most anything for someone who treats her kindly. For heaven's sake, be nice to her."

"Since when haven't I been nice to Jamie?"

"You've never been much on sweet-talking the ladies, but

around Jamie you're so brittle I swear I can hear your bones crack.''

Matt didn't realize it had been so obvious.

"And don't go jumping to any more conclusions about that telephone call until you give Jamie a chance to tell you about it," Liz continued. "I still think you're overreacting."

Matt didn't argue. He'd accomplished what he wanted to. He thanked his sister and hung up the phone.

He wished he could believe what Liz had said about that call being something Jamie could handle.

But Liz hadn't seen Jamie's face afterward. Matt had. And every ounce of his experience and instinct told him something was mighty wrong.

# Chapter Three

"I'm just asking for the truth," Matt said, as he paced around the tiny office at the studio. There was only one chair. He had offered it to Jamie but she had insisted on standing.

His last comment planted her feet firmly on the carpet, arms across her chest. He was surprised to see her assume this fighting stance. Not a whole lot of folks squared off against him so readily.

He was beginning to understand what Liz had meant about the deceptiveness of that pretty face and petite packaging.

"Now let's get something straight here, Matt Bonner. I didn't lie to you. It was a crank call."

Despite her combative stance, her voice had remained cool. Matt liked seeing that control in her, just as he liked seeing the fight. Wimpy women had never held any appeal for him.

"I never said you lied," Matt equivocated. "But I think you'll agree that the expression 'crank caller' implies someone who doesn't know you. That caller knew you. He or she asked for you by your maiden name."

"So?"

She wasn't giving an inch. Trying to bully Jamie definitely didn't work. Matt remembered his sister's admonition about Jamie doing anything for someone who was nice to her. He tried to put a gentler touch to his tone.

"Did Liz explain to you why I'm concerned?"

Jamie said nothing for a moment, but Matt thought he

sensed a lessening of the tension in those lovely straight shoulders.

"Liz said you care a lot about doing your job right. She seemed to think that you cared a lot about doing right by me."

Jamie stopped to smile. "She also told me you still consider me family like she and Cade do, and that's why you're so worried. She was doing a good job of convincing me until she mentioned that last part."

Matt watched the gleam of amusement enter her eyes. He always liked the fact that laughter never seemed far away from Jamie, no matter what other emotion might claim her at the moment. Of course, Jamie would be far away from that laughter if she knew how accurate Liz had been in that last statement.

"So even though you didn't believe what Liz said about my motives, you still decided to show up tonight?"

Jamie unfolded her arms and leaned her back against the wall. "Oh, you must know how hard it is to say no to Liz. I'd face a dozen mean, ol' bulls rather than disappoint her."

"And that's what I represent to you? A dozen mean, ol' bulls?"

The amusement danced through her eyes. "Naw, just one mean, old bull. But a mighty big one."

He could go on looking at her forever when she smiled at him like that. No woman had ever made him feel like this with just a smile.

Damn. Matt recognized that their conversation had begun to take on a friendly give-and-take quality that he had purposely avoided on all previous occasions. He reminded himself this was not the time to allow his guard to drop.

In the past he had solved the problem by avoiding her. Since he'd taken on her case, that was no longer an option.

Friendly was not going to do. Neither was gruff. He had to be polite and professional when he talked to Jamie, like he was with all his other clients. Nothing less. Nothing more.

He leaned against the edge of the small studio desk, his

hands at his sides. He concentrated on putting that formal but civil quality into his expression and his tone.

"So who was the call from?"

Jamie gave a small shrug and uncrossed her arms. "I don't know. He or she didn't give a name."

"You want to tell me what was said?"

"I was told Tony didn't want to see me and didn't appreciate my putting his name and picture on TV."

"Anything else?"

"Something about the fact that the caller was in a position to affect my future health and welfare. And that I was placing them in jeopardy."

Matt felt his anger surging. His fingers curled beneath the rim of the desktop. He concentrated real hard on keeping his voice emotionless and even. It wasn't easy. But he'd just promised himself he was going to remain in control with her. And damn it, he was going to.

"And the implication of this threat was that you would be doing so by continuing to look for Tony Lagarrigue?"

"Yes."

"Why didn't you tell me this last night?"

"Because it was a crank call."

"Was it? I think you suspect who this caller is. I just don't think you want to accept it."

"No, Matt. It wasn't Tony."

"Why would anyone else go to this kind of trouble to warn you off?"

Her eyes met his levelly. "Why would Tony?"

"You haven't seen him in fifteen years, Jamie. A body can change a lot during that amount of time. You have no idea who he might have become."

"A person's character doesn't change that dramatically. Look, let's forget the call, okay? It means nothing."

"It turned you as white as the wall."

"I admit I was initially shocked. I wasn't prepared to hear something like…that. I expected—I thought—the caller was Tony."

"Did the voice sound familiar?"

"Not…exactly."

"Translate 'not exactly' for me."

"Just for a second there at the beginning I thought it was Tony I was talking to. I think it was because the person called me Jamie Lee. Not a whole lot of folks outside of Sweetspring refer to me by my first and middle name."

"Maybe it would be better if you didn't go on tonight."

"Why? Matt, you're not taking some half-wit's vague threat seriously, are you?"

"This half-wit knows your name."

"So would anyone who knew me before I married your brother."

"You telling me you left a trail of brokenhearted half-wits behind you?"

"No, of course not."

"Any lover at all?"

"No."

"There was no one before Cade?"

"Matt, this is getting kind of personal."

"Threats do have a tendency to do that. You leave an unhappy sweetheart back in Sweetspring or here in San Antonio before you got together with Cade?"

"No."

"Did you date anyone steady before you met Cade?"

"No."

Matt wondered if she was answering these questions a bit too briskly. He'd managed an even tone up to now. He took a deep breath and reminded himself to maintain it. He chose his next words real careful like.

"You and Cade didn't get married until you were twenty-five. Most women would have acquired a bit of a romantic past by then."

"I was too busy working and getting through school to do more than date casually."

"Did the guys you did go out with get upset with that decision?"

"Why should they? The guys in college just wanted to party. Once they knew I wasn't into that, they went on to someone else."

Matt had a hard time believing a man who had seen Jamie would "go on to someone else." A real hard time. Since the moment he met her, there had been no one else.

A perfunctory knock sounded on the door before it swung open and Randy's curly red mop shot inside. "Show starts in two minutes. We're going to need you and Ms. Bonner on the set."

Matt looked over at Jamie. He was encouraged to see there was no fear on her face or in those lovely deep blue eyes.

He'd rather goad this guy into contacting her again, so he could trace the call, rather than leave him out there and have to worry about what else he might try. Yes, for his own peace of mind, he'd prefer she went on.

"It's your call," he said.

"I'm ready," she said, leaning away from the wall.

Matt placed an extra emphasis of urgency in his voice when he asked viewers to call in to help find Tony. He even added that he was certain Tony would want to see Jamie after all these years. He said these things purposely so that he could goad the guy who had called her into calling back.

After Jamie's short spot, Matt introduced a thirty-five-year-old man who was looking for his twin sister. They'd been separated at the age of five when they went to different foster homes.

As Matt read the story off the prompter, he thought of Jamie and the foster home in which she'd been raised. Had she been separated from a brother or sister when her folks died? And if so, had she ever tried to find them?

Liz said Jamie hadn't been too forthcoming about her early life. Matt knew that folks who didn't talk about things generally had something to hide. What was Jamie hiding?

Matt was distracted from his thoughts when Perry gave him a sign that a call had come in for Jamie. Matt quickly introduced a commercial break. The instant the camera was off him, he made his way to the switchboard.

Matt picked up a receiver next to the switchboard and signaled to Perry to transfer the call to Jamie where she sat waiting in the small studio office.

Jamie picked up the receiver on the first ring.

"Hello."

"Is this Jamie?"

Matt noted it was a woman's voice asking.

"Yes. Who's this?"

"My name is Erline Lagarrigue."

"You're Tony's mama!"

"Yes, Tony's my boy. And, I don't appreciate your saying he took you out and kissed you, when he never did."

"Excuse me, ma'am?"

"Now, I don't know why you're saying things that aren't true, but you got no call to, no matter what the reason. That's all I got to say. Goodbye."

"Mrs. Lagarrigue, please don't—"

Jamie's plea came too late. Erline Lagarrigue had already hung up on her. Matt replaced the receiver on the hook and turned back to his switchboard operator.

Perry seemed to read Matt's mind. He handed over the originating number already recorded on a piece of paper.

"I want to know the name and address by the end of the show."

"You will," Perry promised.

Matt felt Randy moving up behind him. He turned just as the assistant producer arrived at the switchboard. "Ten seconds."

Matt slipped the number into his pocket and made it back to the set in time to introduce the next segment. During the rest of his half-hour show, Matt kept an eye out for another signal from Perry. There wasn't one.

He thanked his crew quickly and went to the switchboard operator. He had the information for Matt on the number from which Jamie's caller had phoned. Matt made his way to the small office where Jamie waited.

When he stepped inside, he noticed immediately that she had that haunted look in her eyes. He realized it only came in connection with Tony. He didn't like what that realization was doing inside him.

"You want to tell me about the call?" he asked.

Jamie sighed. "She said her name was Erline Lagarrigue. She said she was Tony's mama."

"Was she?"

"I don't know."

"You didn't recognize her voice?"

"I only spoke to Tony's mama once."

"Would you recognize her face?"

"Yes, I'd know her face."

"Then, I'll pick you up at your place at seven tomorrow morning."

Jamie's startled eyes turned to his. "To go where?"

"To Louisiana. That's where the call came from. It's listed under the name of Oscar Lagarrigue. I'd say we've gotten the lead we've been looking for."

"You traced the call? But how—"

"Seven tomorrow. Good night."

He was out the door before Jamie could make a sound, much less ask any more questions.

He didn't want her questioning him. He didn't want to see that haunted look in her eyes another second and know it was another man she was hankering after. He just wanted this over.

"Matt?"

Matt turned around at Randy's call.

"The network guys want us in their office tomorrow morning at ten," his assistant producer said.

"Can't make it, Randy. Have to be next week."

"Are you crazy? I'm not going back to these guys and telling them they have to wait until next week. Do you have any idea how many local cable programs ever get this kind of a shot?''

"You have that startling statistic at your fingertips, do you, Randy?''

"Well, I don't have the actual statistic.''

Randy never did. Matt's assistant producer was a man of lots of sweeping generalizations and few facts. Fortunately for Randy, he was a competent producer.

"But I can tell you it's damn few—and I mean damn few,'' Randy said, his voice riding high on the scales.

Matt knew Randy was young and eager. Too eager. "Look, Randy, when it comes to spelling out our terms, it's always better to do it on our own time and our own turf.''

"You think you're going to spell out terms to a network?''

A confident smile drew back Matt's lips. "If you place a small value on what you got, nobody is going to up the price. Tell them we'll squeeze them in a week from this coming Wednesday. Six o'clock in my office. That way they can take us out to dinner after the deal is done.''

Matt turned to go.

"You don't want the show to go to the network!'' Randy shouted. "You want it to fail. You want out.''

Matt halted. True, he thought the syndication stupid. But he never would have tried to sabotage it. There was only one way Randy could have known he wanted out. Matt slowly walked back to him. Randy's tongue nervously slid over his lips. When Matt reached him, he rested his big hands on Randy's thin shoulders.

"Randy, give a listen here to some real good advice. Going over my head to talk to Cliff Nevelt isn't a real smart career move. Matter of fact, it's downright suicidal. Get my drift?''

Randy's Adam's apple bobbed up and down.

Matt withdrew his hands, turned and walked out.

As soon as Matt had left his small studio office, Jamie picked up the phone and punched in a number. Liz answered on the first ring.

"Liz, I want you to tell me honestly. I can take it, I swear. Why doesn't Matt like me?"

"Uh-oh. What has he done?"

"He just told me he'd pick me up tomorrow at seven and then stomped out of the room before I could say a word."

"What does he want to pick you up for?"

"He thinks he may have found Tony's folks in Louisiana."

"Jamie, that's great! Didn't I tell you Matt's the best!"

"I'm not saying there's anything wrong with his P.I. skills. But I swear sometimes I could cheerfully string him up by that stiff neck of his. What would have been so terrible about his staying around to see if I was ready to go tomorrow?"

"The way Matt acts around you is passing strange, Jamie. He's never been a ladies' man, but he's normally real polite. Matter of fact, most women find him so attractive that he's generally having to fight them off."

"Yeah, but *this* woman married his brother."

"Naw, that can't be it."

"I'm convinced it is. He's been like this from the first moment we met. He didn't think I was good enough for Cade. Compared to the kind of roots the Bonners have—the kind of roots that count in a Texas town—I'm just a tumbleweed."

"Jamie, Matt doesn't think like that."

"I think he does."

"Don't forget, Jamie, I've known him all my life. He's not small-minded. Whoever Cade or I brought home, Matt was always hospitable to them. And you should have seen some of the guys I used to bring home! Well, you did see Hank, so you know."

"What is it about me, then?"

"I don't think it has anything to do with you. I think it's probably a love affair that went bad and has soured him on women."

"Who was she?"

"I've no idea. It was when he came home from that military-intelligence assignment five years ago that I started to notice the changes. He moved out of his wing at the ranch and rarely came back even for dinner. He started up his P.I. firm and buried himself in work. I don't even think he's dated since.''

"Liz, I just want to be friends. It makes me so mad that he won't meet me halfway.''

"Still, you got to admit he got you on his show in record time, and now he's set aside all his other work to fly to Louisiana to find Tony for you.''

"That's true,'' Jamie said, more puzzled than ever. "He has been real accommodating.''

"It's going to be all right, Jamie. Trust me. Matt has a real soft heart beneath that tough exterior. And he's just as competent as hell. It's not going to take him long to find Tony for you. Remember, you're family, and family means everything to Matt.''

Jamie didn't believe that last bit about Matt considering her family, but she loved Liz for saying it. Liz had been her first real friend in the world. And her best.

"Did I ever tell you how much you mean to me?'' Jamie asked.

"And right back at you, Jamie Lee Bonner. Come on out to the ranch for supper Sunday if you can break free. Cade will still be out of town, but Mama and Daddy would love to see you. And we're all going to want an update on the Tony search.''

"I'll call and let you know if I can make it. Thanks, Liz. For everything.''

Jamie hung up the phone feeling a lot better. Liz was the sister she had never had but had always wanted. What's more, Liz had made Jamie part of the kind of family she had never had but had always wanted.

If Jamie had had to give up the other Bonners when she divorced Cade, she knew she'd probably still be married to him.

She'd fallen flat in love with the bunch of them because each and every one of them had accepted her from the first with open hearts.

Well, all of them except Matt.

That long-legged son of a gun hadn't once sent her even one of those half smiles of his. He still stared at her with steel-gray eyes as cool as a March moon.

Well, she was tired of trying to warm them up. If he wanted to be as ornery as an old longhorn, then let him be.

Besides, Liz was no doubt right. Matt was going to find Tony real soon, and then she wouldn't have to be around that big, ol' ornery bull anymore.

It should have been a comforting thought. Finding Tony. Losing Matt. But for some reason, it wasn't comforting at all. Matter of fact, it turned the smile right over on Jamie's lips.

ROLLO PICKED UP THE phone and dialed the number. It rang several times before Val answered with a sleepy hello.

"Val, I've seen him!"

"Rollo? What in the hell are you doing calling me in the middle of the night?"

"Didn't you hear me? I've seen him!"

"Seen who?"

"Well, now who in the hell do you think?"

Rollo heard Val's startled intake of breath.

"Where?"

"On TV. They ran his picture on this late-night cable show. 'Finder of Lost Loves' it's called. Reyenna puts it on sometimes. I watch it with her when I spend the night. It comes out of Texas."

"What was his picture doing on the show?"

"Turns out a broad in Texas is looking for him."

"What broad?"

"I don't know. When Reyenna turned it on, his picture was on the screen. I nearly choked on my beer."

"You didn't blab to Reyenna about him, did you?"

"Val, sweetie, give me a break. The only redhead I shared both a bed and my secrets with was you."

"Knock it off, Rollo. It's not amusing. What good is any of this if you didn't get her name?"

"Hey, I got the station number. The show's out of San Antonio. I can call them and get her name."

"Is it an 800 number?"

"No."

"Good," Val said, sounding relieved. "Eight-hundred numbers always capture the originating telephone number. Still, you better use a pay phone just to be on the safe side. Find out her name, how she knows him and why she's looking for him. Do it now."

"Now?" Rollo asked.

"Right now. And be smart about it. Don't say anything that could leave a trail back to us."

"Give me a break, Val. I'm always careful."

"You weren't with him when it counted."

"Are you still blaming me for that?"

"It was all your fault that he gave us the slip. Call me back when you get the information. And be ready to leave in the morning. I'll pick you up at nine."

"We're going to Texas?"

"Of course, we're going to Texas. This woman is our lead. You know how many years I've waited for this? I swear to you, I'm going to get him. If it's the last thing I do, I'm going to get him!"

# *Chapter Four*

"I never figured you for a Cadillac man," Jamie said as she slipped onto the passenger seat of a big bronze El Dorado. It was plush and as comfortable as a couch. Matt said nothing in response to her comment, just closed the door and circled around to the driver's side.

He'd been on time and on his usual reserved behavior. He even refused to come in for a cup of coffee. He'd stubbornly stood on her doorstep until she had collected her things and then corralled her out to the car.

But Jamie had promised herself she was not going to be upset by it. She'd thought long and hard on what Liz had said the night before. She decided that it wasn't her, after all. Matt had been disappointed by some previous experience with a woman. She was going to have to remind herself of that whenever that rough edge of his mashed against her nerves.

She watched as he maneuvered his long legs into the car. His huge hands expertly spun the wheel as he drew away from the curb. She remembered what else Liz had said— about how women found Matt attractive.

He was attractive. Okay, attractive was an understatement. His rugged profile and well-packed frame projected a straight shot of unadulterated maleness that could be downright dizzying. If a gal was into that sort of thing.

Jamie wasn't, of course. She'd always been drawn to men with big hearts, not big biceps.

Not that Cade hadn't had some bulk, too. But that was just an added feature, like a nice accessory on a car.

"So what kind of car did you think I'd drive?" Matt asked suddenly, surprising her with how closely his question mirrored her mental ramblings.

"A tank, at least," Jamie said with no hesitation. "Certainly not this plush, comfortable, normal car."

She watched his profile carefully in hopes of a smile. She didn't get one.

"Cade drives a Seville," Matt said.

"Yes, but Cade is normal. Now you..."

She let her voice trail off deliberately and waited. And waited some more.

"What about me?" he asked, finally taking the conversational bait just about when she was ready to give up. Was she imagining a speck of interest in his gravelly voice?

"You are a man no one would ever dare call normal. So, how long will the flight be to Louisiana?"

"About three hours. We change planes in Houston. Why wouldn't I be called normal?"

So, he was interested. Well, maybe he was human after all.

"Because you're not an experience for the fainthearted, Matt Bonner. I remember that first day I saw you. Suddenly, I looked up and there you were just like an enormous chunk of Texas—ninety-percent sky and ten-percent earth and far too big to be believed."

Jamie waited for a response, but he was quiet after that. It wasn't a comfortable, companionable quiet, which sometimes stretched between two people. It was charged, and made her nerves positively dance. Now what was wrong?

"Matt, I meant no offense by that description."

"No offense?"

His words had come out with just that touch of gruffness that she'd come to recognize with discomfort.

"I was just kicking around a little conversation so as to get you to smile."

Once again Jamie was greeted by quiet, only this time it

was even more charged. She could see what appeared to be a real busy pulse throbbing in his jaw. This conversation had crossed that line from uncomfortable to troublesome real quick.

"So where in Louisiana are we going?" she asked, redirecting the topic back to the much safer territory of business.

"Far end of the Saint Tammany Parish." His voice sounded real cool. "It's in an area called the north shore of New Orleans."

"And that's where Oscar and Erline Lagarrigue live?"

"That's the address that goes with the telephone number she used to call you last night."

"About that call, Matt. I suppose you'd better know that Erline said something...odd."

"You mean about the fact that according to her you never went out with Tony?"

Jamie whirled around in the passenger seat to fully look at him. "You listened in on my call!"

His eyes remained straight ahead, focused on the road.

"Someone calls you up and threatens you, and I'm supposed to sit back and just let him call again without taking any precautions?"

"Why didn't you at least tell me that you were going to listen in?"

"Would you have agreed to let me?"

"No."

"There's your answer."

"Damn it, Matt, I would have told you what she said."

"Just like you would have told me what your last caller said? As I recall, I had to drag every word of that conversation out of you."

Jamie crossed her arms over her chest and took several deep breaths, trying to remind herself the whole time that she'd promised herself not to get frayed on Matt's rough edges. After the way he had grilled her about the contents of the first call, she should have guessed something was wrong when he'd asked so little about the second.

"You haven't answered my question," Matt said. "Why would Erline Lagarrigue deny Tony went out with you?"

"You ask me that as though you think I should know the answer. How could I?"

"Have you considered that Tony might have sneaked out that night to meet you? His folks may never have known."

"Tony didn't have to do something like that. His folks were nice. Real nice."

"I thought you said you only met them the one time."

"It doesn't take long to determine who's mannered and who isn't. And while we're on the subject of manners, the next time you want to listen in on one of my telephone calls, Matt Bonner, I strongly suggest you ask me first."

He sent her a scowl and she sent him one right back. Damn him. Well, there went all her good intentions. Rough edge, nothing. This man was a full-fledged, prickly cactus.

Jamie had never sought anyone's approval before. Why did she keep trying to be friends with Matt? And why did it bother her so much when she failed?

MATT'S ANGER KEPT licking at him all the way through the flight to New Orleans. Jamie ignored him, her nose stuck in the latest John Grisham thriller she'd purchased at the airport.

The polite professional distance he'd been working at so hard just wasn't working.

As much as he tried, he couldn't refrain from trying to find out what she thought of him. When he heard the warmth of approval in her voice when she finally described him as a big chunk of Texas sky and earth, it had nearly stopped his heart.

He never imagined she'd ever noticed him in any way or with any warmth.

For one wonderful moment she'd fooled him into believing that she might have thought of him as someone special. That would have meant so much to him. He wanted to be someone special to her because she was someone real special to him.

But she hadn't thought of him that way. It had all been just a conversation piece. To make him smile.

Well, he wasn't smiling.

Anger was a good shield to disappointment. Matt wrapped it tightly around his thoughts. Way he figured it, he needed all the protection from Jamie that he could get.

It was just about fifty miles from the Moisant International Airport in New Orleans to the north shore and the Lagarrigue home. Matt drove through rolling hills and past cypress swamps, wisteria, palmettos and trees dripping Spanish moss.

"This is pretty," Jamie said. It was the first thing she'd said to him in over three hours. Matt tried not to feel so happy to hear the husky sweetness of her voice again.

"Have you seen Louisiana before?" he asked.

"The coast, when there was an oil spill in the gulf. I was with a team that was fixin' to evaluate the impact on the waterfowl. This looks like something right out of a book. Why these trees are so thick sometimes you can't even see the sky."

"Just as well. It's coming up a cloud."

"It is a mite sticky. So, is the plan that we just drive up to the house and knock on the door?"

There was an eagerness in her voice. She was fingering the large, gaudy locket that she'd been wearing that day she came to his office. And every day since.

"That's the plan," Matt said, feeling torn. On the one hand, finding this guy was what he'd dropped everything else to do. On the other, he still had a big problem with getting her together with this lost love.

"After the way Erline spoke to me on the telephone, I'm not sure she'll even open the door to us."

"I'll talk us inside," Matt assured.

"And how are you going to do that?"

"Private investigators are good at that sort of thing."

"It would sure solve a lot of problems if Tony were there."

"Seeing as how he's thirty, I rather doubt he's still living with his folks."

"Cade and Liz still live out at the ranch with your mama and daddy."

"Yes, but the ranch is a business to them, as well as a home. Besides, the separate wings that have been added on are more like separate houses."

"That being the case, why did you move out, Matt?"

"I'm not fond of commuting."

"But your business wasn't even started up before you took off for San Antonio."

"This is the house," Matt said, avoiding a response.

He pulled up in front of a comfortable-looking home sitting on half an acre on a tree-shaded corner lot. They walked up the long pecan-tree path to the door. Matt knocked on the screened-in porch.

A tiny gray-haired woman who looked to be somewhere in her fifties came out of the house a moment later. She squinted up at Matt through the screen as she dried her hands on a dish towel.

"Something I can do for you folks?"

"Yes, ma'am," Matt said. "We're looking for Erline Lagarrigue."

"You found her. And who might you be?"

"My name's Matt Bonner, Mrs. Lagarrigue. I'm a private investigator."

"Matt Bonner?" Erline got on her tiptoes to squint up at Matt some more. "You're that fellow who has that TV show?"

"Yes, ma'am."

"I'm not wearing my glasses or I would have recognized you right off. Ought to, seeing as how I watch your show all the time. Well, Matt Bonner here. Imagine that."

"Can you spare us a moment of your time, ma'am?"

"Since you come all this way, I guess you got something important to say. Step on inside."

Erline unlatched the screen door and gestured Matt and Jamie through the entry into a large living room.

Matt's mama had been collecting antiques all her life.

Which is why he knew the leaded-glass table lamps he walked past, as well as the cherry candle stands on which they sat and the sidechairs that surrounded them, were all extremely valuable.

He stepped carefully, just as he had done growing up, as if he were moving through a field of land mines.

"Make yourselves to home while I go look for those pesky glasses," Erline said bustling out the room.

Matt was relieved to see that there was a couch in the living room that had a sturdy look to it. As he made to take a seat on the end opposite to the one Jamie was heading for, he noticed the unopened mail on the Chippendale tea table.

Sitting just behind a telephone bill from South Central Bell and a letter from the Heritage Antiques and Collectibles Company was a pair of glasses.

Matt picked up the glasses and studied them. They were bifocals, with strong lenses both top and bottom. Matt wondered how Erline saw at all without them.

"Excuse me, ma'am, I believe I've found your glasses," he called out.

Erline came bouncing in from the back room. "Well, saints be praised." She took her glasses from Matt's outstretched hand and set them on her nose. Her eyes grew enormous behind them as she looked up at Matt.

"Now that's a heap better. It's great to have a clear view of this old world again."

"I can imagine it would be, ma'am," Matt said, treating her to a smile. "Here, let me hold that chair for you."

Matt circled around to the back of the delicate antique chair that Erline was heading her behind toward and held it steady for her.

"Much obliged, Mr. Bonner. Always such a pleasure to be around a mannered man."

Matt took the opposite end of the couch, where Jamie was seated, and faced their hostess.

"You come here because of my call to the station last night, is that it?"

"Yes, Mrs. Lagarrigue. You spoke to Jamie here."

Erline looked over at Jamie and studied her face. Matt saw the sudden stiffening of her posture. Her arms hugged her sides as her hands folded tightly at her waist. Her tone was just as wooden as her body.

"Oh, so that was you. I didn't get a clear look at your face last night on account of I didn't have my glasses then. But I'm telling you again. My Tony never went out to any dance with you, you hear?"

"Mrs. Lagarrigue," Matt said, quickly interjecting, "why are you so sure of that?"

Erline's magnified bug eyes swung back to his.

"Because my Tony was never in Texas a day of his life. He was born and raised right here in Louisiana."

"I...see," Matt said, not really seeing but beginning to wonder. "Then you and your husband, Oscar, have never lived in Texas, either?"

"'Course not. My granddaddy was a sharecropper on this land. My daddy bought it. My husband and I have lived in this house all our married lives."

"Yes, ma'am. If you don't mind my asking, how old is Tony?"

"Don't mind at all. He's thirty. Born December 3, 1967."

"And where is he now?"

"Why, at work at the brewery in Abita, of course. Been there ever since he came out of high school."

"And your husband?"

"Working right alongside him. I have to tell you when I heard you saying last night that this woman was looking for Tony Lagarrigue, son of Oscar and Erline Lagarrigue, you gave me quite a fright, even though I knew right off it weren't true."

"I can understand how you'd feel that way, ma'am," Matt said, carefully. "Do you have a picture of your son that I might see?"

"There's one right up there on that mantel. You just help yourself."

Matt retrieved the framed portrait that Erline had pointed to. He scrutinized it while standing by Jamie's chair so that she could study it, too.

"That's me and Oscar and Tony," Erline said. "Belinda—she's Tony's wife—is taking the picture. They were married last year. She's going to be having my first grandchild soon. She called me up last night after hearing you talk about Tony. It upset her to think that some woman could be looking for him."

Matt skipped over the faces of Erline and Oscar to concentrate on that of their son, Tony. Other than the fact that Tony Lagarrigue possessed dark hair and eyes, he did not resemble the picture Jamie had given Matt at all.

Erline would have obviously recognized this, too, if she had had her glasses on the night before when she was watching his show.

"Ma'am, did your daughter-in-law mention the picture I ran with the story?" Matt asked.

"She said it didn't look at all like Tony, which was a puzzle to her—seeing as it's his name and all."

Jamie rose from her chair. "Mrs. Lagarrigue, Belinda didn't recognize Tony's picture because it wasn't a picture of her husband. I apologize to you for any distress my appearance on Mr. Bonner's program has caused you or your daughter-in-law. You are quite right, of course. Your son never took me to a dance. I've never even met him."

"Well, then, why did you say you had?"

"It was a case of mistaken identity, ma'am," Matt said as he returned the picture to the mantel. "We're not looking for your son. We're looking for someone else."

"Another Tony Lagarrigue? But you said Tony's mama and daddy were named Erline and Oscar!"

"I regret any misunderstanding, ma'am. I will be sure to broadcast on my next Wednesday show that the staff at 'Finder of Lost Loves' is not looking for Tony Lagarrigue of Louisiana. How does that sit with you?"

Erline's ruffled feathers appeared to be dampening down

some. Her hands came unclasped from around her waist. "You'll say it wasn't my Tony? You'll make it quite clear?"

"Yes, ma'am. Quite clear. Simply a mistake."

"Well, now, I suppose that mistakes do happen."

Matt sent her another smile. "That's right understanding of you, ma'am. Much obliged."

Erline actually smiled back. Matt took hold of Jamie's arm and made a quick exit.

"This makes no sense at all," Jamie said with a voice full of disappointment, when they were in the car and back on the road.

Matt turned to look at the haunted expression on her face. He turned his eyes back toward the road.

"You'll feel better after a good lunch," he said. "There's an old plantation house on the bayou, just a mile or so from here, that's been converted into a restaurant. It's a picturesque step right back into the past with lots of high-octane seasoning and wrought-iron railings. Better yet, it's the best little eat 'em up in this particular part of Louisiana."

"You seem to know this area well. When were you here last?"

"Couple years ago."

"A case brought you here?"

"Yes."

"But your practice is in San Antonio."

"P.I.'s get around."

He felt her eyes studying his profile again. He could always feel when she did that. Each time he wondered what she was seeing, thinking. Each time he told himself it was better he didn't know.

A couple of fat raindrops hit the windshield just as Matt pulled into the parking lot of the restaurant. They raced to the entrance, just making it in time before the deluge broke out from above. A chubby-faced woman wearing a happy smile showed them to a corner table right off the balcony on the second floor. From it, Matt could hear and smell the rain coming in through the open windows.

He ordered the homemade gumbo without looking at a menu. Jamie followed his lead. It was full of French roux, African okra, American Indian filé, Spanish peppers, Cajun sausage and burned his throat as only real good gumbo could.

He was so intent on the food that it wasn't until he was half through that he noticed Jamie had only taken a few bites.

"Not to your taste?" he asked, realizing that it would disappoint him if she didn't like it.

"No, it's perfectly good. I just can't figure out what's going on. That picture of Erline's son looks nothing like the Tony I knew."

"What about Erline?"

"She's nothing like the Erline Lagarrigue I met, either. I know it's been fifteen years and folks do change, but no one could change that much."

"What did the other Erline look like?"

"She was tall, lots of pretty red hair, big boned. And as you saw, this Erline is small."

"And the other Oscar?"

"He was nothing like the picture Erline showed us of her husband. Tony's daddy was more like Tony, dark haired and slender. This is definitely not the Lagarrigue family that was in Sweetspring, Texas fifteen years ago."

"So it would seem."

"But how many thirty-year-old Tony Lagarrigues can there be with a mama and daddy named Erline and Oscar?" Jamie asked, mirroring Matt's thoughts closely.

"I'd say the unusualness of those three names appearing together narrows the pickings down a piece."

"I don't know what to make of this, Matt. The strongest lead I had on Tony was his name and that of his folks. I was so sure they were Oscar and Erline. Did I remember wrong?"

Matt hated hearing the tone of defeat in her voice. He was suddenly overcome with a strong need to take it away.

"We've hit a dead end here," he said. "But that doesn't mean we won't spot another trail up ahead. Don't worry. I'll find this Tony for you. In the meantime you might as well eat that gumbo, because it's going on my expense account for this trip."

Her eyes met his and she smiled. "That's about the nicest thing you've ever said to me, Matt Bonner."

Her smile slipped inside him, warmer and more filling than any food. He wanted to reach across the table to touch those smiling lips. But instead he put a note of gruffness in his voice.

"I didn't know you'd be so pleased to be reminded you're paying for this somewhat less than satisfactory excursion."

"Not that. It was the confidence with which you assured me that you'd find Tony. It sounded real good when you said it. I was getting discouraged."

"Oh, that," Matt said, pretending not to know that was what she meant. "P.I.'s are trained to cheer up clients."

And then he concentrated on his gumbo, because he could feel her eyes were once again studying his face.

WENDY MCCONNELL WAS not happy. Nope. Not happy at all. She glared at her husband, Jerry, across the table.

And Jerry could feel that glare. He'd been feeling it for the past twenty-five years.

"I really wish you'd put that newspaper down when I'm trying to talk to you."

Jerry McConnell knew there was no ducking it anymore. It had reached the stage where it would have to be dealt with if he was going to get any peace.

He put down the paper and looked up at Wendy with as attentive a look on his face as he could manage.

"I shouldn't have listened to you," Wendy said. "I should have called that TV show the other night."

"Look, Wendy, we agreed. No more toll calls. Last month's long-distance charges were more than the mortgage. And it wasn't me on the phone to your sister half the day and night."

"Now, Jerry, you know Maddy's been going through difficult times since her divorce. I've just been trying to be supportive.''

''You should have sent her the money for a shrink. It would have cost less.''

''You spend your share of the budget, Jerry. Don't think I don't know you got all those sports-bloopers videos in the mail last week. Forty bucks each. What a waste!''

''Waste? They're classics! And I don't order them every month. They're a one-time thing.''

''And my call to that station would have been a one-time thing, too,'' she retaliated. ''I feel awful about not helping Jamie find her Tony. And I could have, too!''

''It's probably not even the same guy.''

''Of course, it's the same guy. I recognized his picture right away. You even agreed it looked exactly like him.''

''A lot of people look like a lot of other people.''

''But this one is her Tony. I just know it.''

''What do you want to go getting involved for?''

''Oh, isn't that just like a man. If she were looking for some guy because he played wide receiver on some football team fifteen years ago, you wouldn't have been able to rush to the phone fast enough.''

''What are you talking about?''

''I'm talking about the fact that it doesn't touch you at all that this Tony made her life special by taking her to a dance and being the first boy to kiss her, does it?''

''Damn it, Wendy. We're not going to get into one of those conversations again, are we?''

''We are already in one of those conversations again. I'm talking about feelings, Jerry. Those annoying little things of mine you do your best to ignore.''

Jerry knew when he was licked.

''Oh, all right, I give up. Go call the station. Stay on the phone an hour, for all I care. And when they deliver the next telephone bill in a truck because it's so heavy with charges, you can get the loan from the bank to pay it.''

''Funny, Jerry. Very, very funny. And how magnanimous

of you to encourage me to call now, when you know perfectly well I didn't write the number down.''

Jerry let out an internal sigh of relief. "Well, guess that's that then.''

"Of course, they'll broadcast the number again on next Monday night's show," Wendy said, a bit of hope rising in her voice.

Jerry should have known he'd counted his blessings too soon.

"Still, that's four whole days away!" Wendy lamented. "Who knows what could happen to Jamie and Tony in the meantime. I've waited far too long.''

"You've been watching too many of those soaps again, Wendy. There's nothing urgent at stake here. She's waited fifteen years. She can wait four more days.''

"Not if I can help it." Wendy got up from the table.

"Where are you going?" Jerry asked.

"To call Maddy. She watches the show all the time, too. Maybe she remembers the number.''

Jerry's eyes shot to the kitchen clock. "It's not after seven yet. You won't get the lower rate.''

Wendy grabbed the receiver of the kitchen wall phone and turned back to glare at her husband. "You want to know what you can do with that lower rate, Jerry?''

Jerry recognized that look in his wife's eye. He buried his head back in the newspaper where he could focus on subjects with more uplifting topics such as arson and murder.

"I'LL SEE YOU INSIDE," Matt said as he opened the car door for Jamie.

Jamie appreciated the gesture. Matt's rough, gruff exterior might be right out of the Wild West. But today Jamie had begun to see that beneath this wild-as-the-west tough Texan was a man of real old southern charm.

The way he had handled the ruffled Erline Lagarrigue so smoothly had been real surprising and downright revealing.

She knew he had been attempting to make her feel better

at lunch, too, when he assured her he'd find Tony. She didn't believe a word of his denial that it was just what private investigators were trained to do.

Yes, it had been a revealing day, even if it had led to a dead end in her search for Tony.

Jamie glanced at her watch. It was nearly nine at night. The traveling and disappointment about Tony were taking their toll on her. All she wanted now was some food, a bath and her bed.

When they reached her door, Jamie was surprised to see a large white envelope taped to its front. "Jamie Lee" had been sprawled across it.

"What's this?" she mused aloud, pulling the taped envelope off the door.

She slit open the back and pulled out the card from inside. It had a big red heart on it, just like a Valentine's Day card.

"One of your admirers must have missed you today," Matt said from just behind her.

"I don't have any admirers," Jamie answered absently, her fingers tracing over the velveteen heart.

"I believe your dates would disagree," Matt said, a slight edge to his typically cool, gravelly voice.

"I haven't dated anyone since Cade and I divorced two years ago. This is a beautiful card. I can't imagine who could have sent it. Just one way to find out."

"No, wait!"

She heard Matt's warning just as she started to open the card. It came too late. The contents were already exploding right in her face.

# *Chapter Five*

Jamie coughed and choked, trying to get the soot out of her nose and lungs. She was still holding the booby-trapped card with the word BANG written in big capital letters inside it.

Her hands were covered in the black soot that had shot out of the card when she opened it. So was her ice-blue silk dress. She didn't even want to think what her face must look like.

Matt stepped close. She felt his warmth like an enormous blanket wrapping around her. An odd sensation rippled through her and she was suddenly shaky inside. Was it the shock catching up with her?

"Jamie, are you all right?"

His voice had a somewhat unusual sound to it. She tried to look up at him, but the soot sticking to her lashes wasn't making it easy.

"No, I'm not all right," she said. "I'm mad. What kind of sick joke is this?"

Matt's head came closer as he read what was written inside the card. He smelled spicy clean and sultry warm, even better than the scents of the rain shower and their dinner in Louisiana. Vaguely expectant quivers began to break out inside Jamie.

"Anger's a good, healthy response," Matt said. He stepped back. "A lot better than fear."

Jamie thought his comment sounded strange. And then her eyes focused on the other words written inside the card.

*You're not getting a third warning.*

"This is from that caller at the studio the other night," she said, a rush of breath escaping her lungs as shocked surprise wiped out every other sensation.

"He would get my vote."

A shiver ran down her spine. "Who's trying to discourage me from finding Tony? And why? This isn't making any sense."

"Let me have that card. I'll need it and the envelope to check for prints."

Jamie realized that Matt was holding a pair of tweezers. He fastened them on the card. He adroitly slipped the card into a waiting cellophane bag and repeated the process with the envelope.

"Where did you get those cellophane bags?" she asked.

"I generally carry a few in my pocket."

"Why?"

"They come in handy."

"But how would you know you were going to need them?"

"Private investigators are always ready."

"You yelled out a warning just as I was opening the card. You knew the card was booby-trapped, didn't you?"

"I guessed it could be."

"Why would you guess something like that?"

"You come home to find a card on your door that looks to be from a lover. Yet you say you aren't going with anyone. Three nights ago you got a threatening call telling you not to do something. You did it. It's not such a leap to consider the card might not be from a friendly source."

"But how could he find out about my last name, much less my address? I'm not even in the telephone book."

"For someone determined to do so, these things are easily obtained."

"How?"

"I can think of half a dozen possibilities."

"Give me one."

"He could have been at the studio last night and seen you come out to your car. If he didn't follow you here, all he had to do was call to find out who the car was registered to and your address."

"Who would give out that information?"

"We're in a computerized society. You'd be amazed at the amount of data that's already been gathered on you and is sitting in various computer files just waiting to be accessed. Do you recognize the printing on this envelope or inside the card?"

Jamie peered at the envelope encased in the cellophane, which he was holding up for her to see.

"No."

Jamie looked away from the offensive card to her grimy hands, her ruined dress. The ends of her bangs were black. She could taste the soot in her mouth. She could feel it on her cheeks, clumped on her eyelashes like thick mascara. Some of it was working its way into her eyes and stinging them.

"I have to wash off," she said, digging in her purse for her keys. But as soon as she pulled them out, Matt took them from her.

"I'm going in first. Stay behind me. Close and lock the door as soon as you're inside. Do it as quietly as possible."

Jamie was appalled at the message in his words. "You don't think someone's in there?"

"I'm going to find out."

"Matt, it doesn't seem logical—"

"This isn't a debatable issue, Jamie. I'm simply telling you what I'm going to do."

And was he ever. Jamie had once thought Cade stubborn. But Cade couldn't hold a candle to the stubbornness she was finding in big brother Matt.

Under the circumstances, however, she didn't take offense.

He unlocked the front door so silently that she wouldn't have known he'd done it if she hadn't watched. She followed him inside and closed and locked the door behind her as instructed. He motioned her to remain in the entry. He didn't turn on the light.

She tensed as she watched him open the door to the hall closet, crouching just as though he expected an armed intruder might come barreling out from inside.

The closet was empty. Matt switched on the hall light.

She stayed put while he moved through the rest of the rooms with an intensity and swiftness that told her he has done this kind of thing before. And he took it seriously.

That thought was quite comforting.

When he returned to the front door, he towered over her like a mountain. It was something else that was beginning to strike her as comforting. More than comforting.

"You can go wash up now," Matt said. "I'll wait."

Her heart skipped one beat too many.

"You're waiting?"

"We have to talk about the plan for tomorrow."

"Right," Jamie said, heading for the bathroom. Of course, he wanted to talk business. What else? Where had her mind been?

When Jamie looked at herself in the bathroom mirror, a soot-splattered mess stared back at her. Unbidden images of another time when she'd stood in front of a mirror with a black face began to break through from the back of her mind.

She'd been running. Again. But this time she hadn't been fast enough to get away. And this time it hadn't been that man and woman after her.

This time it had been Wrey Kleinman. He had grabbed her just outside the school yard, thrown her to the ground, shoved her face down in the mud and sat on her. And then he had laughed. And laughed. Until Jamie had finally passed out from his weight crushing the breath out of her body.

Jamie resolutely looked away from her reflection, hating the taste of fear that coated her tongue. She took a deep, steadying breath and willed the vivid images to fade. She would not live memories and let them control her. She would live her life—the life she had made for herself and which she controlled.

By the time she had showered and shampooed her hair, she had washed away not just the soot but the past.

She wrapped her hair turban style in a towel and soothed her face with moisturizer. She tied her terry-cloth robe around her, slipped on her fuzzy slippers.

She returned to Matt to find him pacing the length of the living room. He stopped when she entered, and stared.

"Not exactly formal garb, I realize," she said, quickly surmising the reason for his stare. "I hope you don't mind."

Matt looked away. "Whatever you wear is fine."

"I'll fix us something to eat," she offered. "You must be hungry. Dinner was hours ago."

"I can't stay."

Jamie fought down the disappointment that had arisen at his words. "I thought you wanted to talk?"

"This won't take long. Do you still want to find this Tony Lagarrigue?"

His question surprised her. "Of course."

"That could have been a letter bomb he taped to your door."

"Tony had nothing to do with that card."

"Even if he didn't, that doesn't change the fact that you could have been hurt."

"Are you saying I'm in danger because I'm looking for Tony?"

"Whoever found out your last name and your address and rigged that card to spew out soot is going to a lot of trouble to try to warn you away."

"Okay, Matt. I hear what you're saying. But I think this is just the work of some half-wit. He's not going to do anything serious."

"And if you're wrong?"

"Would you live your life kowtowing to some creep's scare tactics?"

"I can take care of myself, should the necessity arise."

"And I can take care of myself. There's a good lock on my door. The windows are wired to an alarm system. I've been taking self-defense lessons for years. And if all that fails, I have a gun in the bedroom, which—thanks to Liz and my time out at the Bonner ranch—I know how to use quite well."

"You going to strap it to your hips and tote it with you wherever you go?"

"Matt, I need to find Tony. You assured me today that you'd find him for me. Have you changed your mind?"

He looked at her long and hard. Jamie sensed that he was testing her resolve. She was determined he would not find it wanting.

Still, it wasn't easy returning his steely-eyed scrutiny. Every time she met Matt's eyes squarely, her nerves started to dance up a storm again. She couldn't quite put her finger on why, but it felt as if she were actually close to danger. Of course, she knew that was silly. Matt was no danger to her.

"All right," he said finally. "Tomorrow we go to Sweetspring."

Jamie's stomach lurched.

"Sweetspring? Why?"

"Because that's the last place you saw Tony Lagarrigue. There should be some records there that will help us to trace him."

Jamie walked past the overstuffed cream couch in her living room and sat on the matching chair, dotted with bright lemon and cinnamon throw pillows. She pulled off her slippers, curled her bare feet beneath her.

"What's wrong?" he asked.

Jamie took a deep breath and let it out slowly. "I'd rather not go to Sweetspring."

"Most folks never miss an opportunity to visit their hometown. Something about Sweetspring you don't like?"

"There is plenty about Sweetspring I don't like."

"For instance?" he said.

The weak laugh that began in her throat rose up to disintegrate into a nervous, thin sigh.

"They say it's hard to tell which smells worse, an oil well or a feedlot," she said after a moment. "I'm here to tell you it's a feedlot. Sweetspring has a dandy one that reeks right through every inch of town. First day I ever got a lung full of clean air was the day I left. I never planned on going back."

"Looks like your plans have changed."

She glanced over at him and saw he had retreated to the far end of the room. He was casually peering out her drapes.

"I don't suppose you could do this part alone?" she asked.

"Nope."

"Why not?"

He turned back to look at her. "Because I might just come back with no leads at all if you're not there to answer a crucial question when it comes up."

"It appears I don't have a choice here."

"You can stop looking for Tony Lagarrigue."

"No."

"Then I'll be by at eight tomorrow."

Matt started for the door. He already had his hand on the doorknob by the time Jamie had risen from her chair.

"Just a minute, Matt," she called out. He turned and waited until she had joined him.

She realized it was probably just the fact that she was in her slippers, but he seemed so incredibly towering and so far out of reach as she stood beside him.

"I appreciate your coming inside and making sure everything was secure. It was real thoughtful."

"Private investigators are trained for this sort of thing."

Jamie smiled. "So it was all just a matter of training?"

"That and the fact that if Cade or Liz or Mama or Daddy read about your murder in tomorrow's newspaper, I'd have never heard the end of it."

Jamie laughed, rather delighted to find this funny side of Matt. At least she thought it was a funny side. Come to think of it, she was the only one laughing.

Big, powerful, puzzling Matt.

"Lock this behind me," he said in that quiet, serious voice of his.

And then he just slipped out and was gone.

IT WAS A SWEET AND SUNNY kind of spring day. The land was low and flat and went on forever. Matt had been the world over, but his heart had never left West Texas's wide-open spaces. It never would.

They'd been driving with the windows down. But fifty miles outside of Sweetspring Jamie had insisted that the windows be zipped up and the air conditioner turned on.

Matt figured it was memories of the feedlot that had prompted her request.

He wore comfortable jeans and boots and a western shirt— what he deemed appropriate for a long drive through the dusty southwest on a warm late spring day.

He'd been surprised when Jamie answered the door in the kind of well-tailored suit dress that was far more appropriate to city work. Her matching heels were three inches high.

Jamie had always been a sophisticated dresser. She reminded him of the ladies of Dallas who didn't do a whole lot of shopping outside of Neiman Marcus. But today he could see she had made a special emphasis to look even more well dressed.

He wondered why.

He'd seen her wearing pants plenty of times out at the ranch. She looked as good in them as she did in her fine suits and dresses. But then she looked good in everything.

He had a sudden mental vision of her walking into her living room the night before, scrubbed and shiny faced and covered top to bottom in terry cloth and fuzzy slippers, just as sweet and warm and cuddly as a newborn baby chick.

A baby chick who had informed him she had a gun she was prepared to use in the bedroom. He knew she could use it, too. He'd surreptitiously watched her practice out at the ranch. She was a fine shot, even better than Cade.

Matt's mental musings had him almost missing the Welcome to Sweetspring sign.

"We're here," he said as he looked over at Jamie. She said nothing, just wore that familiar frown that had taken over her forehead the night before when he told her they'd be coming here.

He slowed to the requested twenty-five miles per hour as he drove down the main street.

It wasn't much of a main street. A couple of restaurants, a few stores. It looked like the biggest industry was bars. There had to be a dozen of them, all with beer signs hanging outside the front and beat-up pickups with gun racks parked out back.

Matt certainly wouldn't have picked this as Jamie's hometown. She possessed a classy elegance and self-assurance that seemed at odds with whatever this place had to offer.

"Where do your foster folks live?" he asked.

"They don't live here anymore. Take the next left. I'll show you where Tony's family stayed."

Matt followed Jamie's directions and found himself drifting into a more residential section of town, greener and cleaner than the main street. He turned down Kleinman Lane at Jamie's signal.

The homes lining the block were small and modest and about twenty years old—all except for one on the very end.

It was an elaborate Victorian shingle, two stories with latticed attic windows, a balcony off the second floor, and a gambrel roof reminiscent of late 19th-century architecture. The nicely landscaped lot around it was at least three times the size of any other.

"That's not the one," Jamie said, obviously having caught the direction of Matt's eyes. "Tony's house was this one, here."

She was pointing to one of the more modest homes halfway up the block. Matt pulled his car to the curb, but left the engine running. All the house told him was that the Lagarrigues were middle-class in terms of this town.

"Who lived in that big Victorian?" he asked, pointing to it.

"The Kleinmans," Jamie said.

"Did the Lagarrigues rent?"

"I don't know."

"Maybe the local real-estate office can tell us. I didn't see a sign for one as we drove through town. Do you know where it is?"

"When I was here, the sheriff's deputy also had himself the real-estate license."

"Where was his office?"

"One street south of Main next to the library. It's probably still there. Nothing much changes in a town like this."

Jamie was right. The sign said Sweetspring Realty and Sheriff's Deputy. It was clear to Matt which occupation was foremost in the mind of the occupant.

Matt parked the car. The minute he stepped out to circle around to let Jamie out, he got a whiff of the feedlot.

Matt had been born and reared on a ranch. He'd gotten used to all kinds of smells. But he had to admit, Jamie hadn't exaggerated this one.

They found Deputy Plotnik sitting behind his gray metal desk, a telephone sticking out of his ear and a Polaroid picture of three homes pinned up on a corkboard behind him. Soon as he saw Matt and Jamie step inside, he cut his conversation short.

"Gotta go, Maylene." He hung up the phone and rose to his feet with a big smile.

"Well, howdy. And how you folks today?" he said eagerly, as he hitched his pants up over his hefty belly.

Plotnik was fleshy faced, about forty-five and balding just a bit. Matt knew he had clearly mistaken them for prospective real-estate buyers.

And despite the fact that he'd included Matt in his greeting, the deputy clearly only had eyes for Jamie.

Matt didn't blame him none. He couldn't imagine a man

in his right mind who wouldn't prefer looking at her. He held out his hand. "I'm Matt Bonner. And this is—"

"Mrs. Bonner," Jamie said quickly.

Matt looked over at her in surprise. He'd never expected that Jamie would introduce herself that way.

"Well, Mr. and Mrs. Bonner, now you just set yourselves level in those chairs and tell me what I can do you for," Deputy Plotnik said, beaming happily as he pointed to a couple of worn wooden specimens in front of his desk.

Matt and Jamie sat. Plotnik was trying real hard not to stare at Jamie. He obviously didn't want to offend Matt, since it was also obvious he thought Jamie was his wife. But Matt could tell it was taking a lot of the deputy's effort to be polite about it.

"I'm a private investigator," Matt said, pulling his identification out of his wallet and handing it to Plotnik. "We're here to consult you in your capacity as deputy, not real-estate agent."

Plotnik's smile dribbled into disappointment. He took a good look at Matt's ID before handing it back. Then he eyed Matt a moment more before leaning back in his squeaky chair and sticking out his stomach.

"Who you looking for?"

"A family who lived here briefly fifteen years ago. Name of Lagarrigue."

"Why you looking for 'em?"

"They appear to have some relatives in Louisiana who never even knew about them," Jamie said, before Matt could respond. "Sweetspring is the only lead we have."

Matt once again looked over at Jamie. She was just full of surprises today.

"You and your husband work on investigating together?" Plotnik asked.

"Not on every case," Jamie said. "But this one has become special to me. We'd sure appreciate any help you could give us."

And Deputy Plotnik was sure appreciating that smile Jamie was giving him. He leaned forward in his chair.

"Yep, I remember the Lagarrigues all right," Plotnik said. "He sold life insurance. They had a boy, high-school age. I arranged for them to rent the Mason house while the Masons were up visiting their new granddaughter in Oklahoma. The Lagarrigues were going to buy their own place in town and settle in Sweetspring. They weren't Texan, of course. But nice enough folks."

"You have a remarkable memory, Deputy," Matt said.

"I've been the law here in town for close to twenty-five years. Nothing gets past this old boy. I know'd everybody who's been and gone. Besides, the Lagarrigues were here during the time of the murder, and that sort of makes everything around it stick in a man's mind."

Matt came forward in his chair. "The *murder?*" he repeated.

# Chapter Six

Deputy Plotnik rubbed his hands together in obvious anticipation.

"Y'all don't know about the murder? Biggest thing that ever hit this town, I can tell you. Up until that time, all the peacemaking I had to do was keeping the cowboys from stomping each other too hard when they come in to whoop it up on Saturday nights."

"Who was murdered?" Matt asked.

"Kyle Kleinman, richest man in these parts. He owned the feedlot on the west end of town. Left a widow and a boy. Real sad thing, that. Wrey never did get over his daddy's death. I've had to make a lot of allowances for that boy over the years."

"How did the murder happen?" Matt asked.

"Kyle come home to surprise a burglar. He and the missus was over chaperoning a dance at the school. Kyle gave it up early and walked on home to get a whiskey. Kyle was a man who liked his booze. Naturally, no alcoholic beverages were allowed on the school grounds."

"What happened when he surprised the burglar?" Matt asked, wondering why Jamie had said nothing about this.

"Kyle got a round off at the guy with his shotgun. Not that it did any good. Dang fool never could hit the broad side of a barn. Only went hunting with him once. He come near to shooting me!"

"What happened after Kyle shot at the burglar?" Matt prodded.

"Well, way I figure it, must have been a struggle. 'Cause Kyle ended up dead. The murderer hightailed it out the back of the house, leaving everything he'd sacked up to steal."

"What kinds of things?" Matt asked.

Plotnik scratched his chin. "Don't rightly recall. But some nice stuff. The Kleinmans were well off. Still are. Only now there's just the widow, Wrey and Wrey's wife, of course."

"Did his family find him when they returned home?"

"No. Neighbors found old Kyle with his throat cut just a minute or so after the deed was done. Before that, folks never even locked their doors around this town."

"Did you find the murderer?"

"Not fast enough."

"Meaning?"

"Oh, I know'd who did it. But before I got the evidence to prove it, he was long gone."

"Who was it?"

"A no-count, name of Lester Wilson. He'd just come home to Sweetspring after doing a two-year stretch for a robbery in San Angelo. Bad seed clear through."

"He was a resident of Sweetspring before he went to jail?" Matt asked.

"Not in town proper. He was part of some trash down the road a piece. He'd been camping out near the creek since his return. He was just out of the town's limits or I would have run him off. And the rest of them, too. Anyway, Lester went over to the feedlot looking for a job. Kyle told him he didn't hire no ex-cons. Lester cussed Kyle out."

Plotnik paused to lean back again in his chair. "Next thing we knew Kyle was getting his throat cut. Didn't take being bent over double in intellect to know'd who'd done it."

"I thought you said Kyle surprised a burglar?" Matt said.

"Way I figure it, Lester was just planning on robbing him at first. But Kyle come home unexpected like and then started shooting, so Lester jumped him and cut him."

"The evidence supported that?" Matt asked.

"Not right off. When we found Lester sleeping in the alley behind a bar the next morning, only blood on him was his own, from a fist fight he had with a couple of cowboys."

"You have a forensic lab in town?"

"Naw. Sheriff came in from the county seat and had the boys from his lab take the samples, real official like. Now, you cut a man's throat, Mr. Bonner, you wear his blood. Those lab boys couldn't find a trace of Kyle's blood on Lester. So there it was. We had no knife. We had no bloody clothes. That boy was just as crafty as a coyote in covering his tracks."

"What did he say?"

"He said he was in that bar when Kyle got it."

"But you didn't believe him."

"Nobody in that bar could say when Lester came in that night. Way I figure, Lester cut Kyle and then lit out the back of the house when the neighbors come running to investigate the shooting. I figure he washed off in the creek, changed clothes, hid the bloody ones where we'd never find them and went to pick a fight with a couple of cowboys in a bar so's he could get that alibi of his."

"What happened to Lester?"

"I kept him in jail until the forensic reports came back. Then I had to let him loose."

"Where did he go?"

"San Angelo. He knew better than to stay around this town. Feelings were running pretty high. Folks were talking about lynching him, proof or no proof."

"You said you did find evidence later?"

"Three months later a couple of kids came across the knife buried in the creek mud, right near where Lester had been camping. Lab boys said it had Kyle's blood on it all right. Lester had sunk it in that mud to hide it. Trouble was by then Lester was long gone. Damn, if this town didn't blame me for it, too. But, hell, I couldn't keep him in jail until I could find some proof. Law don't work that way."

"Did you ever catch up with Lester?"

"Naw. He got himself killed in a holdup a year later. The way most folks figure it, though, justice got done."

"We've strayed from the subject of the Lagarrigues, Deputy Plotnik," Jamie said.

"It probably seems that way, ma'am," Plotnik said, "but it does all tie in with the Lagarrigues."

"How's that?" Matt asked.

"Well, the murder was why they left. No more than a day or so later, old Oscar come to see me and said he wasn't going to be staying in town no more. This whole thing about Kyle getting killed had spooked his wife good. And if truth be told, it appeared to me as though it had spooked Oscar good, too."

"He was afraid?" Jamie asked.

"Couldn't blame him none, ma'am. He was one of them neighbors who heard Kyle's shotgun and come running. Got to Kyle's place right after Old Man Sistern and his son, Judd. Judd runs the town's newspaper. So he was right glad to be on the scene so soon. But not poor Lagarrigue. Not a nice thing to see, a man's throat cut. Particularly when you ain't born with a strong Texas stomach."

"Where did the Lagarrigues go when they left here?" Matt asked.

"Back east, I reckon. Yeah, now as I recall Oscar did mention something about his company arranging for him to take a desk job."

"What was the name of the insurance company he worked for?" Matt asked.

"He never told me. I had to charge them a full month's rent, but they didn't squawk none. His wife even thanked me, she was so scared. Her face weren't much to look at, but she had real pretty red hair and she were real polite."

"Do you remember her name?"

"Gotta have it around here some place."

Deputy Plotnik turned his chair around and rummaged through a two-drawer file cabinet with Real Estate written on a three-by-five card in front of it. After a minute he pulled out a manila folder and turned back to plop it on his desk. He opened the folder and shifted through its contents. Matt was aware Jamie was giving them a once-over from her vantage point. He was studying them, too.

"Yep, here it is. Oscar and Erline. Tony was their boy. No pets. No trouble. Left the place real clean. No forwarding address."

"Did they pay by check?" Matt asked.

"Nope. Cash." Plotnik closed the folder. "Sorry I can't be of more help, folks."

Matt thanked Deputy Plotnik, and he and Jamie left. As soon as they were back in the car, he started up the engine and put on the air conditioner. After a breath or two of somewhat cleaner air, he turned to Jamie.

"It would have been helpful if you had told me that you intended to hide the fact that you come from this town," he said.

"I wasn't thinking about your having to introduce me, Matt. I realize now I should have, but I wasn't."

"Is it just the deputy that you plan to keep in the dark?"

"I'd prefer everyone we talk to here knows me simply as Mrs. Bonner. I'm not telling a lie. My name still is Mrs. Bonner, if I care to use it."

"You told Plotnik a lie when you said that relatives in Louisiana were looking for the Lagarrigues."

"I didn't actually say they were looking for them. If you'll recall, I said the Louisiana Lagarrigues didn't know the Texas ones existed. And that's true."

"Why the subterfuge? Why don't you want these folks to know who you are?"

"I wasn't even the person the people in this town thought I was fifteen years ago. Reminding them of that inaccurate memory wouldn't help them to see me as who I am today."

"Someone's bound to recognize you sooner or later."

Her laugh surprised him. "No. I seriously doubt that. Deputy Plotnik saw a lot of me during that time. You were just a witness to the fact that he didn't recognize me, despite his brag about knowing everyone who's been in or out of this town."

"Did you have plastic surgery?"

"No, something far more effective and life altering."

"And what would that be?"

She turned to smile at him. "The freedom to be who I am."

Her blue eyes held a lovely light when she said those words.

"Why didn't you tell me about the murder?" he asked.

She looked away from him, straight out the windshield. The frown returned in full force to her brow.

"It didn't have anything to do with Tony. There was no reason to."

"It was the reason the Lagarrigues left town."

"I didn't know that until Deputy Plotnik told us just now."

"The murder happened on that night he took you to the dance, didn't it?"

"Yes."

"What was the reason Tony gave you for leaving town?"

"He didn't. A few days later he was just…gone."

Matt studied her lovely face, once again seeing that unmistakable haunted look in her eyes that appeared whenever she talked about Tony leaving.

Damn it. How good could one kiss have been? Or had it been more than just one kiss?

Matt gunned the engine and pulled away from the curb, more than disturbed by the rushing train of that thought.

"Where's the newspaper office?"

"It's next to the post office. Why?"

"I want to read about what was going on in the town during the time the Lagarrigues were here. And I'd also like to talk to Old Man Sistern and his son, Judd."

"I told you the murder has nothing to do with finding Tony."

"Oscar Lagarrigue moved his family out of town because of it. At least, the murder was the reason he gave."

"You say that as though you think there was another reason."

"Jamie, doesn't it seem peculiar that Deputy Plotnik didn't know what insurance company Oscar Lagarrigue worked for?"

"Not particularly. Why?"

"Ask yourself this. If you were a life-insurance salesman, who would you be pitching your product to?"

"Just about anyone I met, I suppose. Oh, I see. You're thinking that Oscar should have tried to sell Deputy Plotnik some life insurance. What makes you so sure he didn't?"

"Because Plotnik said Oscar didn't even mention his company's name. The first thing a life-insurance salesman does is tout the reliable reputation of the company he represents. The next thing he does is hand you his card."

"So why didn't Oscar Lagarrigue try to sell Deputy Plotnik some life insurance?"

"That's what I'm wondering about. Now, where's the newspaper office?"

"It's three blocks down and two over. I'll show you where to turn."

Matt opened the door to the newspaper office for Jamie a few minutes later. They stepped into the large window-lit room to find it contained an old-fashioned printing press and a short, chubby, mustached man whom they had interrupted setting type by hand. He was dark, in his late forties. He looked up at them with unabashed interest.

"Something I can help you folks with?" he asked, wiping his hands on his black apron.

Matt introduced Jamie as Mrs. Bonner and then handed the newspaperman his card.

"Well, well," he said. "A San Antonio private investigator." He held out an ink-stained hand and Matt shook it. "I'm Judd Sistern, Mr. Bonner, editor of the *Sweetspring Star*. She's not big-time, but she's all mine."

"Mr. Sistern—" Matt began, after releasing his hand.

"Now you just call me Judd. Everybody does. So, what's a big city P.I. doing here in Sweetspring?"

"We'd like to look through your editions of the paper from fifteen years back."

"I should've known. Even after all this time, folks are still interested in that murder."

"I'd also like to see the papers from about six weeks before it happened."

"Now why would you be interested in them?" Judd asked.

"Just to help me get a flavor for the town happenings before the murder."

"Wasn't much. Just births and deaths and town meetings to complain about this and that. But you're welcome to judge for yourself. Come on into the back and I'll pull out the roll."

Matt and Jamie followed Judd into the back room. He stopped in front of a long, deep closet.

"I know a lot about this murder. My daddy and me were the ones who found Kyle Kleinman."

"Why don't you tell us about it," Matt said, knowing the newspaperman was just waiting for an invitation.

Judd leaned his back against the closet door. He crossed his arms and looked like he was settling in for a spell.

"Well, it was like this. We were watching television when we heard the shotgun. It was so loud we knew right away it had to be coming from Kyle's place."

"How far away did you live?"

"Next door. We went right on over to check it out. I thought at first Kyle had shot himself."

Judd stopped to heave his chest and shake his head sadly.

"There was so much blood it was hard to know what had happened. And Kyle was lying on his stomach in it."

"When did you realize the wound wasn't self-inflicted?"

"When Daddy and I turned Kyle over on his back and saw the gash in his neck. Daddy's retired now, but he was still doing most of the doctoring in town then. He tried to stop the bleeding. Wasn't any use."

"You both touched the body?"

"Had to. Kyle was six-two and at least 240 pounds. Daddy could never have handled him by himself."

"I see."

"Anyway, when I straightened up was when I saw the open window and the bag near it. Right then I knew this was going to be a whole different shooting match. Daddy was still working on Kyle, so I started toward the phone to call Deputy Plotnik. Then one of the neighbors up the block came in all out of breath asking what the shooting was all about."

"Who was it?" Matt asked, as though he didn't know.

"Oscar Lagarrigue."

"Did you know this Oscar Lagarrigue well?"

"Naw. He and his family had only moved in a few weeks before. He sold insurance. Real timid sort."

"Yet he came to investigate a shotgun blast," Matt said.

"It was his wife who sent Oscar to investigate the shooting. On his own, I doubt he would have done it. As it was, old Oscar took one look at Kyle lying there in all that blood and he passed out cold."

"Mr. Lagarrigue fainted?" Jamie asked.

"Yes, ma'am. Dead away. I dragged him out and waited with him a minute or so until he came to, just to be sure he was all right. Then I sent him on home to his wife, went back inside and called Plotnik."

"No one else showed up in response to the shotgun blast?"

"Not right off. They were having a to-do over at the school. Most of the neighborhood was there dancing up a storm to a live band while pretending to chaperon the kids. Unless someone was outside of that auditorium, he wouldn't even have heard the shotgun. Deputy Plotnik went over there about an hour later to tell Kyle's wife and son the news. Sad thing, that."

"Was there anything you saw that night that didn't make it into the newspaper, Judd?" Matt asked.

"Well, I never told my readers that Lagarrigue had passed out. Figured it would have embarrassed him. Needn't have worried. He moved his family out real quick. The rest of what I saw and Deputy Plotnik's investigation is all written up in detail. I reckon you heard it was Lester Wilson who did it?''

"Did he?" Matt asked.

"No doubt in my mind," Judd said. "No doubt in the minds of any of the folks here in town, either. Sold out every paper that came off the press about that business."

"Did you get some out-of-town competition when the news hit?" Matt asked.

"Several reporters drove into town interviewing folks and taking pictures and all."

"How about national coverage?" Matt asked.

"Oh, sure. Made the wire services. But it was a one-time shot for them. Sixty-second blurb and they were onto something else. Only the *Sweetspring Star* carried the story right on through to the end."

"So even though no one was ever caught and tried for the murder, you still believe it had an end?" Matt asked.

"The day Lester Wilson got his due in that shoot-out put it to rest in the minds of most folks here in town. Except for Wrey Kleinman. He ain't never going to forget that Lester Wilson died before he got a piece of him."

"Did Lagarrigue ever try to sell you life insurance, Judd?"

"Well, now, that's a mighty strange thing to ask."

"Is it? I thought he was an insurance salesman."

"Well, yeah, he was. But he never tried to sell me any insurance. Oscar was a quiet, polite kind of man, not at all pushy about poking into folks' personal finances and such. Why you interested in Oscar?"

"Just background details. Being a newspaper reporter, I'm sure you understand what I mean."

"Yeah," Judd said, trying to sound knowledgeable, when it was clear to Matt that in reality Judd didn't have a clue as to what he meant.

Judd leaned away from the door and opened the closet. He rummaged through an interior full of what looked like large long rolling pins. He pulled out the one with the label 1982 on it. He laid it across a long wooden table in the back room and beckoned for Matt and Jamie to take a couple of the chairs.

Judd unraveled the editions of the four-page weekly newspaper that had been wrapped and stored on the long rolling pin.

"They're sequential, January on top," he said. "Help yourself. I have to get back to work. You need anything, just holler."

Matt thanked Judd and held out a chair for Jamie to take.

Together, they flipped through the yellowed weekly editions of the *Sweetspring Star*. Judd was right. Until the murder had come along, things had been pretty dull around town.

Matt found what he was looking for in the services column, two weeks before the murder.

Need Life Insurance?
Come see Oscar Lagarrigue
109 Kleinman Lane

He pointed it out to Jamie.

"Pretty uncreative ad," Jamie said. "Not at all enticing. He didn't even put in his telephone number. If someone wanted to buy from him, they had to go see him. How did he expect to sell insurance that way?"

"Interesting question. This is where the murder coverage starts."

Matt could sense Jamie's interest flagging. She sat back as he perused the stories of the murder, which took up all the space of every newspaper for four weeks straight.

He thought he understood. She was probably bored. He imagined she had gotten her fill of this murder fifteen years before, when she was a teenager in this town.

Most of the stories consisted of interviews with the locals.

It looked like anyone who had ever even talked to Lester Wilson had been asked to give his opinion. And none of those opinions had been favorable. It didn't take a rocket scientist to see that public opinion had clearly tried and convicted Lester Wilson long before the knife had made its appearance.

The only thing new Matt learned from looking at the newspapers was what was in the sack left by the interrupted burglar. They were antique rifles and guns—some of them one of a kind, all extremely valuable.

"They were the cream of my husband's collection," Mrs. Kleinman had been quoted as saying. "He had acquired some of them only six months before. It would have ripped the heart out of Kyle to have lost them."

So he fought for them and got his throat ripped out instead.

"You finished?" Jamie asked.

Matt realized that he'd been staring at the filing cabinet on the opposite wall, his mind absorbing and trying to make sense of what he had read. He turned to her.

"How well do you remember the murder?" he asked.

"Too well."

Her husky, even voice was at odds with the sudden look in her eyes. Matt began to realize that he had been wrong. She was not bored. This murder still affected her quite strongly.

"You knew the Kleinman family, of course?"

"Yes."

"Did you think Lester Wilson did it?"

Jamie exhaled a long breath. "Lester was violent. It certainly was the kind of thing he could do."

"You knew him?"

She rose. "Everybody knew everybody in this town. Can we go now?"

Matt rolled up the newspapers and returned the enormous rolling pin to the closet where Judd stored it. They retraced their steps to the front room of the newspaper office and thanked Judd for his help.

Matt was opening the car door for Jamie when he asked his next question. "Where's the junior high?"

"Combined with the high school on the street behind

Kleinman Lane. But you can't get to it from Kleinman Lane
because it dead ends into the big Victorian.''

"The Kleinman house. Where Kyle Kleinman was killed.''

"Yes.''

"Did anyone at the dance that night hear the shotgun?''

"It's like Judd Sistern said,'' Jamie answered. "If you
were inside the auditorium, you couldn't have heard over the
music.''

Matt followed Jamie's directions and found himself in front
of an old wood-slatted two-story building set back twenty feet
from the street by a thirsty brown lawn.

"That's the auditorium where the dance was held that
night?'' he asked pointing to the two-story building on the
far right.

"Yes. The administration office is in the building to the
left, second floor up those stairs,'' Jamie said. "I'll wait for
you here.''

"You're not coming in?''

"No.''

"Why?''

"Because you don't need me to ask questions about Tony.
I might even prove a hindrance to that smooth Texas charm
of yours, seeing as how this school has always been run by
women.''

Matt saw her words were accompanied by a smile. She had
meant her comment as a compliment. But the smile didn't
reach her eyes this time. There was another emotion there
that blocked out all others. It accompanied that now familiar
frown that had settled in from the moment they drove into
Sweetspring.

"I could be a while.''

"It's all right.''

Matt turned off the engine and got out of the car. Just
before he entered the school building, he looked back at Jamie. He noticed the frown was still on her brow.

She had kept the windows rolled up despite the pleasant
warmth of the day. Matt supposed that if a body lived in

Sweetspring long enough, the feedlot smell would just become part of the background.

Except Jamie never seemed to have gotten used to it. She said the first fresh air she had was the day she left. Unless she was speaking metaphorically. What was it about this town that bothered her so much? What had happened to her here?

In a way he was glad she had decided not to come with him. Now he could ask a few questions that he wouldn't have been able to had she been along.

Matt approached the counter. It was unmanned. At a desk in a far corner sat a thin, thirtyish, dark-haired woman chewing voraciously on some gum. She had her shoes off and was painting her toenails bright red to match her fingernails and lipstick. Her shoulder-length earrings bobbed as she listened to some music through the earphones over her head.

"Excuse me, ma'am," Matt said, waving to try to get her attention.

She looked up wearing a bored expression. But as soon as she saw Matt, her eyes went wide. She recapped her nail polish, and set it quickly on her desk. Matt could see the gum she was hastily swallowing traverse down her thin neck.

"Lordy, I don't believe it. You're Matt Bonner, that guy on 'Finder of Lost Loves'!"

Matt smiled at her, happy not to have to go through introductions. "Yes, ma'am."

She scooted out of her chair and bounded barefooted, toes up, toward the counter. Her bony hand shot across it for a shake. Matt obliged by taking it.

"Etta Oates Kleinman. But everyone just calls me Etta. I'm the assistant principal. You come about Tony Lagarrigue now, haven't you?"

"Yes, ma'am. I assume you watched the show?"

Matt was doing his best to retrieve his hand. It was a challenge. Etta's hold was more like a death grip.

"Never miss it, Mr. Bonner. Never, never, never. Soon as I saw Tony's picture, I elbowed Wrey—he's my husband—

and I says, 'Honey, there's that foreign boy who was in school with us, remember?'"

"Foreign?"

"Well, he weren't from Texas now, was he? Anyway, Wrey said he didn't remember him. That's probably because Wrey's a year older. But I was in the same class with Tony fifteen years ago. Yep, I remember him real well."

Matt finally reclaimed his hand. "I could use your help in trying to find Tony."

"Mine? But I would've called ya if I knew anything. The thing is that Tony wasn't in this town all that long."

"But you were in his class. Surely you talked to him?"

"All the girls did. He was the best-looking thing to ever come to Sweetspring, I can tell ya. He weren't backward like the other boys, neither. He could talk so fine like."

"Did he say where he was from?"

"Just back east somewhere is all I recall."

"Would you still have his records from fifteen years ago?"

"I reckon. We never throw out anything here."

"I'd like to take a look at his transcripts."

Etta looked behind her and then scooted closer, lowering her voice.

"Now, Mr. Bonner, as ya probably already know, these are confidential records I got here. I'm not supposed to show them to anyone outside of the school system."

No, she wasn't supposed to, but Matt could see that she was just dying to. "You can trust me," he said in his most confidential tone.

Etta leaned toward him and smiled seductively. "My mama always told me never to trust a man."

Matt didn't like this change of direction the conversation was taking. Etta was apparently one of those insecure women who had to give every man she met a come-on to reassure herself she was attractive.

He reminded himself he needed Etta's assistance and forced a smile to his lips. "Your mama was right."

Her laugh was harsh and grated on Matt's ears.

"You just give me a minute, honey," she said as she turned and swiveled her bony hips out of the room.

Etta was good to her word. She was back just a minute later with a green folder in her thin hand. She slipped it across the counter to Matt as though it were the secret formula to a new doomsday weapon.

The telephone on her desk rang. She scurried over to answer it. Matt quickly surveyed the contents of the file. There wasn't much.

In the three weeks' time that Tony had been a student at Sweetspring High, he had earned an A in math, English, geography and history, and a B in sociology and physical education.

Matt's eyes then focused on the transcript that had been sent from the Saint Tammany Parish public-school system in Louisiana for Anthony Mercedes Lagarrigue, born December 3, 1967. The home address in Louisiana matched that of the Erline Lagarrigue he and Jamie had spoken to the day before. Tony had received all his required immunizations.

At the Louisiana school, Tony had earned C's in all his academic subjects and an A in physical education.

Matt looked up to see Etta was hanging up the phone.

"Is this the entire file?" he asked.

"Yep."

"If a request came in for a transcript to be sent to Tony's new school, would that request be shown in this file?"

"Well, sure. Any time a copy is made of a student's file, it has to be noted where it was sent. That's one of our rules."

"Then why isn't there a notation of a request from Tony's next school?" Matt asked.

Etta returned to the counter to look at the file. "Well, now, that's right strange. Somebody must of screwed up. They should have written it down and kept a copy of the request right here in this file."

"Could it have been filed somewhere else?" Matt asked.

"Nope. Right here in this file. Nowhere else."

"I see."

"Now is there anything else I can take care of for ya this morning, honey?"

Etta's suggestive voice and smile left no doubt what she was offering.

"Matter of fact there is," Matt said. "You must remember a girl by the name of Jamie in your class?"

"You can't be talking about Jamie Lee Lamay?"

"Yes, that's her."

Etta's smile slid off her face real fast. "Hold on a minute here. Am I getting this right? Are ya telling me *hers* was the face you ran next to his? *She's* the Jamie looking for Tony?"

"You seem surprised." Actually Etta seemed more than surprised. She seemed downright astounded.

"But it didn't look anything like her!"

"Folks do change. Was your class pictured in a yearbook that you can show me?"

Etta snatched Tony Lagarrigue's file off the counter and clutched it to her bosom. She glared at Matt, all vestiges of flirty friendliness gone from her sharp features.

"Ya not getting one blessed thing more out of me. If I'd known ya was working for Jamie Lee Lamay, I never would have let ya see anything."

"Why is that?"

"I got nothing more to say to ya, Mr. Bonner. Now ya just get on out of here before I call the deputy and have him throw ya out."

Matt knew of no appropriate exit line he could offer a woman with the kind of lemon-sucking look that Etta Kleinman wore.

He made a quick retreat. When he stepped outside the administration office and closed the door behind him, he glanced back through the window. He saw Etta making for the telephone on her desk, Tony's file still clutched to her bosom. She was in an all-fired hurry to call someone. He wondered who.

Actually, he was wondering a lot of things at that moment. As perplexing as the information he'd gotten on Tony was, the reaction he'd just gotten from Etta at the mention of Jamie's name was even more perplexing.

And he meant to get unperplexed real quick.

As Jamie sat in the car by herself, she kept fighting the flashes from the past. They'd come on her the second Matt had driven into Sweetspring. And each one reminded her of all the reasons she had vowed never to return.

She looked over at Matt as he slipped into the driver's seat. The slight frown on that bold brow told her something was up. He didn't start the engine, but turned to face her.

"Did you find out where Tony went from here?" she asked.

"Before we talk about that, I want you to tell me why the mention of your name to an assistant principal just managed to get me thrown out of the administration office."

Jamie felt the irritation rising inside her. "Why did you mention my name? I told you I didn't want anyone to know I was here."

"No, what you told me was that you didn't want anyone to know who you were. And I didn't tell her you were here. I just mentioned your name."

"To whom?"

"Etta Oates Kleinman."

"Etta Oates Kleinman?" Jamie repeated. "So she married Wrey. Well, I can't say as I'm surprised. They were always two of a kind."

"You didn't answer my question," Matt said.

"I would think the answer is pretty obvious, Matt. Etta doesn't like me. Matter of fact, I don't think you'd find a soul in town who would react kindly to hearing my name."

"Why?"

"Let's just say I had the wrong roots for the folks in Sweetspring."

"You mean because you lived with a foster family?"

"Something like that," Jamie said, her attention riveted on the window of the administration office. Even from this distance, she recognized the sharp features of one of her chief tormentors from fifteen years before. Etta stood at the window staring at the car. Anger suffused her face as she gestured and jabbered away on the telephone stuck in her ear.

"Matt, are you sure you didn't tell Etta I was with you?"

"I'm sure."

"Well, she's figured it out. She's staring at us from the window of the administration building."

Matt turned around to look.

"No doubt she's alerted the whole town by now," Jamie said. "Can we go?"

Matt turned back to her. He wore his sober no-nonsense expression. "Why? Are they likely to come tar and feather you?"

"I suppose you mean that to be funny. Just my luck you picked now to develop a sense of humor. Is there anything else in town you wanted to see?"

Matt started the car. "No, I suppose not. We'll stop at the café, have some lunch and be on our way."

"The café in town? No, thank you. I'd rather eat someplace else."

"Where?"

"About a hundred miles from here."

"It's a long drive to the next town," Matt said. "Let's at least stop off at a grocery store and pick up a couple of cold drinks."

Jamie nodded. As she showed Matt the way, the images kept coming. How she used to walk with her back bowed, her head down. Trying not to call attention to herself. Before the murder, she had only the two in the trailer to avoid. Afterward, the list had expanded considerably. She remembered hurrying up and down these streets. She had always been hurrying in those days—running as fast as she could to grow up.

So she could get away and get control over her life.

And here she was again, letting these memories be her life. She was angry at Matt for making her come here. And she was angry at herself for letting these memories take over. What was it going to take to release their hold on her once and for all?

Jamie automatically directed Matt to a small grocery store that she had always gone to as a youngster. It was on the other side of town, a full ten-minute walk out of her way home from school.

But the old woman who owned it didn't speak English, so she wasn't in on the town gossip. Jamie had been safe there.

It was hot in the little store, much as she remembered it being. The little old woman was nowhere in sight. A teenager sat behind the cash register, dressed in shorts and a tank top, her feet bare. She was leafing through a fashion magazine.

"Help you?" she asked, with no enthusiasm and no Spanish accent.

"Just a couple of cold drinks," Matt said.

"Co-cola's out back in the freezer," the teenager said. "Compressor got too noisy to keep in the store."

Matt went out the back door looking for the freezer.

Jamie's eyes lingered on the chocolate candy. She remembered the countless times she had stood in this exact same spot and looked at them. The grocery lists she'd been given each week had never included a chocolate treat for her.

Jamie had a sudden impulse to splurge. She was just reaching into her handbag to pull out some change when she heard some heavy boots stomping into the store behind her.

"Jamie Lee!"

Jamie whirled around in surprise at the sound of her name being yelled. The big man who yelled it stood like a windbag of bad news in the doorway of the little store.

He had a prominent beer belly and his nose was red and bulbous. His dark hair was a matted mess and his triple chins needed a shave. His shirt and jeans were filthy and he smelled of things that should be buried. The sneer line he once had to add consciously to his mouth was now a permanent fixture.

It had been a lot of years since she'd seen him. But she would have known him anywhere.

Wrey Kleinman.

Wrey was looking her up and down as though he couldn't believe his eyes. Jamie knew why. She was no longer that scared little fifteen-year-old who bowed her shoulders and kept her head down and wore ragged, scratchy clothes and butchered hair.

When Jamie thought of the mean-spirited, ultrafastidious Etta Oates tied to this coarse, dirty man for life, she knew that there was such a thing as justice in the world.

It was that knowledge that had Jamie standing straight and tall and confident and smiling.

Wrey Kleinman knew Jamie wasn't smiling at him. The acknowledgment entered his facial features, blurred by fatty flesh, and balled the hands at his sides.

"Damn, it is you! You got some gall coming back here!"

Jamie felt every one of her muscles automatically tensing. When she was fifteen, they would have been preparing her to run. And run fast.

But the day she left Sweetspring she had promised herself that no one would ever brutalize her again. If she ran now, she would be letting it happen. She wasn't going to let it happen.

Jamie stood her ground, calmly preparing herself. She replayed every self-defense move she had learned. She visualized kicking Wrey in the shin and groin. Slamming his nose with the heel of her palm. Even reaching for one of the beer bottles on the counter and breaking it over his head.

She'd do every one of these things if he dared to touch her. Adrenaline percolated through her, washing away the memories of fear, changing her as she faced him.

Wrey must have read those confident feelings in her face.

She saw the surprise enter his eyes. He was hesitating, clearly uncertain as to what to do next. And then something new entered his eyes, something Jamie could have sworn looked almost like fear.

In her preoccupation with facing down Wrey, she had almost forgotten Matt was with her. She hadn't heard him reenter the store. Suddenly, she simply felt him at her side.

"Someone you want to introduce to me, Jamie?" Matt asked evenly.

Jamie purposely turned her back on Wrey to look at Matt. "He's no one important. Did you get the cold drinks?"

Matt lifted up a can in each hand. But Jamie noticed that even as he did so, he didn't take his eyes off Wrey.

"How much?" Jamie asked, turning to the clerk.

The clerk was staring at Jamie wide-eyed. Her eyes darted to Wrey and Matt. Wrey probably was carrying around at least 250 pounds of flab on his six-four frame. He no doubt outweighed Matt.

But Matt had two inches on him, and he was packing solid muscle, not fat. Jamie knew neither of those facts was escaping Wrey's attention.

"Will a dollar do it?" Jamie asked the clerk calmly.

She nodded mutely.

Jamie reached into her billfold. She heard Wrey's boots stomp out the door and smiled to herself. She suddenly had no desire to get the candy. The impulse to fill a craving from the past had just walked out the door.

The clerk rang up her purchase. "That's the first time I ever saw old Wrey get that angry and retreat. Who's your friend?"

Jamie glanced over at Matt, who was standing calmly in the aisle of the dark, hot store looking as big and solid and deadly cool as a mountain lion. Her insides tingled.

She turned back to the clerk and smiled. "He's kin."

"Sure wish I had some kin like him. What's Wrey angry at you for? You're a stranger."

"Well, you know Wrey. It doesn't take much to rile him up."

"Ain't that the truth. He come on to you, didn't he? And you turned him down."

"He comes on to a lot of women, does he?"

"All the time. Thinks cause he owns the feedlot he owns

everyone in this town. He's just a bully, always out looking for a fight.''

Jamie smiled at the clerk. Well, at least some of the folks of Sweetspring seemed to be getting wised up when it came to Wrey Kleinman. Not that they would probably end up doing anything about it. Excuses always got made for rich men like Wrey in small towns like Sweetspring.

"I have to be going now," Jamie said. "Much obliged."

"You take care now. And come back real soon, hear?"

*Next cold day in hell,* Jamie thought. But she sent the clerk a smile and wave as she and Matt headed for the door.

Jamie was blinded as she and Matt stepped out into the bright sunshine after being inside the dark store. Which is why she had no forewarning of the danger.

By the time she knew what was happening, she was already in the dust and it was way too late for her to do anything about it.

# Chapter Seven

Matt sensed the shadow bearing down from the left even before he saw the tire iron in Wrey's right arm. He dropped the cold drinks in his hands at the same instant he pushed Jamie out of harm's way. The tire iron connected hard with his left shoulder, the force of the blow vibrating through Matt's bones.

Matt swung around, grabbed Wrey's arm and wrenched the tire iron from his grasp. Then he threw him facedown into the dirt and pulled his arm up hard behind his back.

Wrey let out with a sewer stream of curses. Matt dug his knee into Wrey's kidney. Wrey howled.

"There's a lady present, Mr. Kleinman," Matt said evenly. "You will kindly watch your language."

"She's no lady, she's—"

Matt dug his knee into Wrey's kidney a little harder. Wrey howled even louder.

"And speak only when you are spoken to," Matt said.

Matt kept a tight hold on Wrey as he looked up at Jamie. She was standing no more than five feet away, her face white, her eyes huge. Her beautiful suit dress was soiled. He knew she'd landed in the dust when he'd pushed her, trying to get her out of harm's way.

"Are you all right?" he asked.

She nodded. She appeared composed, but he didn't miss the excessive brightness of her eyes.

"Jamie, why don't you make yourself comfortable in the car for a few minutes," Matt said, careful to keep his voice even and conversational.

"What are you going to do?"

"Mr. Kleinman and I have some things to discuss."

Jamie didn't say anything. She just looked from Matt's face to Wrey's beet-red one in the dust and then back to Matt's. And then she did two things that Matt didn't expect at all.

One, she smiled. And two, she turned toward the car.

Matt felt more than relieved by that smile. It assured him like nothing else that she was okay. He was also rather relieved by her compliance with his request. It came at a time when he didn't need an argument, and she hadn't given him one.

As soon as she was safely inside the car, Matt got off Wrey and pulled him to his feet. He kept the man's arm behind his back and steered him toward the side of the store. They walked all the way around to the back near the loud compressor running the big freezer where Matt had gotten the cold drinks earlier.

Matt took a look around. This was a sparsely populated side of town. This time of day, no one was about. What with the rickety fence all around and the noise of the compressor, not a whole lot could be seen or heard.

"Now this is how it is going to go," Matt said to Wrey. "If you mind your manners and answer my questions real nice like, I'm going to let you walk again sometime soon. You'd like that, wouldn't you?"

Wrey called Matt a foul name in response. Matt twisted Wrey's arm. He howled.

"You don't learn real quick like, do you, Wrey? Good thing I'm a patient man and you got so many bones in your body."

Jamie waited in the car. It was getting uncomfortably warm. The only thing that saved her was the fact that the car was parked facing away from the direct rays of the sun.

She took off her suit jacket and brushed off the dust she'd

tumbled into when Matt shoved her aside to protect her from Wrey's attack. And found her hands were shaking.

She knew it was a reaction to the fight. Watching Matt move against that savage attack by Wrey had been one of the scariest experiences of her life. His lightning reflexes had subdued that bully and had his nasty red face in the dust even before she'd gotten to her feet.

She had grown up a victim of violence; had learned to defend herself as an adult, to try to wipe away the childhood memories of the fear it had bred. But she had never had someone stand up for her like that. The impact of what Matt had done was still unfolding new feelings inside her.

She checked her watch. Matt had been gone five minutes. She'd witnessed how well he could handle himself. She shouldn't be worried. But she was. If something happened to him now...

She was just reaching for the door handle when Matt came strolling out of the store. He was alone, carrying two new cans of cold drinks, looking just as cool and composed as always. Her heart did a happy, little leap.

Matt opened the car door. She didn't know how to thank him for what he'd done. She didn't have the words.

"I'm glad you're back," was all she could think to say.

"Hold these a moment, Jamie."

Jamie took the drinks he placed in her hands. "Where are you going?"

"Just over there. Be back soon."

Just over there proved to be a big red Range Rover with a personalized license plate that read "Wrey."

As Jamie watched, Matt fiddled inside the cab for a minute or two and then returned to the Cadillac and got in. He started the engine and backed out to turn onto the road leading out of town. During the entire time, Jamie didn't see Wrey make an appearance.

"What happened?" she asked, unable to keep the curiosity down any longer.

"Let's just say we fell into a vigorous discussion from which he won't be recovering anytime soon."

Jamie grinned.

"He told me Lester Wilson was your brother. Is it true?"

Jamie's grin overturned. Dear Lord, here it was. Again. She took a deep breath and let it out slowly, soundlessly. "Yes."

"Damn it, Jamie, you could have told me Lester was a member of the foster family who took you in. I couldn't have been less prepared to face this town if I had rode in backward."

"This is not something that's easy for me to talk about."

Matt's eyes darted in her direction. His voice instantly gentled. "Jamie, I'm not going to repeat what you tell me. You can trust me."

Yes, she could. She knew that now. Slowly, in a voice whose volume was no more substantial than feathers blowing in the air, she found herself relating Wrey's terror campaign against her in the long year and a half that followed the finding of Lester's knife and led to the day she left Sweetspring. When she got to the part when Wrey threw her into the mud and sat on her, she saw Matt's hands tighten on the wheel.

"Where were your foster mama and daddy?"

"They weren't welcome in town, so they didn't come into it. But I had to go to school, so he targeted me."

"Couldn't you turn to someone for help?" Matt asked.

"There wasn't anyone willing to stand up to Wrey. Everybody felt sorry for the boy who'd lost his daddy. 'Course, they knew he was inheriting the feedlot, which meant he was rich and a major employer. And I was, well, I was just…"

"Part of some trash down the road a piece," Matt quoted Deputy Plotnik's words when her sentence trailed off.

Jamie heard an amazingly earthy oath come out of Matt's mouth followed by Plotnik's name. But the one that preceded Kleinman's name both shocked her ears and warmed her heart.

Matt apologized for his language as he popped open his

soft drink. They zoomed past the Welcome to Sweetspring sign. He raised his hand in a mock toast.

"Good riddance," he said.

Jamie clicked her can with his and smiled.

She was no longer upset that he had made her come to Sweetspring. As a matter of fact, she was glad.

She had finally faced Wrey and not let him intimidate her. For the first time in her life, Jamie knew that the emotional hold of those long-ago memories of fear had been broken.

She popped open her can and enjoyed the cold, frosty root beer as a heart-roping Texas ballad played on the radio.

"So where did Tony go when he left Sweetspring?" she asked a little later as she stored their empty drink cans in the litter basket in the back seat.

Matt told her about Tony's school transcript from Louisiana and the fact that no new transcript request had come through.

"I don't understand," Jamie said. "Where would Tony have gone that he didn't need a new transcript?"

"I don't think that should be the first question we ask," Matt said.

"What question would you ask?"

"Whether or not the boy you met was even Tony Lagarrigue."

Jamie turned to stare at him. "Run that one by me again?"

"The transcript from Louisiana was for the Tony who never left the Saint Tammany Parish. His birthdate, his address, his folks' names—they all match. But we've met Erline Lagarrigue and seen a picture of her husband and her Tony."

"And they're not the Lagarrigues who were here in Sweetspring," Jamie said, nodding. "So you're saying that Tony and his mama and daddy borrowed the Louisiana Lagarrigues' names and identities?"

"Yes."

"That doesn't make any sense at all. Why would they do something like that?"

"I can think of several reasons. Most folks assume another identity because they are fixin' on escaping the law."

"No, Matt. They weren't that kind of folks. I met them, remember?"

"Did you think they were the kind of folks to take another family's name and pass themselves off as that family?"

"Well, no. But I don't see that they harmed anyone, and I'm sure there must be a reasonable explanation."

"You're right quick to come to their defense. You only met Erline and Oscar once. How can you be so sure?"

"Because I'm sure of Tony. You will be, too, when you find him for me."

The blast of a big eighteen-wheeler behind them drowned out Matt's response.

"What?" Jamie asked.

Matt was looking in his rearview mirror as he pulled over to the right. "The driver of that truck behind us is apparently in an all-fired hurry to get somewhere."

Jamie looked over her shoulder. The huge tractor-trailer rig was right behind them. Its horn blasted again in her ears.

"Could it be his brakes have given out?" Jamie asked.

"We're on a slight upgrade. If he lost his brakes, he'd be slowing down, not picking up speed. Besides, there are no cars coming in the other direction. He could pass using that lane."

"Then what in the hell is he doing?"

The horn blasted again, just as the truck whacked the bumper of the Cadillac. Jamie pitched forward. Her spine went rigid and she gripped the door handle and held on.

The Cadillac lurched as Matt floored the accelerator. Jamie looked at the speedometer. It was pointing past a hundred. Her heart was racing with it. The road ahead was clear, but even on this country road, they were bound to be moving up on some car soon.

And then what? She looked over at Matt. He had both hands on the wheel. That telltale pulse throbbed in his set jaw.

"Can you take a side road?" Jamie asked as one whizzed by.

"We'll flip if I turn the wheel at this speed." Despite the danger of their situation, his voice was wonderfully calm. Jamie instantly felt steadied by it.

The eighteen-wheeler whacked the bumper of the Cadillac once more.

"Looks like I should have gotten that tank," Matt said. "Jamie, open up the center console and get out my gun."

"Gun?"

"We don't have much time, Jamie."

Jamie told herself she shouldn't be surprised to learn that Matt carried a gun with him. He was a private investigator after all. She opened the console and pulled out the serious-looking .38 she found there.

"Now what?" she asked.

"Now I'm going to open the sunroof. I want you to get up there and shoot at that guy."

"You want me to shoot him?" Jamie repeated, shocked at Matt's words.

The horn blasted behind them again. Once again, Jamie's neck snapped forward, then back as the rig behind them whacked the bumper of the Cadillac.

"Don't shoot him, Jamie. Shoot *at* him. Aim carefully. Try to get a bullet through the passenger side. That should give him something to think about."

Matt's hand shot off the steering wheel and back again as he hit the button to open the sunroof. But even in that instant, Jamie felt the car careen slightly. She realized then that a side wind was buffeting the car quite strongly. It was probably taking all Matt's concentration and steady hands to keep the car on the road at this speed.

Jamie's hair instantly began to whirl around her head as the sunroof came open. The smell of dust and heat and exhaust assailed her nose. She heard the roar of the road and the unmuffled blast of the truck behind them. Her eardrums reverberated with the vibrations.

Jamie's pulse skittered as her sweaty hands slid back and forth over the cold steel of the gun.

Target practice had been one thing. But shooting in the direction of a person was another. Still, Jamie understood this was something she must do.

"I'm going to open her up, Jamie," Matt shouted over the roar of the road. "We should leave him behind long enough for you to get into position before he can catch up to bump us again. Ready?"

Jamie slipped off her high heels and steeled herself.

"Ready."

She felt the Cadillac leap forward with a new burst of speed. She didn't waste time looking at the speedometer. She unbuckled her seat belt and quickly straddled the console on her knees, facing the back of the car. She held the .38 firmly with both hands, just as Liz had taught her.

The wind blew her hair every which way. She ignored it as she focused on the big tractor-trailer rig. Matt's last burst of speed had left it several car lengths behind. But it was coming up again, and coming up fast.

"Wait until he's about a car length behind," Matt shouted over the roar of the road. "No longer."

Jamie rested her wrists on the opening of the sunroof to steady them. Her heart was pounding against her ribs like a sledgehammer. The eighteen-wheeler was coming closer, closer.

The black windshield of the red cab stared at her like the engorged pupils of an angry beast. It was almost on them. Another second or two and it would be ramming them again.

Only this time she wouldn't have a seat and shoulder belt to keep her from going through the windshield.

"You aim for that exact point you want the bullet to go, Jamie," she heard Liz's voice say inside her head. "Then you just start squeezing that trigger real slow and gentle like and let that critter go off when it's ready."

The loud blast of the gun and the kick from its recoil surprised Jamie. It surprised the driver of the eighteen-wheeler a lot more. Jamie couldn't tell for certain, but she was pretty sure she'd hit the windshield.

The big rig that had been just inches away a moment before dropped back so fast it appeared as though it had just stopped cold. She could see the smoke bursting out of the brake linings.

Relief flooded through her, making her feel as weak as water. She dropped back into her seat, her hands trembling as she replaced Matt's gun in the console.

"Nice shooting," he said. "Although you did call it a bit close."

Jamie looked over at Matt to see him smiling at her. She had no idea how good one of those wonderful half smiles of his could feel. Until now.

It lasted only a fraction of a second, though. His eyes were instantly back on the road.

"Jamie, buckle up. Quick."

There was a sudden, urgent note in Matt's voice that caught Jamie's attention immediately. She snapped her seat and shoulder belts into place as she felt the car decelerating rapidly.

"What is it?" Jamie asked at the same instant she saw the sign whiz by. *Deep bumps ahead—slow to 25 MPH.*

They were going way too fast and there simply was no time to slow down. Dread squeezed her stomach like a fist. She gripped the edge of the console and the handle on the passenger door and held on for dear life.

The first bump launched them into the air. They landed in the deep depression of another. Hard. Jamie felt one of the tires explode. Then another. Sparks flew out from underneath the chassis as the metal rims screeched over the blacktop. Then the car hit another bump, flipped off the road and turned over and over.

A big mushroom cloud pressed her back in the seat and swallowed her whole. She couldn't see. All she could hear was a deafening roar.

Then the air bag deflated and her view returned. The world

passed by as a great cloud of dust and breaking glass and tipping earth and sky. She'd never been a screamer, but at that moment she wanted to scream her lungs out. She might have, too, but she needed all the air in her body just to breathe.

And then the car whipped around and she hit her head on something and a deep, sweet blackness swallowed her whole.

WHEN THE CAR STOPPED pitching in the dust and settled, Matt unbuckled his seat and shoulder belts and reached for Jamie. She was slumped over on the passenger door, out cold. An icy knife stabbed him in the chest.

"Jamie?"

She didn't answer. He quickly released her from the restraints of her seat and shoulder belts and checked her pulse. It was steady. He couldn't figure out why she was unconscious until he noticed the skin on her right temple was abraded.

She had hit her head. She needed medical attention right away.

He had turned off the ignition the second they'd hit the first bump. He had no fear of the car catching fire. He reached for the cell phone and put through an emergency call.

When he knew help was on the way he tried to push open the driver's door, but the metal was too bent and compressed to yield. Every window in the car was a spider web of shattered glass. Matt repositioned himself in the driver's seat and kicked out the web over the driver's door. It fell away to the dust. A welcome breeze drifted in.

The car was a wreck. There was nothing to do now but wait until help arrived.

He drew Jamie's unconscious body into his arms. He rested her head on his shoulder and held her close to him to keep her warm and ward off the possibility of shock.

She had to be all right. He couldn't allow himself to think of the alternative. Unconsciously, he stroked her long hair, barely aware of its refined silk sifting through his roughened, calloused hands. Her face was white, so awfully white.

"Damn it, Jamie, wake up."

When she stirred in his arms, Matt's pulses took an incredible leap.

She opened hazy eyes and blinked up at him. "Matt? That you?"

Matt controlled the sigh of pure relief that was escaping from his lungs. "It's me. Jamie, how do you feel?"

She raised a hand to her temple and winced. "My head hurts some. Are you okay?"

"Getting better by the second. Help is on the way."

She still looked dazed. "Help? What kind of help?"

"Someone to get us out of here and take a look at you."

Her eyes were beginning to focus. Her head turned as she took in the shattered glass, the deflated air bags, the bent metal of the car's frame impinging on them.

He felt her small shudder. "That was some ride. I sure wouldn't want to be you when you explain the condition of this car to an insurance adjuster."

He smiled. She started to pull herself up and swayed. He gently eased her back into the cradle of his arm.

"You'd best stay put for a spell."

She sighed. "Maybe I'd best." She relaxed against him, nestling in closer. Matt could feel the side of her breast nudging his chest wall. He closed his eyes and swallowed hard.

"Are you sure you're all right?" Jamie asked.

He opened his eyes. "Oh, yeah." Now that his fear for her had receded, his senses were filling with her warmth, her scent. He gripped the driver's door with his free hand and held on. He knew if help didn't get here soon, his insides weren't going to be in any better shape than his car.

"It must have been Wrey in that truck that rammed us."

"It wasn't Wrey," Matt said.

"How can you be so sure?"

"Because I didn't leave Wrey in any condition to walk, much less drive a truck."

Her eyes grew wide.

As soon as Matt saw her reaction, he realized he'd spoken without thinking. "Sorry. I didn't mean to shock you."

She sent him a smile of pure approval that slipped past every defense he ever had to settle deep and warm inside him.

"I've always thought emceeing a show that finds lost loves a mite too tame for you."

Matt's pulses took another incredible leap at the warmth and meaning in her words. "You thought that, did you?"

"Cade always fit right into the big, softhearted veterinarian persona, and Liz, the sophisticated and sharp accountant, but I always pictured you as the type to be roping steers and riding the range like the leather-faced cowboys on your mama and daddy's ranch."

"You're talking about the ones who are always doused in eau de cow manure?"

She laughed, light and warm. "The romantic image does rather tend to relegate the practical considerations."

The romantic image. She thought of him as a romantic image. He took a deep breath and tightened his hold on the driver's door.

"Even if it wasn't Wrey, he could have called someone to do his dirty work for him, Matt."

"Wrey wasn't in any condition to be picking up a telephone or talking anytime soon. Besides, the store didn't have a phone. I checked. I also made sure neither his truck nor the phone inside it was in operating order before I left. No one from Sweetspring could have caught up with us so fast, anyway."

"So it was just a random attack?" Jamie asked.

"I seriously doubt it. The way I see it, that truck was waiting for us outside of town."

"Waiting for us? No, that can't be. Who would want to run us off the road?"

"Maybe someone who figured you'd go looking for a trail to Tony in Sweetspring and followed you here."

"This can't have anything to do with my looking for Tony."

"Can't it? I don't believe in coincidences. Twice before you've received warnings to back off the search. It seems pretty obvious to me that our being rammed was designed to scare you real bad, so you'd stop looking for Tony."

"Why would someone go to all this trouble just to stop me from looking for Tony?"

"Jamie, face it. You know virtually nothing about him, not even his real name. We have no idea what his family was doing in Sweetspring fifteen years ago. Or what any of them might be doing now. There could be a lot of reasons why he doesn't want you finding him."

"He isn't the one doing these things."

*Damn it, what had this guy done to earn this kind of belief?* Anger rode Matt's tone. "End of the trail, Jamie."

"What do you mean, end of the trail?"

"In case you hadn't noticed, you were just almost killed. You're letting this matter go."

An irritated eyebrow flew up her forehead. "Excuse me?"

Matt knew his tough routine had not worked on Jamie before and wasn't going to work now. But he was just too angry and frustrated to care. "You heard what I said."

She reached up to the steering wheel and pulled herself into a sitting position. She scooted over to the passenger seat. This time she didn't wobble. On the contrary. Her reflexes were smooth, her movements agile.

And boy, was her color back. She had a dangerous glint in her eyes. When she tossed her windblown hair it crackled across her shoulders as though filled with an electrical charge.

"Just because you decided you don't want to go looking for Tony any more, that does not mean the end of the trail for me. I'm not letting this matter go."

Matt knew she meant it, too. She was a damn headstrong, stubborn woman. She was going to go on looking until she probably got herself killed.

He grabbed her arms and held them tightly. "Damn it,

Jamie, what is it with you and this Tony? Is it worth your life to find him?''

"He's not connected with that eighteen-wheeler, Matt. He's—''

"I know," Matt said, not letting her finish. "He's a good kisser. Well, I'm tired of hearing how good the bastard can kiss. Good kissers can be gotten on any damn corner in Texas.''

Matt pulled her into his arms and brought his mouth to hers with all the angry frustration that had just overwhelmed all his good sense.

But all the anger and frustration fled the instant he felt her softness crushed to him and the incredible sensation of having her mouth molded to his.

Her lips parted with an intake of surprise. He dipped his tongue into the heat and softness inside her mouth and came out with a taste so sweet it burned all the way to his soul.

In the next heartbeat he was kissing her deeply, wantonly, madly, greedily sinking into all the sensual heat and textures of her mouth and body. She was everything he'd ever dreamt she would be and more.

He no longer had any thought for the past. The future. Family. Honor.

With her in his arms he had no thoughts at all.

The blood hammered through his ears so hard he couldn't hear. He couldn't breathe. It didn't matter. He didn't need to hear. He didn't need to breathe.

All he needed was her. All he had ever needed was her.

He ran his hands up her back, over the soft, smooth heat of her body and tangled them through the silk of her hair. With every new demand of his mouth he found himself pouring out all the ache and longing and hunger he'd carried in his heart for her for so long. He was soaring way out of control. He didn't care. She was heaven, and he never wanted to come back to earth again.

But he did. With a crash.

Because she was suddenly putting her palms against his chest and pushing back out of his arms. Hard.

The last thing in the world he wanted to do was let her go. The absolute last. But he did. Barely.

And then fought for breath. For sanity. He could find neither looking into her beautifully flushed face or the sensual blue heat swirling in her shocked eyes.

He closed his and fought again for that superb control that had once been his to command. But his body was the one in command now. He'd been way too hungry for her, way too long.

If she hadn't stopped him, he knew nothing else would have.

He had gotten a taste of the kind of passion with her that bred an exquisite kind of madness. That kind of passion that only came once in a man's life—if he was lucky or cursed enough for it to come at all.

Matt's body was one big, throbbing ache and it was all for Jamie. But his feelings for her had never been just physical. And they weren't now. She had pushed him back. With all the force of his discipline and resolve, he willed his body and his blood to cool.

Still, it was another moment or two before Matt heard Jamie saying something. He opened his eyes. She was pointing toward the dented roof of the car. He realized now that she had been saying something all along, and he hadn't been hearing it. He forced himself to concentrate on listening to her words.

"Matt, the helicopter. They've been calling your name over and over."

Matt realized then that not all the roaring in his ears was coming from his blood. He listened and heard the whirling of the rotor blades. And then the electronically enhanced voice.

"Matt Bonner, are you inside that damn vehicle or aren't you?"

Matt recognized the voice immediately. He poked his head

and shoulders out of the window frame on the driver's door and looked up to see the helicopter circling above. He waved at the silver-haired man holding the portable loudspeaker, signaling him to set the helicopter down.

Two guys with an assortment of tools and torches were out first. A medical team with a stretcher came next. They all made directly for the car. Matt shielded Jamie with his body as they cut a hole in the driver's door.

Matt crawled out of the car when they were done. A paramedic immediately climbed inside to check Jamie out, despite her protests that she was fine.

While she was being examined, Matt walked over to the stocky man with the leathered skin and silver hair who was standing at the back of the chopper, keeping a watchful eye.

Matt held out his hand. "I appreciate the rescue, Keele."

"Well, seeing as how you've pulled me out of a few tight spots along the way, I'd say I owed you this one," the silver-haired man said as he took Matt's hand for a shake. "This feels real good, like old times, Matt."

"Yep, it sure does. Riding a desk all day gives a body the wrong kind of saddle sores."

"Don't know how you do it. If I were tied to a chair, I'd be going as crazy as an anthill what just been stepped on. The office said you've taken a couple of days' leave. You want to tell me how you ended up out here?"

Matt gave Keele a brief description of his run-in with the eighteen-wheeler.

"Curious thing is, Keele, on the way into town, there were at least three signs a mile ahead of those deep rivets in the road. On the way out of town, no warning signs appeared at all. I was on those bumps before I knew it."

"Sounds to me like someone took 'em down, Matt. It's time you told me what you're doing out here and who the looker is."

Matt glanced in the direction Keele was pointing. Jamie had come out of the wreck. Her high heels were off. She was arguing with the paramedics who loomed over her. They were trying to get her to lie down on the stretcher. She was having none of it. And she was getting her way.

Not for the first time that day, a smile for that gutsy spirit of hers stole over Matt's face.

"She's the reason I'm out here," Matt said, "and she's the reason I'm going to be needing more of your help."

"Are we talking about an official kind of help here?"

"Unofficially, yes."

"Matt, you know I cannot commit the Firm's resources to something that isn't its business. Why not just let the local sheriff track down your fender-bashing cowboy?"

"Because I need the best. You have to find that tractor-trailer rig for me, Keele."

"Dang if you didn't do yourself proud on that arm twist. Okay, you got me. What was the license number?"

"Hell, Keele, if I knew the license number I could find it myself. All I know is it wasn't a Texas plate."

"Well, now, Matt, that's real helpful. There are what, a few thousand interstate rigs traveling around West Texas roads today? Why, just as soon as I fly you and the lady on to San Antonio, I'll be sure to come back and check out each and every one of them."

Matt grinned at the sarcasm. "Come on, Keele. I know you're one of those good ol' boys who just thrives on a challenge. Besides, I can narrow this rig down for you some. It has a bullet hole in the windshield."

"You got off a shot?"

"Not me. My passenger."

Keele looked over at Jamie with new respect in his eyes and a long whistle on his lips. "A gorgeous petite blonde and she can shoot, too. Hot damn, but I just love Texas womanhood."

"Well, don't go getting any ideas about this Texas woman. Her name is *Mrs.* Jamie Bonner."

"You trying to kick dust in my face, Matt? I know you're not married."

"She's my brother's wife."

Matt had purposely misstated Jamie's marital status. He had no intention of telling Keele she was technically free. Keele was far too likely to come on to her.

Keele shrugged. "The soft-spoken veterinarian I met that time out at the ranch? Well, now that's a heap of disappointing news. How fond are you of this brother of yours?"

There was no humor in Matt's tone when he responded. "You make a move in Jamie's direction, I'll have to kill you."

"That fond, huh? Well, damn, it don't look like this is going to be my lucky day."

Matt didn't kid himself. He wasn't protecting his brother's claim on Jamie. Just the idea of any other man touching her was enough to make him crazy.

Even if that man was his own brother.

The realization hit Matt like a blow. What the hell was he thinking? And doing?

He'd gone way over the line back there when he'd kissed Jamie. Way over.

And now that he was taking a good look at himself, he sure didn't like what he was seeing. He was going to have to get back on the other side of that damn line. And damn quick, too.

Before he lost his head completely. And his brother forever.

# Chapter Eight

Jamie could barely sit still on her flight back. Matt's friend, Keele—who was also obviously the boss of the crew—insisted that Jamie sit next to the pilot and let him explain the controls. Matt sat in the back of the helicopter next to Keele. Jamie saw their heads together over a map, obviously discussing something about it.

Her curiosity and emotions were running wild.

There was no insignia on the helicopter, nor on the white-and-gray uniforms its crew wore. Jamie had no idea who these people were. She was determined to find out, however.

"How do you know Matt?" Jamie asked the pilot after he'd finished his short course in Chopper Aerodynamics 101, none of which she was paying attention to.

"We've met a few times here and there," the pilot answered.

"He and Keele seem to know each other quite well."

"They've met a few times here and there."

"Were they in the military together?"

"Can't say, ma'am."

"Where does this helicopter come from?" she asked.

"It was built in the good old US of A, ma'am."

"I meant, is it part of the military?"

"Can't say, ma'am."

This conversation was proving to be a challenge.

"You mean you won't say."

"Can't say, ma'am."

"Some regulation prohibits you from answering my questions?"

"Can't say, ma'am."

Jamie laughed at the conversational runaround, not taking offense, despite the lack of information. At the moment, she was finding it extremely difficult to take offense at anything.

Because no matter where her outward attention was directed, Jamie's inward thoughts were all for Matt and that unbelievable kiss they had shared.

She felt suspended in an ecstasy compounded of incredible joy and insight. She understood now why it was that Matt's unfriendliness had so disturbed her for so long. His kiss had revealed to her a depth of feeling she had never even imagined could exist. Her whole body tingled with it, reveled in it, radiated it like a beacon.

She had never known that a man could want her so hard or make her want him so hard right back. The things that Matt had communicated in that kiss had shaken her to her soul and still had her quivering and quaking and soaring inside.

The helicopter set them down on a hotel rooftop in San Antonio. They got a taxi out front. Matt was quiet all the way to her townhome. He didn't touch her, but she could feel the solidness of him beside her. She understood why her nerves had always danced when she was around him. And why they always would.

Once the taxi pulled up out front, Matt got out and came around to open her door for her. When she had stepped outside, he leaned into the open window.

"Wait for me. I'll be right back."

Jamie was both startled and disappointed. "You're not coming inside?"

"I have things to do."

All that cold, aloof distance was right back in his voice. He stood in front of her as if he were at attention, as if nothing

had happened between them. Jamie wondered what in hell
was wrong.

She put her hand on his arm. "Matt, are you all right?"

He slowly but deliberately moved his arm away from her
touch. "I'm fine. You'd best go in now."

Stunned, she turned and walked toward her townhome, trying to sort through his behavior, to understand it. When she
reached the door she turned back to him.

"You've hardly said a word to me since your friends rescued us. What's wrong?"

"Jamie, there's simply nothing to say."

"Matt, you kissed me."

"So I did," he said with no emotion whatsoever. "Did
you enjoy the kiss?"

He had a doubt? Was that the problem here? She smiled.
"I'm still tingling from it."

"Glad to hear it. Now maybe you can forget this Tony or
whatever his real name is, and get on with your life. Like I
said, there's a good kisser around every corner in Texas."

Jamie lost her smile. All the beautiful brightness of the day
instantly dimmed, as if the batteries were giving out.

"Matt, are you saying that's all it was? Proof to me that
you're a better kisser than Tony?"

"Did you think it was anything else?"

A sluggish ache began to emerge on the side of Jamie's
temple where she had struck her head. It had probably been
there all along, but she had only just begun to notice it.

She couldn't look at Matt's remote, passive face another
second. She dropped her eyes to her handbag and dug inside
for her keys.

As she fumbled for them, she swallowed an ocean full of
disappointment.

She pulled her keys out of her bag and put them into the
lock. "I would appreciate it if you would send me your bill
as soon as possible."

"Does this mean you're finally going to drop the search?"

She kept her face to the door. "No. It means I'm going to hire another private investigator."

She pushed open the door and started to step inside.

Matt's hand shot out to circle her arm. "Jamie, wait."

The warmth and strength of his touch charged through her body. The force of it was so strong it left her feeling dizzy. She was horrified to find herself wobbling.

His other hand came out to steady her. Suddenly she was surrounded by his warmth and strength. Her knees went weak. She wanted nothing more than to lean right back in his arms and let them enfold her. The thought shocked her. This was not like her. No, this was not like her at all.

"I told Keele they should keep you under observation today. Concussions can lead to dizziness, double vision, not to mention a numbing fatigue. Come on. I'll help you inside."

"No!" Jamie grabbed hold of the door frame to anchor herself. She held on tightly to it, as if it were a lifeline. Which it was. A lifeline to her strength, to her independence, to her dignity, to her pride. To everything that defined her.

"I'm just a little dizzy because I neglected to eat breakfast this morning," she lied. "I'll be fine. Goodbye, Matt. Much obliged for everything."

She stepped inside, forcing him to release her. She quickly closed the door and locked it behind her.

A few seconds later, she heard his boots retreating down the walkway back to the taxi at the curb.

Jamie slumped against the door. Her whole body was throbbing with the ache in her head…and her heart.

Oh, how could he have been so heartless as to open up a dazzling new world of feeling to her only to tell her it wasn't real?

She wanted to hate him but she couldn't. She had gotten to know him too well over the past few days to ever hate him.

He had stood by her side today—emotionally as well as physically. She'd never get over that wonderful feeling.

But she would get over him. She had to.
He didn't want her. That left her no other choice.

"WHERE HAVE YOU BEEN?" Charlene demanded as soon as Matt walked into his office.

"I've been on vacation, remember?"

"Some vacation. You look terrible."

"Careful. You're up for a raise."

"Idle threat. I know you already put it in the budget."

"It can come out again."

"That's aunt abuse."

"Remind me again, Charlene, why did I hire you?"

"Because you thought it would give your P.I. firm a homey look to have your aunt around, and because you have a soft heart."

"It must have been my head that was soft that day. Has Keele called?"

"No. But I got this urgent fingerprint-check request back from the lab. I didn't know you were having a greeting card and envelope evaluated. Since when did we get one of those cases?"

Matt took the report out of Charlene's hands and quickly scanned it. The only fingerprints the lab had found were Jamie's. Damn.

"Put Keele right through if he calls," Matt said heading for his door. "Hold everything else."

"Where did you go that you didn't get any sleep? And couldn't you be reached? I tried to get you all yesterday afternoon. You didn't even answer your car phone."

Matt exhaled a heavy breath as he turned back to her. Charlene was worse than his mama sometimes. Actually, all the time.

"I have a new car and phone."

"You traded in the Caddy? I thought you loved that big, old gas guzzler."

"Charlene, was there something else?"

"A bunch of stuff. Randy said you were right. Those network boys are real eager now to meet with him and you next Wednesday. And they already offered to buy that dinner."

"No surprise there. What else, Charlene?"

"Perry talked to Sarita's birth mama yesterday. He checked her out. She's the real thing."

"What did she have to say?"

"That she was married now and had two sons and she'd never told her husband of what she referred to as her 'youthful disgrace.' She also said that she has no intention of revealing it now. She doesn't want to see her daughter. Not ever."

"So why did she even call?"

"Because she apparently doesn't want Sarita to go on looking for her. Didn't want to get the girl's hopes up, she said."

Matt shook his head. "Instead she wants us to tell her daughter that her own mama doesn't want her in her life."

"You going to do that?"

"Do I have a choice? Damn, but there are days when I hate this job so much I just want to chuck it all in."

"Don't do it yet. Perry sent a package over from the studio. It's regarding Jamie."

"Where's the package?" Matt asked.

"Right here," Charlene said removing it from her desk drawer. She handed it to Matt. "There's a tape of two telephone calls that came into the station while you were gone. Perry said Jamie has become one of those cases. Where did he get that idea?"

"I told him she was."

"On whose authority?"

"On mine. You have any other questions, Charlene?"

Charlene put up her hands. "No sir, boss nephew. My, but you are testy this morning. What is it about our Jamie gal that always gets you so riled up, huh?"

Matt opened the door to his office and closed it behind him. He stomped over to his desk and slumped into his chair. Lord, he felt like hell. Trying not to think about Jamie had kept him awake all night.

When she had told him that she was still tingling from his kiss, he'd nearly lost his head again and taken her right back in his arms. The idea that she might want him to kiss her again...

Matt put the thought right out of his mind. Because if he didn't, he knew he'd do something about to. And he couldn't.

He couldn't betray his brother.

Only now she was going to hire some stupid P.I. who was probably going to screw up everything and maybe even get her hurt. Damn. Matt rubbed his throbbing temples and tried not to wince when he moved his bruised shoulder.

The intercom on his desk buzzed. He leaned over to press the button. "Yes, Charlene?"

"Cade's on the line."

Matt looked over at the framed photo sitting on his desk. It was of him and Cade, just before Matt went off into military service. Matt's arm was around his brother.

Cade's arm was around a half-starved hound he'd just rescued from the pound. For as long as Matt could remember, Cade's heart had been as big as the whole outdoors. He took a deep breath before he reached for the telephone receiver.

"Cade, how you been?" Matt asked.

"Fair to meddling, Matt. I'm in Tulsa. Don't mean to rush this none, but I got to get back to some doings here in just a minute. Liz said you had some questions about Jamie?"

Matt had learned some things from their trip to Sweetspring. But there were other questions still weighing on his mind.

"Did she ever mention this Tony Lagarrigue to you before this sudden urge to look him up?"

"Not as I recall."

"What did she tell you about her growing-up years?"

"Not nearly enough."

"What do you mean, Cade?"

"Just what I said. Jamie kept a lot to herself for a long time. Too long. I guess she thought she had to. Her growing-up period was a painful time in her life. Poor kid."

Matt had thought of Jamie in a lot of ways, but "poor kid" was never a description that would have entered his mind.

Yes, she'd had to endure difficulties when she was a youngster in Sweetspring. But the cool woman he'd watched stand up to Wrey Kleinman and fire a bullet into the windshield of that eighteen-wheeler had grown into one resilient, gutsy gal.

"Cade, you've never talked about what broke up you and Jamie. Why?"

"Because I'm not sure Jamie would want me to."

"She was the one who divorced you though, right?" Matt asked. "It wasn't your idea?"

"It wasn't my idea."

"You weren't playing around on her. I know you better than that."

"Yes, you do."

"And she's not the kind of woman to play around—"

"No, she's not, so stop fishing for the answer, Matt. If you want to know, ask Jamie. If she wants to tell you, she will. Now, how's the search going for this Tony?"

"Not quite as smoothly as I hoped. You sure you want me to find him for her?"

"It's obvious she has some unfinished business with him, Matt. I want whatever she wants to make her happy. I'll always want that."

Matt shook his head. Cade must be in a lot of pain over losing Jamie, but he was showing a lot of class about it. Matt knew if he were in Cade's position, he'd never be able to do it.

Matt suddenly realized that what with his military stint and then Cade's marriage to Jamie, he'd missed out on a lot of his brother's maturation. He was proud of Cade and the man he had become.

"When you get back from this trip, give me a call, Cade. We need to do some catching up."

"Sounds like a winner to me. Why don't you come on out

to the ranch? Mama's always complaining she never sees you enough.''

"Then it'll become a whole family thing. I thought we'd try for some time with just the two of us. We could catch a ball game somewhere.''

"Well, sure. I'll give you a holler. Hey, I gotta go now. They're calling me for a seminar. Now you take care of my little Jamie for me, hear?''

Matt hung up the phone with a heavy exhale. Take care of "*my* little Jamie.'' Matt hadn't missed the possessive pronoun in that sentence.

He had to do right by his brother. And that meant he couldn't let Jamie go to another P.I. He couldn't trust her with anyone else.

But could he trust himself with her?

Damn. He put his head in his hands. Somehow, he had to keep his distance. He had to come through for Cade…and Jamie.

Matt reached for the package Perry had sent over. He dumped the contents onto the desk. There were two tapes. He unraveled the sheet of typed paper that had been rubber-banded to the first tape.

The call on the tape had been placed from a pay phone in Florida. It had come in Wednesday night about an hour after Matt had left the studio.

Matt removed a tape recorder from his desk drawer. He slipped the first tape inside and pressed the play button. A man with a distinctive nasal tone was the first voice he heard.

"This is that 'Finder of Lost Loves' show, right?''

"Yes, sir. How may I help you?'' Matt recognized Perry's taped voice right away.

"I watched the program tonight, and I think I know this Tony Lagarrigue guy.''

"And your name, sir?''

"What does it matter? I'd just like to learn a little more about the woman who's looking for him.''

"And why is that, sir?''

"'Cause I think I might know him. If it is the guy I'm thinking of, I'd like to look him up, too."

"Where do you think you know him from, sir?"

"That picture you ran looked just like a Tony Lagarrigue I went to school with. So who's the looker who wants to find him?"

"Her name is Jamie."

"What's her last name?"

"That's confidential, sir."

"Where did this Jamie go to school?"

"I'm not acquainted with all the details of the case, sir."

"Well, then let me talk to Jamie. She's the one looking for Tony. She should know."

"I'm sorry, sir. Jamie's not here right now."

"Well, then give me her telephone number."

"Where are you calling from, sir?"

"Why are you asking?"

"I'd like to take down your number so that I can have Jamie call you."

"Just give me her number."

"We are not allowed to give out the number of our program guests."

"She's local to San Antonio though, right?"

"I will be happy to check to see if I can find out that information for you, sir. What's your name and telephone number?"

"Oh, forget it. It probably wasn't him, anyway."

The caller's line abruptly ended in dial tone.

Matt stopped the tape. The caller wasn't a Texan. That was clear in his speech. Matt also got the distinct impression that he was more interested in Jamie than he was in Tony.

No surprise there. A beautiful woman appears on camera looking for someone who kissed her fifteen years before. Hell, probably any guy watching was wishing it was him. Matt was just surprised the switchboard hadn't gotten a dozen calls from men like this fixin' to find out more about Jamie.

He ejected the first tape and tossed it aside.

The information sheet rubber-banded around the second tape had much more detail. The caller was a Wendy McConnell of Reno, Nevada. Perry had included her address along with the note that he had verified the number she had given to be hers. Ms. McConnell had called late on Thursday. Matt put the second tape into the recorder and pressed the play button.

"I'm Wendy McConnell and I want to speak with Jamie."

"I'm sorry, Ms. McConnell, Jamie isn't here right now," Perry responded.

"What do you mean she's not there? It took my sister and me half a dozen calls each to finally locate someone with your number. You must get a hold of Jamie for me."

"Does this concern the person she's looking for?"

"Well, of course, it concerns Tony. Why else would I be calling? Tell her I recognized his picture. I know where he is."

"I'll be happy to take down his location and get that information to Jamie."

"Oh, no. I know better than to entrust information like this to a man. I want to tell Jamie myself."

"All right, Ms. McConnell. I'll ask her to call you."

Matt stopped the tape. Wendy McConnell might be confusing Tony's face with someone else's, but at the moment she was the only lead he had. Matt picked up the phone and punched in Jamie's number.

He had memorized it the day he looked at her check. Just as he had memorized everything else about her.

She answered on the second ring. Matt identified himself and then hurried into his explanation before she could ask any questions.

"We've gotten a call from a Ms. McConnell who says she recognizes Tony's picture. Can you meet me at the studio in an hour?"

A long, quiet pause blared at him from the other end of the line. Matt waited it out.

"I thought you dropped the case?" Jamie said finally.

"I was trying to get you to drop it."

"Why do you want me down at the studio? Can't I just call her from here?"

"I want to listen in on the call and tape it."

"And the reason for that?"

"Should be obvious. Since you started looking for this Tony, you've been subjected to threats and an attempt has even been made against your life."

"We've no proof that eighteen-wheeler episode had anything to do with my looking for Tony."

"I don't need proof."

"We should have reported the incident to the police. I wasn't thinking straight yesterday."

"The proper authorities have been notified," Matt said.

"You told them? What did they say?"

"That you should forget this Tony," Matt said.

Matt stopped to take a deep breath, knowing his voice was getting gruffer by the second. "You want to take that excellent advice, or do you want to come down to the studio and call Ms. McConnell?"

Matt didn't think he had a chance of convincing Jamie to take his first option. He was right. She didn't hesitate in making her choice. "I'll be there in an hour."


ALL DURING THE DRIVE to the studio, Jamie's emotions had her on a roller-coaster ride. She was excited about what this Ms. McConnell might say. She was worried that it would be just another dead end. She was mad because Matt was still working on the case and she had to continue to be around him.

And she was so damn happy that he was still working on the case and she had to continue to be around him.

The thought of having to employ another private investigator had begun a slow drip of seeping depression into her veins all morning. She'd drunk three cups of coffee as she stared at the yellow pages. But she hadn't called another P.I.

Instead, she'd kept seeing Matt holding Wrey as he asked

her with a worried frown if she was all right. She'd kept remembering his incredible, soul-claiming kiss. And she'd kept losing her breath.

What might have happened had she not heard the helicopter overhead and pulled back? Would he have stopped with that kiss?

Later, his words had said no, but at the time his body had...

She was losing her breath again, and her hands were shaking on the wheel.

*You have to get a grip. He told you. He doesn't feel anything for you. He was just proving a point.*

She forced herself to take a deep breath. Slowly she let it out. She was more disciplined than this. Resolutely she redirected her thoughts to Tony.

For fifteen years, she had replayed her wonderful night with him. Sometimes, during the bad times, it was all that got her through the pain.

So maybe the warmth of Tony's kiss had been nothing more than a firefly compared to the solar flare she'd found beneath Matt's lips. At least when Tony had kissed her, he meant it.

Jamie pulled into the parking lot at the back of the studio. There was only one vehicle there—a Jeep Cherokee. When she rang at the back door, Perry opened it to greet her.

"Come in, Ms. Bonner. Matt will be here shortly. You can use his office to make the call." He led the way to Matt's office and then swung open the door.

Jamie was about to step inside when she stopped dead in her tracks, absolutely stunned.

The desk drawers had been dumped unceremoniously on the floor. The steel file cabinet in the corner had been overturned on its side and its contents were spilled everywhere. Even the pictures on the wall had been taken off and smashed. Someone had obviously searched the office and none too gently.

"What the hell?" she heard Perry say beside her.

She knew the precise second Matt came up behind her. She

hadn't heard him. But she could feel his presence in the way her pulse suddenly leapt. She took a steadying breath and then turned slowly to look at his face.

He was staring at the interior of his office, an expression containing both surprise and concern covering his rough features. He turned to Perry.

"Check the rest of the studio and get a team down here. Quick."

Perry scurried away without question.

"A team?" Jamie asked.

"Forensic types."

"Oh, you mean the police."

"We should get out of here, Jamie. The longer we stay, the more we'll contaminate the scene for them."

"Won't the police want to talk to us?"

Matt's hand gently pressed at the small of Jamie's back as he urged her to the rear door. The sudden intimacy of the contact actually made her knees weak.

"There's nothing we could tell them. Perry will handle it."

"What would someone be looking for in your office?"

"Information. The only thing of monetary value in the studio is the equipment. It wasn't touched."

"You don't have an alarm system?"

"Apparently, not a real good one. I have some recording equipment at my place. We'll go there to make your call to Ms. McConnell. Follow me in your car."

When Jamie stepped out into the parking lot, she smiled to see Matt getting into the black Ford F350 one-ton truck parked next to her car. It looked like a tank to her, if she ever saw one.

She followed Matt to a good-sized contemporary home on a big lot in a nice residential neighborhood a few minutes later. He pulled into the driveway. Jamie didn't know of any bachelors who considered themselves settled enough to invest in a home. She parked her car at the curb and walked up to the door just in time for Matt to open it for her.

The inside was as spacious as the outside, with light oak

floors and an open beamed ceiling. He led her into a living room filled with sun tubes pouring in light from above. One whole wall was sliding-glass doors leading out to a lush backyard where the blue waters in a lap-sized swimming pool gleamed invitingly.

Jamie's voice climbed in surprise. "How long have you lived here?"

"Mortgage company and I partnered up five years ago."

Jamie whirled around the living room, taking in the earthtone colors, the geometric patterns in the large Indian throw rug and the immense sofa that a body could really sprawl on.

"So this is where you came to when you left the ranch. I've never known a bachelor who was this neat."

"Cleaning service deserves the accolades. Recording equipment is in the other room. I'll be right back."

Within a minute he was back with the electronics and busied himself with the setup. He placed two phones side by side on the coffee table. One he connected to a recording machine on the right. Matt gestured Jamie to take a seat in front of the other.

She didn't miss the fact that he kept three feet between them when he sat on his edge of the couch.

Matt picked up his phone and dialed the number. She heard the tones echoing into her receiver. Then the ringing. The call was picked up in the middle of the third ring.

"Hello?" It was a woman's voice.

"This is Jamie from 'Finder of Lost Loves' in San Antonio. Is Ms. McConnell there?"

"This is Wendy McConnell," the woman said, excitement making her voice rise. "Oh, Jamie, I'm so glad you called. You must get here immediately. Tony's straying."

"Excuse me?"

"I saw him with another woman this morning!"

"Ms. McConnell—"

"Please call me Wendy, dear. Ms. McConnell sounds so formal."

"Of course, Wendy. How do you know Tony?"

"Well, I don't really know him. But I've seen him plenty of times. That's why when that picture of him flashed on the screen last Monday night, I knew right away he was your Tony."

"Where have you seen him?"

"Right here in Reno. Me and Jerry—he's my husband—we step in to play the slot machines on our way grocery shopping. Not that we're compulsive gamblers or anything like that. We set aside five dollars each in quarters to wager. It's fun and we figure on losing it, so it doesn't matter when we do. Although a couple of times we've actually won enough to finance our next few weeks. Anyway, win or lose, by eight o'clock we're off to the grocery store to do the week's shopping."

"Wendy, I'm confused. When and where do you see Tony?"

"Well, at the casinos, of course. He's been in there off and on for years. First time I saw him I pointed him out to Jerry and remarked about how he was wearing the same sweater we'd bought for our nephew, Neal. Tony looked so handsome in it."

"Which casinos have you seen him in?"

"Different ones. He was at the Flamingo Hilton this morning. And he was with a woman. She's this big-busted brunette with sticks for legs. It upset me so much to see how she was hanging all over him. You have to get here right away."

"You feel certain it's him?"

"Absolutely. Come to dinner tonight. I can tell you all about what's been going on then."

"Thank you, Wendy, but I'm not sure—"

"Please, Jamie. It would be such a pleasure to have you here. Knowing that I'm the one bringing you together with your Tony is such a thrill for me. After dinner, I'll show you the casino route Jerry and I take on the way to the grocery store. That way you'll know where you'll most likely see Tony."

"I'll have to call you later to let you know if I can arrange it."

"I'll give you my address, just in case. Have you got a pencil and paper?"

Jamie didn't bother writing the information down since the tape was picking it up. She thanked Wendy McConnell for her call and promised to get back to her just as soon as she had made a decision.

"Please hurry," Wendy said. "You're much prettier than that brunette, but she's a real predator, if you know what I mean."

Jamie thanked Wendy for her concern and hung up the phone.

"Isn't that just like a man?" she said, shaking her head dramatically. "Just because he's been away from you for fifteen years, he thinks he can take up with another woman."

She smiled over at Matt and was rewarded when she caught the small half smile on his lips.

For the first time she realized that his eyes weren't just gray but were filled with mercurial silver slashes and shards of vibrant turquoise. She stared, finding herself suddenly mesmerized by the unexpected discovery.

Matt quickly got to his feet and stepped to the other side of the couch. He plowed his hands into the pockets of his jeans and gazed out the glass wall to the serenity of the backyard.

"Wendy McConnell seems sure this man is your Tony," he said, gruffly. "What do you think?"

What Jamie thought was that Matt seemed mighty uncomfortable sitting next to her and even more uncomfortable when she looked into his eyes.

Well, no puzzle there. When a woman stared at a man, it generally was a way of communicating that she might be interested in doing more than just looking. And Matt had retreated. How many other ways could he tell her he wasn't interested?

Jamie sighed as she got to her feet. "Appears as though

I'll be taking a trip to Reno. I wonder how good Wendy McConnell's eyesight is."

Matt looked at his watch. "We'll soon find out. I'll make the arrangements for Reno. I suggest you go home and pack."

Jamie started toward the door. "It's pretty late. What if everything is already booked?"

"I'll find something."

She had absolutely no doubt that he would, too. The more she was with Matt, the more she recognized the sure and certain competence that permeated his every pore.

As usual, he kept his distance as he walked with her to the door.

Still, the warmth and strength of him registered on her senses every step of the way. Since he had kissed her, it seemed every nerve fiber in her body had been sensitized to him.

She paused to look up at him as he held the door open for her.

"I know you don't understand why this is important to me, Matt, but I'm obliged to you for sticking with it anyway."

He nodded but made no direct comment. His expression was cool and professional.

"I suggest you lock yourself in until I come to pick you up to go to the airport. Don't relax your guard for a moment. I doubt whoever has been trying to keep you from finding Tony has given up yet."

Matt's words stayed with Jamie all the way home. Whether it was his caution or some sixth sense, she could have sworn she was being followed.

MATT USED THE CAR PHONE to book them on an airline flight leaving at four-thirty as he drove toward his office. He next arranged for a car and hotel accommodations for them in Reno.

And all the time the image of Jamie's look of delight when she saw his home kept playing through his mind. He had never allowed himself to picture her there.

He knew it would be impossible for him to stand beneath the sun tubes in his living room and not see her sunlit hair and smile. Or sit on that sofa again without remembering the focused intensity with which she had studied his eyes.

It was becoming harder by the moment to stay close and still maintain his distance. When she joked about Tony and the brunette, showing absolutely no jealousy or discomfort, he'd been so relieved that the desire to kiss those smiling lips had driven through him like a nail.

Reining in all these galloping reactions was getting to be harder by the second. But rein them in he would. Because rein them in he must.

Thinking about her wasn't helping. He purposely put his mind to work elsewhere. The way all the records at the studio had been dumped on the floor told him that whoever had broken in had been looking for information.

The only information there related to the names, addresses and telephone numbers of the guests on the show. And not one of their cases dealt with a sensitive issue.

Except Jamie's. Still, it didn't appear logical that the break-in had anything to do with her. The person trying to warn her away from Tony already knew her name and home address. There would have been no reason for him to break in.

So who had?

Whoever it was knew how to get past a standard alarm. And that spoke of a professional.

Matt picked up the cell phone and punched in his office number. Charlene answered right away.

"There's been a break-in at the studio. Don't leave the office even for a second without making sure that both alarms are on."

"You think we're next?" Charlene asked.

"Whoever it was might not have gotten what he was looking for the first time."

"If someone gets to the computers—" Charlene began.

"Without the right password, the fail-safe mechanism will activate."

Once he reassured his aunt, Matt hung up the phone.

He was punching in Jamie's number to tell her about the flight to Reno and other arrangements he had made when he pulled into the lot at the back of his downtown office.

When he saw Keele waiting there, Matt quickly canceled the call to Jamie.

Keele sauntered up to Matt's truck the second it was parked.

"Been waiting for you, buddy. I found that eighteen-wheeler that ran you off the road. And the driver. Interested?"

# Chapter Nine

Rollo smiled at the plain-faced receptionist manning the arrival desk at Harrah's hotel in Reno. She wore no wedding ring and was past the age when youth could have made up for her lack of beauty. Her name tag said Nancie. The yellow-brown stains between her right index and middle fingers said cigarettes.

She was looking very good to Rollo.

"I need a room, Nancie. One night. Two beds."

She returned his smile. "And what is the name, sir?"

"Steven Stedman."

"And the person who will be in the room with you?"

"Stephanie Stedman. My sister."

He could see Nancie was happy to hear it. He'd learned long ago to ignore the beautiful women. Give him a plain-faced one every time. They were always much easier to please.

"Will that be smoking or non-smoking?" Nancie asked.

"Smoking." Rollo pointed toward his pocket where a half pack of cigarettes resided. "When they hook you at sixteen, they got you for life. I've tried to quit a dozen times. No dice."

Nancie coughed into her tobacco-stained hand and smiled again. "Been there. I'll need to see a major credit card, Mr. Stedman."

"Gotta give you cash," Rollo said, slapping the money on the counter. "My credit card is maxed out."

She took the cash, counted it quickly. "Been there, too. Your room is 2316, Mr. Stedman. Here are two card keys, one for you and one for your sister. The elevator is over there. I hope you enjoy your stay with us. Good luck at the tables."

Rollo leaned across the counter toward her. "You want me to have good luck, Nancie, you're going to have to give it to me."

She stared at him in surprise. "Excuse me?"

Rollo held out his hand. "Just touch me, sweet thing, and I'll be more than lucky."

Nancie laughed and gave Rollo's hand a playful slap.

It was the final sign he'd been looking for.

It wasn't like Reyenna was ever going to find out. And knowing he was on a budget, Nancie probably wouldn't even expect dinner.

"See you later," Rollo said as he walked toward the bank of elevators. And he planned to. Of course, it would have to be her place. Val would never understand. Only thing that had ever warmed old Val up was money.

Rollo stopped at the far end next to an enormous plant that sat beside a floor to ceiling window. As he waited for Val to show, he lit a cigarette and took a long drag. Outside, the lights of the casinos turned the Reno night sky into a warm orange hue.

A moment later Rollo caught a glimpse of a lock of distinctive long red hair. "Did you register?" Val asked:

"Yeah. Here's your room key."

Val took it. "You got a smoking room, didn't you?"

"What do you think?"

"I think I'm going to have to spray it. Did you tell them we were married at the desk, like I told you to?"

"Don't I always follow directions?"

"Well, you better follow this. No smoking upstairs. Now, Bonner and the woman have adjoining rooms on the floor above ours. I wrote the numbers down for you. Don't let them out of your sight. I'll relieve you at midnight."

Not until midnight? Well, hell, that could put a damper on things with Nancie. Rollo told himself he'd think of something as he pocketed the piece of paper Val had given him. He took another drag on his cigarette.

"You actually think Bonner's here because they've gotten a lead on him?" Rollo asked.

"If they wanted to gamble, they would have gone to Vegas. It's closer and there's more action."

"It could be a lovers' weekend getaway."

"With separate rooms? Use your head for once, Rollo. Now, go up there and keep a close watch on them. They could be meeting him any time. I'm going to get some shut-eye. We have to be ready."

"COME IN, JAMIE," Wendy McConnell said. "I'm so glad you could come, too, Mr. Bonner." Matt found her to be a middle-aged woman with a generous mouth and a smile to match.

Matt followed Jamie inside the McConnells' modest home. Good cooking smells filled the air, reminding him of how long it had been since he'd eaten. Jerry McConnell waited for them in the living room, dressed in his Sunday suit and standing at a nervous kind of attention. He looked to Matt like a young boy who had promised to be on his best behavior. This was clearly Wendy's show.

When the introductions were completed and Wendy was assured neither of her guests wanted drinks, she bustled them right off to the dining room and brought on the food. Matt's empty stomach growled appreciatively.

Over homemade beef stew and dinner rolls, still hot from the oven, Wendy told Jamie in intricate detail about every time she had seen Tony and how nice he had looked.

"He dresses so well," Wendy said. "Always a clean, crisp shirt and tie and real tailored slacks. And when he wears a sweater, it's a good-quality one."

Wendy took a swallow of food and went right on.

"I guess I told you about the sweater he was wearing that looked exactly like the one Jerry and I gave to our nephew, Neal? A man's personal habits and grooming speak so well about who he is, don't you think?"

Jamie just nodded, smiling, as she ate.

"So many men these days—particularly the young ones—are such sloppy dressers. To them, the height of fashion is a pair of jeans and a T-shirt. Young women, too. It's so nice to see a young woman like yourself wearing such a beautiful dress. It's silk, isn't it?"

"Yes. But I have to confess that the selection of the material has more to do with the fact that I have sensitive skin than a sensible fashion sense."

"Have you ever worn jeans, Jamie? The material is so rough and coarse, why it just cuts into you everywhere. I can't understand such torture pants being so popular. Oh, I do so miss seeing men in well-tailored suits, don't you?"

Jamie nodded and kept on chewing.

Matt wondered if Wendy had noticed his jean-clad legs. Maybe she forgave him because his dress shirt was showing above the table.

Wendy McConnell went on with her continuous stream of mostly one-way conversation peppered with questions that she gave Jamie little or no time to answer.

Matt looked over at Jerry McConnell. He was contentedly focused on his food, probably not listening to a word. Matt imagined that on the nights when company wasn't at the table, Wendy probably carried the conversation for them both. And Jerry was probably just as attentive.

"I don't know how long that brunette has been hanging around your Tony, but she's one of those tight-jean wearers," Wendy went on. "Sticks for legs. And her hair? Why, it was…"

Matt could feel his own mind wandering.

"And this morning I'm almost sure she was talking about you."

Matt's attention quickly returned.

"Why do you say that, Wendy?" Jamie asked.

"She mentioned your name. Well, I think it was your name. We were at the Flamingo Hilton. I was trying to move closer so I could hear their words. Tony called the brunette Sharlyn and told her to stop worrying. And she said something like, 'Jamie see something.' Then this man next to me started yelling because he won a ten-dollar jackpot. Tony turned around to see what all the commotion was about. And that's when Sharlyn saw me looking at them, snaked her arm through Tony's and dragged him away."

Wendy paused to let out a heartfelt sigh. "I'm sorry, Jamie. I blew my cover."

Matt watched Jamie put her hand on Wendy's arm as a humorous smile played about her lips—one she was obviously trying desperately to control.

"I think you did wonderfully, Wendy. Now let's you and me get these two big, strong men to help with the dishes so we can walk that casino route where you've seen Tony."

JAMIE FOUND RENO'S casinos to be noisy, energetic, congenial places full of flashing lights and the jingle of coins hitting the aluminum tray as slot machines spit out winnings.

It was her first time in such places. Gambling had never held a personal appeal. But she found she had an instant bond with these men and women who stood clutching a little cash in their hands and a big hope in their hearts that they were going to beat the odds.

She knew all about hope—and trying to beat the odds.

As they entered and exited the various establishments on the route that Jerry and Wendy McConnell took on the way to get their groceries, Wendy was her usual chatterbox self beside Jamie.

Wendy led the way past the card dealers and the dice tables straight to the slot machines in every casino. She introduced them to Jamie as though they were old friends—and enemies.

"If you talk to this one real nice it will come through for

you. This one likes to be rubbed on the side after you pull the handle.''

"This is the Flamingo Hilton, right? The casino where you said you last saw Tony?''

"That's right. I was playing this machine and he was standing right over there by the bar with the brunette he called Sharlyn. She dragged him off in that direction.''

"He wasn't gambling?''

"I don't ever think I've seen him gambling, Jamie. He's just sort of standing around looking at things, sometimes drinking coffee over at the bar.''

"Have you ever seen him at night?''

"No, but then Jerry and I don't come around to the casinos much at night. Unless we have guests, of course, like tonight. I have a feeling your Tony will be in one of the casinos tomorrow, Jamie. Do you want me to come with you when you look for him?''

Jamie tried to phrase her refusal in as nice a way as she knew how.

"I think I'd best go alone, Wendy. I want this meeting with Tony to be a private moment. But I do thank you from the bottom of my heart for all your help. You've been wonderful.''

Wendy smiled. "You'll tell me what happens?''

"You know I will.''

Wendy gave Jamie a big hug. Jamie hugged her right back. Although a mite overzealous, Wendy McConnell obviously had a romantic soul and meant well.

"Jamie, it wouldn't be a right smart move to be seeing this guy by yourself,'' Matt said a few minutes later as they walked together back to Harrah's.

"You have some reservation about that?''

"A lot of reservation. If Sharlyn mentioned your name, that means she's seen the 'Finder of Lost Loves' program. She knows you're looking for Tony.''

"I think it's much more likely Wendy's eagerness made her overhear wrong.''

"And if she didn't overhear wrong?"

"This Sharlyn could have been telling him about the show. If it is Tony and not a look-alike, that could be the first he's heard that I'm looking for him."

"There's another explanation, Jamie. He and this Sharlyn know you've been looking for him all along, and he is purposely avoiding contact with you."

"I find that hard to believe."

"Would you also find it hard to believe that we've been followed ever since we arrived at the airport?"

"You're not serious."

"Just as serious as a snake bite."

Jamie started to look over her shoulder.

"Don't look around," Matt cautioned.

Jamie managed to mask her half turn by stopping in front of the casino they were walking past and looking through the window. She pretended that something inside had caught her attention.

She felt Matt move closer beside her and lower his voice. "I don't want him to know he's been spotted. If he knows, he might fade into the crowd and disappear before I can find out who he is."

Jamie continued to stare into the window. The bright neon lights illuminated the night sidewalk so well she could see the reflected faces of the pedestrians streaming past.

None of them seemed to be paying her or Matt any particular attention.

"Which one is he?" she asked.

"He stopped when we did. He's at the last corner, staring into a window, too. I haven't gotten a good look at him. He's stayed too far back."

"So what do we do now?"

"We head on back to the hotel and get some shut-eye."

"You're not worried about why we're being followed?"

"This one is watching, not bushwhacking. Come on."

They returned to their adjoining rooms at Harrah's. When

Jamie entered hers, Matt walked in behind her, closing the door and throwing the lock.

Jamie's breath stalled as all sorts of interesting possibilities surfaced in her thoughts.

Matt opened the connecting door and turned back to her. "Don't lock this tonight. I'd hate to have to break it down if someone got in here and started to strangle you."

She noted that he hadn't said he'd hate her being strangled, only having to break the door down. This concern over someone else's property, as opposed to her neck, did not bring a whole lot of cheer to Jamie's heart.

"We'll grab some chow tomorrow morning before making the casino rounds to see if we can spot Tony. I'll knock on the door right about six-thirty. Be ready."

And with that warm parting endearment, he disappeared through the connecting door and closed it behind him.

Jamie sighed in disappointment. It was at herself, though, not Matt. He was acting true to form. It was she who kept forgetting her resolve to wipe out the memory of his kiss.

She checked her watch. It was almost ten-thirty. It had been a long day, and tomorrow would likely be one, too. She got ready for bed, but when she lay down she felt too restless to sleep. Tomorrow could be the day when she found Tony.

And lost Matt.

She had set the locket Tony had given her those many years before on the nightstand. She leaned over to retrieve it. She turned it over in her hand. It was big and chunky and just made of cheap metal.

Still, its value was far beyond measure. She had cleaned and polished it until it shone. The original chain had turned green long ago. She'd replaced it with links of eighteen-karat gold.

The day Jamie told Cade she'd marry him, she'd put the locket away. It was only the week before that it had once again surfaced to become a part of her life.

She opened it and looked inside. But this time it wasn't Tony she was thinking about. It was Matt.

Part of the impetus that had driven her to find Tony after all these years had come from that feeling of missing something vital in her life—a force or energy that should be there but wasn't.

The moment Matt had taken her into his arms and kissed her, Jamie understood what she had been missing.

Passion. In Matt's arms the power of it had filled her, shaken her, brought her to life. She knew that Tony would never be able to do that. Only one man could. And that one man was Matt.

But he hadn't even done it intentionally. And he wasn't ever going to do it again. Somehow, some way, she was going to have to get that message to sink into her thick skull.

Matt said he was going to be with her tomorrow when she saw Tony. He should be prepared for what might happen. Before they went to Sweetspring, she had kept some important things from him. That had been a mistake. She didn't want to make another one. It was time to tell him about the locket. She snapped it closed in her hand.

Jamie slipped her silk robe over her matching nightie and drew it tight at the waist. She stepped into her slippers and approached the connecting door, clutching the locket in her hand.

Would he be upset that she had not told him about the locket before? More than likely. She could almost hear that gruff tone of his voice, see the busy pulse pumping in his jaw.

Well, putting it off any longer wasn't going to help matters. She knocked, ready to face him in whatever mood he chose to greet her.

But there was no answer.

Jamie knocked harder and called out. "Matt?"

When there still was no response, she turned the knob and opened the door. The room was dark. Was he already in bed?

Jamie leaned over to switch on the table lamp. The light flooded the room. Her eyes traveled to the bed. It was empty. So was the room. Matt was gone.

MATT HAD PURPOSELY entered Jamie's room when they returned to Harrah's to give their follower the impression that he was spending the night with her. If their tail was a professional, he still wouldn't leave his post. But if he was sloppy, he'd retreat for the night, figuring Matt and Jamie wouldn't be emerging before morning.

Matt intended to find out which he was. He slipped out of his shirt and pulled on a worn black sweatshirt. He discarded his Stetson and grabbed a black baseball cap. He opened his door just seconds after leaving Jamie to look out into the hall. It was empty. Matt quickly exited his room and rushed toward the elevators.

All he knew of their tail so far was that he was about five-ten and was wearing a gray shirt and slacks. It was enough.

He caught a side view of the man as he got on the elevator going down. Now Matt knew more. His quarry was dark haired, wiry, late forties or early fifties. Matt watched the elevator descend all the way to the lobby with no stops in between.

He took the next elevator going down. His quarry had a good head start. Still, Matt was determined to find him.

Matt was pleasantly surprised a couple of minutes later to see the man he sought leaning over the hotel counter, saying something to the clerk that was making her blush.

This guy was definitely no professional. Professionals knew better than to leave a post and to mix business with a little something on the side. Who was this amateur anyway?

Matt took a small camera out of his pocket and unobtrusively took a few shots of his profile. The clerk said something to another clerk at the desk. She then circled around the counter to join the man. As Matt's quarry wrapped his arm in the clerk's, a group of late arrivals charged up to the counter to check in.

Matt took advantage of the situation by quickly joining the group and swept past his quarry, deftly picking the room-key card and his registration packet out of his pocket. The man never noticed. He was too busy focusing all his attention on the woman on his arm.

As the couple headed for the bar, Matt noted the room number in the registration packet. He also noted the name: Stedman.

Matt stepped into the men's room for some privacy and dusted Stedman's registration packet and room-card key with his portable fingerprint kit. The prints were too smudged to be identifiable.

Matt left the men's room and checked the couple at the bar. Stedman was in a corner booth with the clerk. Full drinks on the table. Cigarettes in their hands. They should be there a while.

Matt made for the elevators.

He wanted to search Stedman's room before the lothario talked the clerk into joining him there.

Matt caught the next elevator up. He was down the hall and at the door seconds later. After making sure no one was around, he slipped the key card in place and quietly let himself inside.

The room was dark and smelled of something heavily floral. Matt was just reaching for the light switch when he heard a noise from inside the darkness.

He froze.

A second later he heard the rustling of covers and an irritated snort, the kind that came from someone whose sleep had been disturbed.

Matt remained perfectly still, barely breathing, alert to the slightest sound. The bed covers rustled again. The minutes ticked by.

Gradually, Matt detected the sounds of deep, rhythmic breathing that told him that the room's occupant had fallen back asleep. He let out a silent, relieved breath.

Matt left Stedman's room even more quickly and quietly then he had entered.

He took the elevator back to the lobby. He took the key card out of his pocket, wiped it of his fingerprints and placed it back in the registration packet. He turned it in to the clerk at the registration desk, telling him he'd just found it on the carpet.

When Stedman found it was missing, he'd probably figure it had dropped out of his pocket.

Matt didn't want to alert these two that they had been spotted. Not until he found out who they were.

Since he didn't want them following him and Jamie tomorrow morning either, he realized a hotel change was in order.

Matt made his way back to his own room. He didn't bother to turn on the lights when he entered. The glowing dial of his wristwatch told him it was eleven. He took off the baseball cap and pulled off the black sweatshirt.

He was reaching for his dress shirt when suddenly the connecting door to Jamie's room swung open. Matt jumped.

She stood there in a diaphanous peach robe, her gentle curves and long golden hair haloed by the light pouring in from her room. She was a soft and supple vision of glowing femininity. Every male cell in his body instantly snapped to happy attention.

"You must be wondering why I dropped in?" she asked.

Her husky tone was sweet and liquid, with just a twist of tartness.

Matt tried to clear his throat to answer. He couldn't.

"I just wanted to let you know that fifteen minutes ago I was being strangled."

Matt was torn between humor at her words and the hum of desire rising in his blood. He tried to clear his throat again. This time he managed to find his voice, albeit a gruff one.

"I'm glad to see all your self-defense classes have paid off."

Jamie leaned over to turn on the lamp. Matt followed the swift gracefulness of her movement. Her long hair flowed past her waist like a glistening waterfall. Then the light flashed in his eyes.

Jamie straightened and crossed her arms over her chest.

One delicate slippered shoe was tapping impatiently on the carpet. There was a good bit of color in her cheeks. And nothing less than a combative sparkle in her deep blue eyes.

If she had come to his room to seduce instead of scold, she couldn't have done a more thorough job. She lured him like nothing else in the entire world ever could or ever would. He wanted nothing more than to go right to her and wrap her in his arms. He forced himself to remain standing where he was.

"Why did you go out without telling me?" she asked.

"How did you find out I had gone?"

"I knocked on the door. When I didn't get an answer, I came inside."

"And why would you do that, Jamie?"

"Because I wanted to see you, of course. I..."

Matt knew the instant Jamie's voice trailed off was the instant that she did see him, really see him.

Her foot stopped tapping. Her arms uncrossed and dropped to her sides. She stood rigid as her eyes widened to stare at his bare chest in surprise.

But the surprise was quickly replaced by an intense, openly frank approval that drained the blood from Matt's head and sent it soaring through his veins. She took a step toward him. Then another.

His heart stopped.

"Matt, your shoulder! Dear, sweet heaven, what did you do to your shoulder?"

Matt was absolutely astounded to see the look of horror on her face and hear the immeasurable distress swallowing her voice.

He followed her stare to look at his left shoulder in a kind of automatic response. Then it dawned on him what she meant. He'd forgotten about the angry bruise that capped it. He opened his mouth to explain, but no words came out.

Because in that instant, Jamie's warmth floated to his side like a lover's caress. Her gown rustled against his pant leg. He drank in the sweetness of her honeyed scent and breath as she exhaled on a long, heartbreakingly sad sigh.

"It was Wrey, wasn't it?" she asked, staring at his purple bruise. "You took the blow he'd meant for me. Oh, Matt! He hurt you!"

Her hair felt like cool fire against his bare arm. The heat of her was licking inside him like an eager golden flame. She was so close. So damn close.

He forced the words through his lips. "Jamie, go get dressed. We have to leave the hotel."

She ignored his words. She reached up to gently trace the bruise that began on his shoulder and spread to his upper chest.

The incendiary feel of the light brush of her fingers on his bare flesh caused Matt to suck in a hard breath.

She instantly withdrew her hands and stepped back. "I'm so sorry! That must have hurt. I didn't think."

Matt closed his eyes and fought for control. No other woman had ever made him want her like this—to the point of pain. And beyond.

"It didn't...hurt," he said carefully, his hands balling into fists by his sides.

"You're only saying that to try to make me feel better. Matt, why didn't you tell me you'd been injured?"

The continuing concern for him in her sweet voice was uncoiling the tight hold he kept on himself with such swift ease that every alarm bell in his brain was clanging. If he remained near her like this much longer, his body's emphatic demands were going to prevail and he'd be molding her to the ravenous length of his body without thought or mercy.

His voice was low and thick and hoarse.

"Jamie, my shoulder is fine. Go back to your room and pack. We have to leave."

"Your shoulder is not fine. I can see that for myself."

Those beautiful, luminous blue eyes of hers were looking right up at him.

He had never begged a living soul for anything in his life before, but he was begging now.

"Jamie, please go back to your room."

"But I wanted to tell you—"

"We'll discuss it later."

"But it has to do with—"

*"Damn it, Jamie, go back to your room."*

She blanched and stepped quickly back, just as if he had struck her.

He felt as if he had. He had never used that tone of voice on a woman before in his life.

But Matt knew that the hurt and shock on her face were nothing compared to what she was going to feel if he lost any more control. And he was so close to losing it now that he was shaking.

She turned and fled through the open connecting door, slamming it behind her.

For the next several minutes Matt just stood where he was and concentrated on breathing in deeply. It was all he could do. When he had recovered sufficiently to move, he stumbled over to the connecting door and locked it.

Then he leaned his forehead against it and swore so hard beneath his breath that he was certain the oaths would be etched on the walls.

# Chapter Ten

"Time to saddle up, ride out and get 'em, Jamie."

It was the first thing Matt had said to her since he knocked on the connecting door between their rooms at the Flamingo Hilton that morning.

Jamie rose from the booth at the coffee shop in the hotel, knowing she should feel excited and expectant that her search for Tony might soon be over. But all she felt was tired. Her coffee cup had been filled and emptied twice. The scrambled eggs and toast remained untouched on her plate.

He'd explained why they had to change hotels. The idea of two people following them should have kept her awake all night. But it hadn't kept her awake all night. Matt had.

Every time Jamie closed her eyes, she kept seeing every smooth muscle ridge and contoured valley of Matt's magnificent naked chest in breathtaking detail. And she kept seeing that awful purple bruise from the blow he had taken to protect her—and never even mentioned. And every time she saw these things, her pulse went wild.

Not even the cold, steely anger in his voice when he had finally ordered her out of his room could cool the heat beating inside her blood.

Lord, no wonder Matt had to fight off women.

Jamie tried to refocus her attention to the business at hand as they left the coffee shop and started on the casino route that Wendy had guided them through the night before. She'd been through a lot to get here. If she was going to talk to Tony this morning, she had to prepare what she was going to say.

But it was Matt she couldn't keep out of her mind.

Jamie skirted around a vacuum cleaner rolling down the aisle as her eyes scanned the features of the men they passed. Tony's computer-aged face had etched itself in her memory. Unfortunately, when she looked at the men trying to find a match, they looked back as though she'd issued an invitation.

She knew if it hadn't been for Matt beside her, she would probably have been having to fight off a lot of unwelcome advances. But Matt—all six foot six of him in boots and Stetson—was right beside her.

And there wasn't one man crazy enough to approach her.

They walked through the first casino. The second. The third. Jamie's eyes kept scanning the faces, looking for that one specific arrangement of features that belonged to a thirty-year-old Tony. But he was nowhere to be found.

It was a few minutes after eight when they entered Harrah's, the second to the last casino on Wendy's route. Matt and Jamie headed as usual for the slot machines, once again having to dodge the early morning march of vacuum cleaners.

Jamie began to realize what a thin trail they were following. It wasn't real likely that Wendy had seen Tony. Someone who looked a little like him maybe, but not Tony. After all, what were the odds it had been him? Pretty slim. She doubted any gambler in any of the casinos they'd been in would have taken them.

Then, suddenly, she looked over and there he was. For a moment, the unexpectedness of seeing Tony made her unsure of her own eyes. She stopped still as a statue and stared.

He was talking to a man. She saw only Tony. His dress shirt and dark slacks. His black hair combed back, neat and shiny beneath the subdued interior lights of the casino. His olive skin smooth, line free. His teeth white. He looked exactly as she remembered him. Exactly.

The age-enhanced photo had been wrong. Tony hadn't changed.

He turned and looked directly at her. She had not expected him to recognize her. Not in a million years. But he did. She saw it in the brief flash of surprise that he instantly quelled.

"Tony."

She didn't even know she'd called his name until she heard the sound of it reverberating in her ears.

He smiled, smooth and impersonal, his face a stranger's mask. "I'm afraid you have me confused with someone else."

He turned to go. Jamie took a step toward him, holding up the big, chunky piece of cheap metal still hanging around her neck.

"Tony, I found a secret compartment in the locket. I have to tell you what's inside."

Even though his back was now to her, she knew he had heard her because of the slowing of his step. But he quickly resumed his stride and walked swiftly away.

Jamie stood motionless, cold, feeling as though someone had dumped an ice bucket over her head. Tony didn't want to see her. He didn't even want to talk to her.

"I'll get him back for you," Matt said.

Jamie grabbed Matt's arm as he moved forward. "No. I couldn't...not now. Let him go."

"He owes you an explanation."

"No, Matt. He doesn't owe me anything. Please. Let's just go back to the hotel."

Jamie felt too disheartened to say another word on the way to their rooms. Her feet dragged as did her thoughts. All this effort and Tony wouldn't even talk to her.

When she opened the door to her room and Matt once again followed her inside, she knew better than to think this time that there was anything even friendly about his actions.

She sat on the bed, kicked off her shoes, then swung her legs on top of the bedspread and leaned back against the headboard.

Matt was standing at the bottom of the bed looking at her with his typically cool, distant expression.

"Something you wanted to say?" she asked, hearing the edge in her voice. "Like I told you so?"

"Do you really think I'd say something like that to you?"

Jamie sighed and rubbed her temples. Lord, she felt tired. And so damn disappointed.

"No, Matt. You're much too much of a gentleman to rub it in when you're right. I should have listened. He knew I was looking for him. He just doesn't want to see me."

"He's a fool."

"No, I'm the fool for letting it...bother me."

Matt pulled up a chair beside the bed and sat on it. "Why didn't you tell me about the locket?"

"I tried to. Last night. But you didn't want to talk about it, remember?"

"I'm sorry about last night. I...had something else on my mind. I'm listening now. Tell me about this locket."

Jamie picked up the locket and looked at it, feeling suddenly as though all the foolish hopes of the intervening years rested heavily in her hand.

"Tony gave this to me on the night he took me to the dance. Just before he kissed me."

"And you've kept it all these years."

"Yes."

"Because it meant so much to you."

"Yes."

"Tell me what was so special about that night, Jamie."

Jamie looked at Matt, trying to understand the emotion behind his request. But all she saw was that continuing polite, cool professional composure of his. And it was more disheartening than even the rejection she'd gotten from Tony.

She sighed, her spirits unraveling to their last thread. "Why, Matt? What does it matter? You promised you'd find Tony for me. You found him. It's over for you."

"It's not over. Someone has been trying to keep you from

finding him. Someone has been following you. Jamie, I have to find out who and why. Help me. Tell me about that night."

"I'm not sure I can."

"Why?"

"Matt, this is real personal and if you don't understand, it's going to—" Jamie stopped herself just in time to hold back some of her pride. "Disappoint me," she finished.

Matt leaned over and rested his hand on top of hers.

The unexpectedness of the gesture made the breath catch in her throat. The feel of his calloused palm was hot and hard. A shiver snaked through her, bringing warmth instead of cold. The pressure of his brief clasp was gentle. When he withdrew his hand, the warmth remained.

"I'll do my best to understand, Jamie."

And Jamie suddenly knew that he would. She stared hard at the locket in her hands. The words came out hesitantly at first as she tried to describe what it was like to be fifteen, sneaking out the back window of a trailer, not daring to draw the attention of the man and woman who were drunk in the next room. And why she couldn't.

Next, she was describing the smell of the feedlot, the feel of the scratchy cloth of the hand-me-down dress, the effort to balance in the chcap, gaudy high heels that were too big for her feet.

But overlaying it all was the excitement of being invited to the dance. Then Tony was putting the locket around her neck and leaning down to kiss her. And they were walking hand in hand.

"When we heard the shotgun blast, I knew it came from the Kleinman place," Jamie said. "Tony wanted to go investigate. I told him Kyle was only shooting at rabbits in his backyard—and missing as usual. So he went in to the dance with me instead."

Jamie paused to take a deep breath. "Deputy Plotnik's wife, Maylene, took our picture with a Polaroid camera as soon as we walked in the door. She was selling the pictures of all the couples that night for a dollar. Maylene and her husband always had this entrepreneurial bent.

"Anyway, Tony bought the picture from her, then tore it up and threw it into the wastebasket because he said it didn't do me justice. When he went to get us some punch, I fished the photo out of the wastebasket and kept it—well, his side of it anyway."

"But not your side of it. Why?"

Jamie laughed with no mirth. "Because it *did* do me justice. Tony and I had a cup of punch and three dances together before Deputy Plotnik arrived to tell Wrey and his mama about Kyle being shot. The dance broke up then, and everybody went home."

"What happened when you got home?"

"It was okay. They were passed out in the living room. They didn't even make it into the bedroom that night."

A moment passed before Matt spoke. "Were your foster folks always that...violent?"

Jamie nodded. "They were ignorant and coarse and cared for little beyond their next bottle of booze. Lester was a genetic twig right off the twisted family tree."

"How did swine like that ever get custody of you?"

Jamie looked up, startled by the sudden, intense anger in Matt's voice. And in his eyes.

"Things were...different then."

He looked away for a moment. When he looked back at her, the steadied coolness in his eyes and in his gravelly drawl told her he had the anger under control. "Didn't you ever try to find any of your blood family?"

"No point to it. There weren't any."

"No uncles, aunts, cousins?"

"None. The only kindred souls that kept me company in those days were the ones I found in books. Their uplifting thoughts and feelings filled in a lot of the empty times. Then I met Liz. From the first, she went about getting the entire Bonner clan to adopt me. She set me up with Cade and kept after him until he proposed."

"I doubt he needed much convincing."

"Truth be told, poor Cade didn't have a chance. There I was, a foundling, just like one of his homeless puppies. He couldn't resist trying to save me."

"Jamie, he loves you."

"I know he does, Matt. I don't mean the comment unkindly."

Matt looked away from her face toward the window for a moment, before his eyes once again found hers. "Did anyone in Sweetspring have the sense not to blame you for your foster family?"

"A couple of my teachers pitied me. But their pity was as bad as the meanness from the other kids."

"I don't understand."

"You would if you'd ever been pitied, Matt."

"Explain what you mean."

"Pity gives you the feeling that you're a victim. Pretty soon you start acting like one and thinking like one and you become one. It's a joyless experience."

"You didn't let that happen."

"I couldn't. Thinking of myself as a victim was not the way to survive. And I had to survive in order to leave that place. A victim could never have escaped."

"So it wasn't his kiss or the locket that has made Tony special to you all these years. It was the fact that he was the only one who saw you and liked you for who you were."

Jamie smiled. "You do understand. I'm much obliged to you for finding him, Matt, even if Tony won't acknowledge who I am."

"I can rectify that. Just say the word."

Jamie saw the look in Matt's eyes, heard the subtle, deadly change in his voice. They both gave her a start.

"No. I thank you, Matt, most sincerely, but no. Tony's acceptance of me as myself got me through a particularly painful period of my life. Whatever his reasons for not wanting to accept me now, I will respect them."

"Why? You must realize that he had to be the one who threatened you."

"No, I don't believe that."

"Jamie, we found the driver of that eighteen-wheeler."

Jamie tensed, her spine suddenly straight and rigid. "Are you saying Tony sent him?"

"His name is Donald Tennisen. He's from Reno."

"I…see. And because he's from Reno, you assume Tony sent him. But you don't know that for sure. What did Tennisen have to say?"

"That he wanted his lawyer. He's intimately familiar with all the roads into Stripe City. But up until now, Tennisen's kept his felonies confined to beating up on his competitors and sabotaging their rigs. This is his first offense that doesn't come off as business related. Unless Tony is part of his business."

"Tony didn't send him, Matt. Not acknowledging me is one thing. But threatening me, having someone run us off the road, that wouldn't be like Tony."

Matt got up from his chair and strode over to the window. He looked out at the clouds that had gathered like thick smoke, blotting out the morning light. The motionless planes and angles of his profile mirrored the somber sky.

But that pulse vibrating in his jaw was moving faster than a rattlesnake strike.

She could sense a tension in Matt that was almost tangible. She didn't know when she had first begun to be aware of it. But now that she had, she realized it was an integral part of him—an almost smoldering energy that lay beneath the cool, professional quality of his control. He turned back to look at her.

"What was inside the locket?"

Jamie unfastened the chain from around her neck. She turned it on its face and slipped her nail beneath a small indentation on the back.

The hidden spring flipped to reveal the secret compartment.

Jamie reached inside and drew out a rolled paper. Matt returned to the side of the bed. She held the paper up to him.

As he unrolled it, Jamie saw his eyebrows raise.

"This is a ten-thousand-dollar note."

"Yes, the discovery rather surprised me, too."

"When did you find it?"

"A week ago I was going through some old clothes I'd stored in a box. The locket fell out on the floor. When I picked it up, I discovered the secret compartment with the money."

Jamie watched Matt hold the wrinkled bill up to the light, studying it more closely.

"At first I thought it had to be play money," she continued. "I was going to throw it out. But just to be on the safe side, I took it to a bank. They verified that it was real."

"Tony must have been more taken with you than you ever knew. He wrote P.S. I Love You on this bill."

"No, Matt. I'm convinced Tony didn't know the money was hidden in the locket or he surely wouldn't have given it to me. The locket itself has no monetary value."

"A cheap metal locket is an odd place to hide ten-thousand dollars," Matt said, still frowning at the bill.

"I've been thinking about how it might have happened. It could be the locket belonged to an elderly female relative of Tony's who passed on. She may have been one of those folks who didn't trust banks. I can see someone like that hiding the money in the locket and not telling anyone about it."

"So returning this money was the reason you wanted to see Tony?"

"Part of it."

"And the other part?"

She couldn't explain to Matt what had been missing inside her—what she had found only in his arms. Knowing that he didn't want her, she could never set herself up for this man's rejection—or worse yet, his pity.

"Sometimes a kiss can be hard to forget," she said simply.

"So you keep telling me," he said, an odd undercurrent in his drawl. "This bill is old. Date on it is 1918."

"The bank told me that 1968 was the last year that the Federal Reserve issued any bills over one-hundred dollars. If this bill was in better shape, it'd be a collector's item. As it is, it's probably worth just the face value."

"Which isn't a bad chunk of change even by today's standards." Matt held the bill out to her.

Jamie took it and returned it to its hiding place in the locket. She slipped the locket into her purse. "I'd still like to return the money to Tony. I suppose that means another round of the casinos tomorrow. Only, if he thinks I might be there, he may avoid them from now on."

"We don't need to repeat this morning's rounds to locate him."

"You're serious?"

"Think about it, Jamie. He frequents different casinos in the early morning on a regular basis, but he isn't gambling. Why else would he be there?"

"If he were an employee," Jamie said. "But he can't work for a particular casino. Wendy says she saw him in the Hilton yesterday morning. We saw him in Harrah's this morning."

"There's another explanation."

Matt was obviously getting at something. Jamie mentally retraced their steps that morning, racking her brain for what it might be.

She had been concentrating on the faces of the men she had seen. But the background lights and shapes, the noises, these were harder to focus on, particularly since they had to compete with the ubiquitous vacuuming machines.

And then it came to her. She leaned away from the headboard. "The cleaning crew. Nearly all the casinos had workers vacuuming and cleaning in the early morning hours!"

"And I wouldn't be a bit surprised if your Tony wasn't there supervising them."

"Matt, you're brilliant!"

Her unconscious burst of enthusiasm spread over his face

in a flash of color. Jamie's mouth almost dropped open in surprise when she realized she had embarrassed him.

The fact that Matt could be embarrassed was amazing enough. But the fact that he could be embarrassed by a compliment from her hit Jamie on a whole new level.

Matt walked over to the phone on the table and picked up the receiver. He dialed the desk and asked to speak to the manager.

As he waited to be transferred, he kept his eyes averted from hers.

A moment later, Jamie heard him identify himself to the person on the other end of the line as the owner of a new carpet-cleaning service in town. She was rather amazed at the extremely polished impromptu sales pitch Matt gave. She didn't know whether to be shocked at how effectively he lied or reassured. After a few questions, he thanked whoever he'd been talking to and hung up the phone.

"The highly competent Timothy Palmer of Palmer's Cleaning Company services the Flamingo Hilton casino and most of the other major casinos in Reno."

"Tony must work for this Palmer."

"Let's find out."

Matt picked up the telephone book and flipped through the yellow pages. "Palmer's Cleaning Company is on the other side of town," he said.

"Let's not call. Let's just try to catch Tony there."

Matt nodded. By the time he had closed the telephone book, Jamie had slid her legs off the bed and her feet into her shoes. She snatched her handbag and beat him to the door.

She hadn't opened it but an inch when two powerful arms materialized on either side of her to shove the door closed again.

"Not so fast, Jamie. Let me check out the hall first."

Jamie felt Matt's breath against her hair, the incredible size and heat of him surrounding her completely, permeating right through her clothing, her skin, her bones. She sucked in a startled breath as a deep, undulating wave of pure, unadulterated desire washed through her.

The feeling was so devastatingly strong that the only thing that kept her standing was the fact that she was now leaning against the door.

The next instant he had stepped back, freeing her from the imprisoning circle of his body, a freedom she did not welcome.

It took another moment for the blood in Jamie's body to rebalance sufficiently in her limbs to allow her to move away from the door. Even so, she was far from steady on her feet. She never knew she could want a man like this.

"Sorry," Matt said, his voice gruff. "I didn't mean to scare you."

Jamie just shook her head, not daring to look at him, afraid he'd see she was anything but scared.

Cade had been her first lover and a wonderfully tender one. But not once in the entire three years of their marriage had she felt anything like this violent passion that threatened to consume her every time she even got near Matt.

This was pure madness. And it was getting worse.

She kept her distance from Matt as she watched him slip open the door and check the hall with swift, silent efficiency. He led the way out into the hall, closing the door behind them.

Matt passed up two elevators that were occupied, before taking the third unoccupied one to the parking garage. They were in the rental car and on the road just minutes later.

Jamie noticed Matt varied his speed, even making several turns to double back over streets they had already traveled. Not once did his eyes stray from the mirrors as he watched the road around them. He seemed even more wary today than usual.

"Are we being followed?" Jamie asked.

"If we are, they're doing it in tandem."

"What do you mean, tandem?"

"One of them follows us for a few blocks. Then he turns off and the other one takes over."

"How can you tell when that happens?"

"It's nearly impossible to know someone is tracking you that way. Professionals use it all the time."

"I thought you said these two weren't professionals?"

"One of them wasn't acting professional last night. When they discovered we slipped out on them this morning, they may have decided to bone up on their surveillance skills."

"You said one of their names was Stedman. Is there any way for you to identify him further?"

"I'm working on it. This is Palmer's Cleaning Company up here on the right."

When Matt had pulled into the parking lot, he made no move to get out of the car. He turned to face her.

"You don't have to see him again, Jamie. If he's in there, I'll get the money to him."

"I'm not comfortable with sitting in a car while someone else takes care of my business. I'll face him—and his rejection, if that's all he has left to give."

Matt nodded his understanding.

Jamie didn't wait until Matt came around to open the door. She opened it herself and got out. When they stepped inside the cleaners', the whirl of motors and the smell of acrid chemicals assailed her nose.

There was no one at the service counter. Jamie rang the bell. It gave out a respectable resonance.

A tall woman with long, rope-like black hair, wearing tight jeans and a T-shirt over an improbable Barbie-doll figure bounced out from the back room. A practiced greet-the-public smile held back her full red lips. But the instant she saw Jamie, the smile disintegrated and her dark eyes tightened.

"You!"

"You must be Sharlyn," Jamie guessed.

"How did you know to come here?"

"I hired an excellent private investigator."

Her deep voice was like a sneer. "How many ways do you have to be told? Timmy doesn't want to see you!"

"But I want to see him. I won't take much of his time. I just need to give him something."

Sharlyn's bloodred one-inch fingernails sliced through the air as her bony arm pointed straight toward the door.

"Get out of here right now or I swear I'm coming over this counter and scratching your eyes out."

"Why so much anger, Sharlyn? You don't even know me. You don't even know what it is I have for him."

"Timmy doesn't want it! He doesn't want you! He just wants to be left alone!"

"Why don't you let him tell me that?" Jamie said.

"You don't care what happens to him! Get out, get out, get out!" Sharlyn screeched, her face turning as red as her nails.

She already had one long, skinny jean-clad leg halfway over the counter when Matt pulled Jamie out of the store.

MATT HURRIED JAMIE into the car and drove away before Sharlyn could get anywhere near her. He'd seen raving lunatics before, and Sharlyn definitely fit the description. Besides, if Tony had been on the premises Sharlyn's raving would surely have brought him up front and center.

"She called him Timmy," Jamie said, a few blocks later. "Tony must be Timothy Palmer, the owner of Palmer's Cleaning Company."

"Appears to be the likely explanation."

"So his family's name was Palmer. They *did* borrow the Lagarrigue name when they were in Sweetspring. I confess until this very minute, I hadn't fully believed it. Could it be he didn't acknowledge me in Harrah's because he didn't want to have to explain why his family was using the Lagarrigue name in Sweetspring?"

"Could be," Matt said, only half listening.

He was concentrating on a gray sedan pulling away from the curb a block back. He recognized it as one that had been parked in front of the Flamingo Hilton when they left the garage there less than forty minutes before.

Jamie turned around to look behind them. "Someone back there?"

"You saw something?"

She straightened in her seat. "Yes. The tensing of your hands, and that telltale pulse in your jaw."

He had been aware of her eyes on him more and more lately. But he hadn't been aware of how much she had begun to see.

"Can you lose him?" she asked.

"We're going to find out." Matt made a signal to go left and slowed. The gray sedan moved from the right to the middle lane a block back and slowed. Matt waited until the intervening red light caught it. Then he quickly changed to the right lane and made a fast turn around the block. He gunned the engine, speeding down the next two streets. He pulled into a casino parking lot, whipping the car into the first available space.

"Come on," he said, jumping out. Jamie was out the passenger door before he circled around. They headed for the back entrance to the casino. Once inside, he led the way toward the hotel entrance.

Matt had to keep his pace moderate in consideration for Jamie's high heels. They took the first cab waiting at the curb.

Matt gave the driver instructions to let them off at a back casino entrance at the Flamingo Hilton. All the way there, Matt checked the windows for pursuit. He saw none.

Once at the Hilton, they caught the first elevator up to their rooms. Matt kept alert, studying every face to see if they were being watched. When they got out at their floor, Matt led Jamie down the hallway in the opposite direction to their rooms. When he was certain no one had followed them, he headed down the right hallway.

He had taken every precaution. He felt sure that he had lost their tail.

The last thing he expected was what greeted him when he opened Jamie's door.

# *Chapter Eleven*

Jamie ran right into Matt's shoulder when he stopped suddenly on the threshold of her room. His huge left arm immediately circled around her body in a protective gesture, keeping her securely in place behind his enormous frame.

"What are you doing in here?" he asked whoever was in her room. The chipped-ice quality of his voice sent a warning chill through Jamie's muscles.

"There's no reason to be alarmed, Mr. Bonner," Jamie heard a man's voice say, with hurried assurance. "We asked the hotel management to let us into Mrs. Bonner's room because we didn't want to look conspicuous waiting out in the hall."

Matt didn't move a muscle. He kept his arm around Jamie. "And who is 'we'?"

"I'm special agent Lane Creighton. This is Special Agent Reg Wilson. We're with the FBI, Mr. Bonner."

The ice in Matt's tone did not melt. "What is the FBI doing here?"

"We'd like to talk to you and Mrs. Bonner about Tony Lagarrigue. That is, if you want to listen."

"I'd like to see your identification," Matt said, still not moving an inch or withdrawing his arm from around Jamie.

Jamie heard the slap of wallets being opened and closed.

"We'll talk downstairs in the coffee shop," Matt said.

An edge surrounded Agent Creighton's words. "Mr. Bonner, as you must realize, this is a very confidential matter. It is hardly conversation for a coffee shop.''

"Folks who have time to pay attention to conversations in coffee shops are standing in lines picking up their unemployment checks about this time of the day,'' Matt said. "Now, are just you two leaving, or are we all going?''

A moment of silence followed before Jamie heard Creighton's irritated voice respond. "Lead the way to the coffee shop.''

"No, you lead the way," Matt said, backing out of the doorway, still holding Jamie in place behind him.

When the two men finally came into view, Jamie found them to look remarkably alike—average height, light brown hair that had seen a barber's clippers quite recently, the same style and conservative cut of dark gray suit, the same dark sunglasses hiding their eyes. The only real difference between them was that the one who nodded in her direction was far more slender than his beefy companion.

"I'm Agent Creighton, Mrs. Bonner," he said. "This is Agent Wilson.''

Jamie nodded in return. She couldn't do much else. Matt still had her circled within the restraint of his enormous arm. The tension in his body was tangible. She didn't understand why he was acting so cautious with these FBI agents.

He let the agents precede them down the hallway and into the elevator. When Matt and Jamie stepped inside, Matt kept his arm around her, close to his left side. He did not turn to face front. He faced Creighton and Wilson.

"Some reason why you don't trust us, Mr. Bonner?" Creighton asked, clearly put out by Matt's actions.

"Some reason why I should?" Matt responded evenly.

Creighton shook his head as though truly puzzled.

The coffee shop was mostly deserted. The waitress showed them to a large corner booth.

Matt waited for Creighton and Wilson to take their seats on one side of the booth. Then Matt gestured for Jamie to slide in on the other end, and he slid in beside her. He still kept her close to his left side, just as he had been doing since he had discovered the FBI agents in her room.

Before the waitress could drop the menus and disappear, Matt told her all they were ordering was four cups of coffee and four pieces of apple pie.

She nodded and left to get them.

"You could at least have asked me what kind of pie I liked," Agent Creighton said, trying out a small smile.

"I could have," Matt said. He did not return the smile.

"I do like apple pie, however," Creighton admitted.

"Then you can have my piece," Matt said.

Creighton shifted in the booth, giving physical evidence to his discomfort with Matt's refusal to respond to the friendly approach. Jamie noticed that Wilson had still not said a word. Both FBI agents still wore their dark sunglasses.

When the coffee and pie arrived, the waitress set the bill facedown and left. Wilson picked up his fork and dug in.

"You appear to be a very cautious man, Mr. Bonner," Creighton said, not making a move to touch either the coffee or pie in front of him.

"And a busy one, Mr. Creighton. It's time you told us about Tony Lagarrigue."

Creighton made a perfunctory look around, as though to reassure himself that no one was within hearing distance. Then he rested his suit sleeves on the table and leaned forward, projecting all the signs that he was about to impart a confidence.

"Fifteen years ago, Oscar Lagarrigue was a bookkeeper in an organization that was taken over by the Mob. When he found out who his company's new owners were, he contacted us. He gave us some valuable information. We gave him the new identity of Oscar Lagarrigue and moved him and his family to Sweetspring, Texas."

"You mean they were in the witness-protection program?" Jamie asked, her voice rising in surprise.

"Still are, Mrs. Bonner," Creighton said. "Always will be. The Mob doesn't forget informants. Not even the children of informants. Tony has to stay hidden, too, and that means out of the public eye. When Kyle Kleinman was murdered right down the block from Oscar in Sweetspring and the media descended, we had no choice but to change their identities and relocate them again.''

"Then Tony isn't Timothy Palmer, either?"

Creighton exchanged quick, uncomfortable glances with Wilson—two pairs of dark sunglasses glaring at each other.

"We didn't realize you'd found out his new name. Mr. Palmer has worked hard to establish himself and his business here in Reno. If we have to change his name and relocate him again—"

"I don't want to expose his past," Jamie spoke up quickly.

"Who else besides you and Mr. Bonner here know that Tony and Timothy are one and the same?"

"No one. We only figured it out this morning."

"How?"

"It's what I do for a living," Matt answered curtly.

"Agent Creighton, Tony was real nice to me when we were in Sweetspring together," Jamie said. "All I want to do is return what I found in a secret compartment of a locket he gave me."

"What did you find?"

"Something private," Matt said quickly before Jamie could reply.

"Give it to us. We'll see that he gets it."

"No," Matt said. "Ms. Bonner has gone to a lot of trouble and come a long way to see Tony. She's not giving up the locket or what's inside it to anyone but him."

Creighton's forehead creased as if he were in deep thought. Wilson's face remained as noncommittal about the conversation as it had from the first. He seemed to be edging toward Creighton's piece of pie now that he had finished his.

"No, sorry," Creighton said, shaking his head after his moment of brow furrowing. "We can't permit your coming in contact with Tony again. This morning's episode was dangerous enough for him."

"In that case, we have nothing more to talk about," Matt said. Jamie suddenly felt Matt's hand pulling her across and out of the booth.

"Just a minute, Bonner," Agent Creighton said.

Matt kept Jamie by his side as they paused at the edge of the booth. "Something else you wanted to say?" Matt asked.

"Before you go, I'm going to need both your and Mrs. Bonner's word that neither of you will divulge anything you know about Timothy Palmer, including what I've told you today. I'm also going to have to have your solemn pledge that neither of you will go near him again."

Jamie was just about to give her assurance on both accounts when Matt surprised her by once again speaking before she could.

"Ms. Bonner is going to see Timothy Palmer again, Mr. Creighton. That's all you have my word on."

"Now hold on here, Bonner—"

"I suggest you talk to Palmer to find out when would be a convenient time. Ms. Bonner and I will be in our rooms for the next forty minutes. You have the number."

And with that, Matt took Jamie's arm and turned away. He did not pause to say goodbye to the agents or give Jamie time to. Matter of fact, he did not break stride once as he all but dragged her out of the coffee shop.

Jamie was prepared to put up a serious argument except that she noticed that telltale pulse was throbbing in Matt's jaw.

They were stepping into an elevator before Matt finally let go of her arm.

"Where's the stampede?" she asked, projecting far more calm than she felt.

"Sorry about the rough ride, Jamie, but there are some things I need to check out. And I don't have a lot of time."

"You were barely civil to those agents. Why?"

"I don't take kindly to having my room broken into."

"Actually the hotel management let them in. But I get your drift. I didn't like that part either."

"There was a part you did like?"

"Learning that Tony and his family were in the witness-protection program explains a lot of what has been puzzling me. Now I know it wasn't me he was rejecting this morning. He simply feared being exposed. Why did you keep the money a secret?"

"Because I didn't want you handing it over to them."

"I can't keep it, Matt. It belongs to Tony."

They were at the door to Jamie's room. Matt slipped the key card through.

"If it does, we'll see that he gets it. Now, let's find out how Creighton and Wilson kept themselves occupied while they were waiting for us in here."

Matt took a quick look inside both rooms before he gestured for Jamie to come in. He closed the door behind her and set the security lock in place.

"Look through your things, Jamie. See if anything's disturbed or missing. Then pack up. I'll be back soon."

He disappeared through the connecting door and closed it behind him.

Jamie was having a hard time envisioning FBI agents searching, much less taking anything of hers. But she'd come to trust Matt so implicitly, she went about looking through her things as instructed. Everything appeared intact. She packed her suitcase.

When she was finished, she walked over to the connecting door and knocked.

"Come in," he called.

She opened the door to find him talking on the phone.

"Since they've already searched our things, that should satisfy them for the present," Matt was saying to whoever was on the other end of the line. "Right. Later."

Matt hung up the receiver.

"They searched our things?" Jamie asked. "I found nothing out of place. How do you know?"

"Private investigators are trained to know. Be ready to go out again when they call to set up the meeting with Tony."

"You seem certain they will."

"They want to know what you found in that locket."

"Matt, do you think it wise to play hardball with the FBI this way?"

"You still want to give Tony back the ten-thousand dollars?"

"Yes."

"Then this is the way to do it."

The call came in twenty minutes later, just two minutes shy of the forty-minute deadline Matt had given.

Matt let the phone ring twice before answering. Jamie only caught the few affirmative grunts that constituted his side of the conversation. He jotted down an address. When he hung up, he turned to Jamie holding up that piece of paper.

"Timothy Palmer will see us now. Get your suitcase. I'll call later and check us out. We're not coming back here."

They took a hotel taxi to an address that turned out to be nothing but a vacant lot. Matt didn't seem surprised, however.

"Park out of sight beneath that tree," Matt said.

Their taxi driver was a chubby, bald cherub who was blessed or cursed with a perpetually pleasant expression that bore no resemblance whatsoever to whatever emotion he might be experiencing. That was dramatically made apparent by the sour note now in his words.

"That's a no-parking zone."

"You get a ticket, I'll pay it."

"I've heard that one before. No dice."

Matt reached into his pocket and pulled out a hundred. He tore it in half and handed one piece to the sour-sounding cherub. "You get the other half when I get back, ticket or no ticket."

Their driver's cheery expression didn't change. But he quickly pulled up to the tree and parked the taxi.

Matt got out and held the door for Jamie.

"This is it?" she asked.

He nodded. She got out.

She couldn't help noticing how he kept looking around,

checking for something amiss. He was like a wary predator, as conscious of what might be lurking behind him as he was of what lay ahead.

She matched his slow pace down the block. He once again kept her on his left side. It was a beautiful neighborhood, upper middle-class.

They passed an expensive new contemporary home with lots of wood and glass and a marble fountain in the front yard. Then a sprawling Spanish-style hacienda surrounded by desert landscaping.

Matt stopped in front of the third house. "This is it."

Jamie did a double take when she realized it was an enormous, imposing, Tudor-style home set back off the street on lush, expansive and beautifully manicured grounds.

"If this is where Tony lives, why did you give the driver the wrong address?"

"Because he has to report the address he takes his passengers to for the official record."

"And you didn't want him to report that we went to Tony's. Why?"

"Just a precaution."

Jamie's eyes took in the impressive Tudor home. "The cleaning business is apparently a profitable one."

Matt made his way casually over to the Mercedes that was parked in front of the garage. The license plate read Clean One. He rested his hand on its hood as he took another slow and careful look around.

"The engine's still slightly warm. Jamie, I want you to stay close to me. Don't leave my side."

Jamie heard that deadly serious sound in his voice. She looked up at him and nodded.

Matt strode slowly, nonchalantly toward the house. But he didn't directly approach the sixteen-foot stone archway that marked the impressive double-door entry to the Tudor.

Instead he headed for the right side of the house, an area hidden by a long, vibrantly healthy and beautifully manicured hedge.

"Are we going in the back way?" Jamie asked.

"We're going to admire the grounds from every angle," Matt said. Jamie understood that he was not admiring the grounds but checking them for something or someone who shouldn't be there.

"Do you think the FBI agents tracked us here to be sure we weren't followed?"

"We weren't followed."

When Matt said it that way, Jamie felt quite certain they weren't.

They were halfway down the side of the house headed toward the back when Matt suddenly stopped. His left arm immediately circled around Jamie in a gesture that was becoming familiar. She felt the tension in him escalating. He stood perfectly still, just like a wild animal sniffing the air.

Jamie looked around, trying to see what had alerted him, trying to listen for a wrong sound.

"Matt, what is—"

Jamie never got a chance to finish her sentence. Matt picked her up, threw her over his shoulder, whirled around and sped away from the house at full and emphatic speed.

The house whizzed by like a blur on one side of Jamie, the hedge on the other. And beneath her she felt the pounding of Matt's muscles like iron pistons plunging up and down.

She had no idea what had warned him. But she understood soon enough why he ran. They had just made the front yard when it happened.

One second Timothy Palmer's beautiful palatial home stood shadowed and still beneath the heavy overcast Reno sky. The next second the walls were thundering and crumbling, the roof flying into the air in a cacophony of roaring noise and exploding fireballs that spit their hellish light into the heavens.

An enormous hole had been blown right in the center of the house.

# Chapter Twelve

The percussion wave of the explosion's force slammed into them like a moving wall, knocking them to the grass. Matt had kept his body between Jamie and the house, taking the worst of it. But what Jamie felt was more than enough to whip the strength and wind right out of her.

She lay on her back, gasping for breath, weak as water. Matt lay across her, balancing his weight on his arms and legs so as not to crush her while his massive body hovered over hers like a shield.

Jamie stared at the house through the open arch of his side in a vague sort of stunned horror. Black plumes of billowing smoke blew out of the hole in the center, filling the sky. Charred debris was falling all around them. A burning piece of roofing landed nearby on a dry wood bush. It burst into flames.

She felt Matt's body jerk above her, hard. She knew instantly that he'd been hit by something.

Jamie's heart gave a huge, hard thump. She put her palms against his chest, pushing to get up.

"Matt—"

"I'll let you up when it's safe."

"But, Matt—"

"Stay still!" He kept her imprisoned beneath him for another full minute. Jamie counted every second against the thinning sheath surrounding her nerves. Then an unearthly stillness seemed to suddenly settle all around them. Matt rolled off her onto his side. Jamie scrambled to her feet.

She dropped right back to her knees beside him when she saw the jagged piece of glass sticking out of the back of his left thigh. Blood was oozing from out the sides, rolling down his jeans.

"Oh, Matt!"

"It's not as bad as it looks, Jamie. I'll take care of it later. We've got to get out of here now. Another explosion could be going off at any moment."

He got instantly to his feet and pulled Jamie to hers. Jamie looked to his face. His eyes were steady. His hand felt warm and hard and strong in hers.

"Hey, I don't know about you two, but I'm getting out of here!"

Jamie looked over to see the taxi driver had backed down the street. He was gesturing frantically out his window at them.

Matt was already on the move toward the taxi, pulling Jamie beside him. How he managed to take a step with that glass in his thigh, Jamie had no idea. But he had the door open for her when she reached the curb.

Jamie jumped inside and Matt jumped in right behind her. Before he'd swung the door closed, their driver was gunning the engine.

They were halfway down the block when the second explosion blew the chimney off the house and sent a fireball into the sky. A second later, literally a ton of bricks was raining onto the patch of grass where Jamie and Matt had been lying.

Jamie shivered when she thought of how close they had come to being buried beneath those bricks.

Their driver let out a muttered oath and crossed himself.

"I've been driving this cab for twenty years and I've never seen anything like that. The fire department is going to have their hands full with that one."

"Have you called them?" Matt asked.

"Right after the first blast. I have a brother on the force. What a fireball that one was. You guys okay back there?"

Jamie looked over at Matt. He was perched on the side of his right leg, his arm extended over the seat, balancing himself in order not to have to put pressure on his left thigh. His expression was calm, but there was a sheen of sweat on his skin. When she thought of the kind of pain he must be enduring so stoically, she could have wept.

"Take us to the nearest emergency room," Jamie said.

"No," Matt contradicted. "The nearest telephone. Then a drugstore, followed by the kind of motel that doesn't mind renting a room for cash to a Mr. and Mrs. Smith for a few hours."

Jamie watched Matt slip the second half of the hundred dollar bill to the driver and then add three crisp new ones.

"And remember that you didn't have a fare when you came back to the Flamingo Hilton," Matt added.

"Yes, sir," the cherub said with enthusiasm, quickly pocketing the money.

"Matt, what can you be thinking?" Jamie asked.

"I'm thinking we just walked into an ambush, Jamie. And I don't intend to walk into any more."


AS SOON AS MATT LIMPED into the new motel room after Jamie, he made sure the door was closed and bolted.

"Why won't you go to a doctor?" Jamie asked.

"Because they'd know the only way to get a piece of glass embedded in a leg like this is through an explosion. These kinds of injuries get reported, Jamie. I don't want to be answering questions from some wet-behind-the-ears police officer who hasn't the faintest idea of what's going on."

"What is going on, Matt?"

"I haven't the faintest idea."

Jamie exhaled heavily. "You can't doctor yourself."

"Private investigators are trained for this sort of thing."

He took off his denim vest and laid it carefully across the nightstand. He picked up the first-aid supplies he'd instructed

Jamie to buy at the drugstore while he was on the telephone. He carried them into the bathroom, closing the door behind him.

He dumped the supplies on the floor in front of the tub-shower enclosure and tried to get a look at the back of his thigh. He couldn't see the wound, but he could sure feel it. It throbbed and burned like hell.

The blood had stopped dripping into his boots, so at least the bleeding had stopped. Shame he was going to have to start it up again. But it was time he got that glass out.

He kicked off his boots, slipped off his socks, removed his shirt and stepped into the shower. He waited until the water was running as cold as a rattlesnake's eyes.

Then he took a deep breath and got a firm grip on the edge of the glass. He wasn't looking forward to doing this twice. With one powerful pull, he yanked it out.

A wave of pain and blood came gushing with it. Matt threw the glass into the trash can beneath the sink. He trained the full force of the shower nozzle at the wound. The icy spray against the burning flesh gave him the seconds of pain relief he needed. As fast as he could, he unzipped his jeans, shucked them and his briefs over his hips and pulled them off.

The dried blood and torn flesh around the wound that pulled away with the fabric brought a violent curse to Matt's lips. The water running down the drain became pink again. He gritted his teeth, watching until it ran clear.

He pulled a towel off its holder, gave his body a once-over. He slung the towel back over the holder. The running water had helped to clean the wound, but he knew it wouldn't be enough. He reached for the bottle of hydrogen peroxide and uncapped it.

He twisted, trying to see the wound.

Matt had doctored plenty of wounds in his time, several of them his own. But not on the upper back portion of his thigh, where he couldn't see what he was doing.

After a couple of stymieing minutes, during which most of

the hydrogen peroxide ended up on the tile floor, he was cursing royally in frustration.

A knock came at the door. "Matt?"

"What?" he called, barely keeping the irritation out of his tone.

When the door opened, Matt was so startled that he just had time to grab the towel off the holder again and wrap it strategically around his middle.

Jamie stood in the doorway. Her eyes moved from his to do a quick, thorough inventory of his body. Their blue was bright with that same frank, intense approval that he remembered from the previous night when she'd walked into his room. His heart began to pound. Hard.

"What are you doing in here?" he asked, hearing the gruffness in his voice, his only defense against her.

She looked at the tile floor, awash in peroxide. Her eyes rose to his. They were clear and lovely and held that glow of determination he'd come to recognize.

"We both know you can't possibly do this on your own. I'm not leaving until I help you, so you might as well just make up your mind to take it like a man."

She moved to his left side, knelt beside his thigh, picking up the bandages he'd strewn across the floor.

Her sleeve brushed the hair on his calf. The sweetness of her scent surrounded his senses. Every muscle in his body tensed. When he heard her sharp intake of breath, he knew she had seen his wound.

"It's deep," she said, her normally full-bodied, husky voice a ghostly whisper.

"I'm tough."

"It must hurt like hell."

"Real tough."

She paused to look at the series of white scars on his legs. Her eyes finally rested on the bruise that still purpled his left shoulder. Her sigh was shaky.

"And I thought your job was too tame."

The sudden whip of sadness in her voice lashed out at him.

He wanted to comfort her, to hold her so badly his hands had begun to shake. He wrapped them around the edge of the towel and held on.

Her eyes returned to the open gash on the back of his thigh. "I should have bought some antibiotic salve at that drugstore."

"Hydrogen peroxide will take care of any germs I missed in the shower."

She picked up the bottle and braced her left hand against his knee to steady herself as she poised the peroxide over the wound.

"I don't know if this is going to hurt."

Matt never felt it if it did. He couldn't feel anything now but the smooth warmth of her hand grasping his knee, the light touch of her breath against his skin and the deep, unrelenting want of her that had every muscle in his body screaming from the pain of it.

When her small, gentle hands skimmed over his flesh, smoothing the large bandages over his wound, Matt's breath came in with a ragged, rippling sound. He closed his eyes and said a silent prayer that the sweet torture would be over soon.

Her voice trembled as she rose. "I'm so sorry. I didn't mean to hurt you, Matt. Or to get you hurt."

He suddenly felt her lips, softly, sweetly brushing against the bruise on his shoulder. Her kiss was a match striking through his blood, setting it on fire. He opened his eyes.

And was ambushed again. For her eyes were so close, so blue, so breathtakingly beautiful, and so full of admiration that they stopped his heart. His voice was nothing but a thick murmur as he reached for her.

"Jamie."

Jamie felt herself picked up as though she weighed nothing more than air. Matt's mouth claimed hers with a groan of hunger so deep she felt it rumbling in her blood and bones. Wild sounds of response burst from her throat as her lips parted beneath the demand of his. The knowledge that he wanted her like this sent her senses soaring.

Arms of steel anchored her hard against his chest as he carried her to the bed. She melted into them, into him. He tasted and felt so impossibly good. She had never been drunk in her life, but she was drunk now with the heat of him and the intensity of her own desire.

He lay on top of her on the bed—naked, heavy, hot, hard. The sudden immense weight and size of him shocked her. Reflexively, she froze. He felt it.

He tore his mouth from hers, pushing his weight to his arms. His eyes were shut tightly. A sheen of perspiration gleamed across his forehead and the magnificent, massive muscles of his shoulders and arms. Jamie panted for breath and realized Matt was battling for breath, too, and for something else. Whatever that other battle, he was losing.

His voice was so thick and slurred, his words were almost unintelligible.

"The gun's on the nightstand in my denim vest. Shoot me in an arm or leg. It's the only thing that's going to keep me away from you now."

He meant it. Dear, sweet Lord, he meant it. The knowledge struck Jamie like a tornado, lifting her up and whirling her into a realm of passion that dwelt beyond reason or understanding.

She grasped his shoulders and brought his lips back to hers with an urgency and force that made her tremble. He sunk into her with a tortured, primitive sound that she had never heard before but recognized on a deep, instinctive level that rocked her soul.

She had never tasted or felt desire so rich, so ripe, so exposed that it could bring pain. But she was tasting and feeling it now because she was tasting and feeling him. It seared her with such force that she felt her insides might shake apart.

When he finally broke off the kiss, she gasped for breath. And then lost it all over again when his hot lips and tongue branded her neck with hard kisses that sent knives of need down her spine. His impatient hands fumbled with the buttons on her blouse. He cursed like a madman and gave up the attempt, pulling up the hem.

He paused for a fraction of a second to stare at her swollen breasts, her taut nipples poking through the thin fabric of her bra. The heat in the look he shot her burned through every inch of her body like a branding iron.

He pulled down her bra and sucked her nipples with such greed that it fired streamers of sensation straight through to her core. Her hands tangled in his hair as she arched her back, feeding her body to him with hungry, incoherent sounds.

He pulled up her skirt with impatient haste, his mouth like steam as he cursed against her breasts at every inch of the fabric that fought him.

His hands felt like molten lead on the cool skin of her thighs. Hot, eager fingers slipped inside her panties to stroke her wet heat.

A deep, eager moan tore from her throat as she arched beneath his touch, wanting, needing, crying out for more.

He was pulling at her panties, desperate to get them off. But they were anchored beneath her garter belt. When he ripped the crotch, she was astonished at how excited she was by the intensity of his need and the sudden rush of cool air against her bare flesh.

And then his hot mouth and tongue replaced the cool air between her legs and her breath caught in her throat. His fingers milked her nipples in ruthless, seductively sweet, torturing pinches as he thrust his tongue into the limits of her self-restraint.

Whether she had been under any semblance of control up until this time, she had no idea. But she did know that she possessed none now. She moaned and panted in a mindless ecstasy as every nerve cell in her body was fused on the sensual pleasures wrought by his mouth and hands.

She began to shudder uncontrollably and then the spasms hit her, strong and racking and almost too intense to be endured. She soared into a mindless pleasure beyond belief.

Then her body fell back against the bed, boneless beneath the aftermath of the onslaught.

She reveled in the full, hot length of him as he once again lay on top of her. His tongue dipped thirstily into her parted lips and he thrust himself against the soft, wet center between her legs. Eagerly, she opened for him. He pushed inside. She wrapped her legs around him, sending him deeper. Her hands grasped his shoulders.

He filled her to overflowing and it was glorious. She moved her hips in a rhythm to the increasing power of his thrusts. The world tilted and turned and spun in streamers of sparkling flashes and the new sensual heat rushing through her.

And then she felt his heavy, powerful body going rigid on top of her, an anguished, crazed cry breaking from his throat into hers as he pulsed warm and wet inside her.

The intimate eroticism of it brought her to another climax, so unexpected that it ripped through her in a stunning shock-wave.

She could feel his heart still hammering, wildly, as he pushed himself up on his forearms to stare at her.

She had barely enough breath for life. She had no words to tell him what this incredible joining with him meant to her, how much sweeter and more important her life had just become. He seemed to have no words for her either.

But what his beautiful silver-gray-and-turquoise eyes were saying as they roamed lovingly over her face was beyond words, beyond anything Jamie had ever seen or heard.

Her heart swelled so much it felt way too big for her body.

He rolled to his side, bringing her with him, still joined to her, his arms holding her fiercely to him. She did not know whether it was a prayer or curse he whispered against her hair. All she knew was that she never, ever wanted him to let her go.

"IT WAS GAS ALL RIGHT," Keele said, over the telephone line. "You smelled it, Matt? That's what warned you?"

"Almost too late," Matt admitted, shifting his weight off

his injured leg as he stood by the motel room's nightstand. "Got a whiff of it coming out of a partially open side window."

"Fire department's preliminary once-over says it must have been a leak in the line," Keele said.

"Have they identified the source of the leak?"

"Too early."

"I don't like that window being open, Keele. Windows stay shut for security in an expensive home like that."

"I hear you. Matt, they found a body in the bedroom. It was beneath the rubble of a brick fireplace and so much shattered glass that they figure the bedroom must have been floor-to-ceiling mirrors."

Matt had been afraid of something like this. "Who was it?"

"White male, maybe five-ten. From his size and the remains of the Rolex on his wrist, they think it's Timothy Palmer."

"Makes sense. It was his car outside, still warm."

"Have you considered this could have been a booby trap that backfired? This Timothy Palmer could have been trying to get you when he miscalculated the explosion."

"If he had decided on a hit, a couple of bullets would have been a lot more accurate, less messy and a damn sight less expensive than decimating his half-million-dollar house."

"I get your point."

"But it could've been someone else who set it up, Keele."

"I can't push this from an official standpoint. And you're going to get your butt kicked if it gets out you've been using the Firm's resources on a case that doesn't qualify."

"Let me worry about that. Run Timothy Palmer's driver's license through the files. What did you find out about Stedman?"

"That picture you sent doesn't match any Stedman we have on file, or anyone else for that matter."

"What about the tie between Donald Tennisen and Timothy Palmer. Anything there yet?"

"Nope. Tennisen's lawyer has shut that old boy's mouth up but good. I do have one piece of news. Seems when Tennisen was given his opportunity to contact his lawyer, one of my buddies here just happened to make note of the unlisted number he called. I checked it out. It belongs to a Sharlyn Beckwith of Reno."

"Sharlyn?" Matt repeated.

"Name sound familiar?"

"If it's the same Sharlyn I'm thinking of, we have our connection." Matt quickly filled Keele in.

"I'll check her out," Keele said. "Where can I reach you?"

Matt heard the shower turn off. He knew Jamie would be coming into the room soon.

"Have to get back to you. That explosion might have been meant to include Jamie and me. We've been followed since we got here. I've lost the tail for now, but I don't want to pick it up again. I have to rent another car and keep moving. I'll call you in two hours."

Matt hung up the phone and turned toward the closed bathroom door. He cinched the towel securely around his waist and prepared himself for all the things that he would have to say.

His heart sank with the weight of them. He'd rather face the tiger than the lady when that door opened.

He was going to have to tell her about Timothy Palmer's death, he was going to have to tell her that everything they had just shared had been a mistake.

For the first time in his life he'd come up against something stronger than his control, stronger even than his honor. He'd let it lead him into committing an unforgivable act of betrayal against his brother.

There would be hell to pay. He was about to pay it. He could never, ever touch her again.

Somehow, he would say this. Somehow, he would get her to understand this. Somehow, he would give her up. Somehow.

The door opened. Jamie walked out, her long hair pinned to the top of her head. She was wearing nothing but a skimpy motel towel tucked above her breasts. It barely reached to the top of her thighs. A triangle of golden curls peaked out beneath it.

"Did I hear you on the phone with someone?" she asked.

He opened his mouth to answer her. But before he could form any words, he had forgotten her question.

She was so damn beautiful. Every time he saw her he knew she couldn't possibly be more beautiful. And then the next time he saw her, she was. Having held her in his arms, made love to her, he knew why he hadn't touched another woman in five years. And why he would never touch another woman.

She smiled when she saw him looking at her.

Slowly, she walked toward him. He knew there was something he had meant to say to her, but his mind had melted. All he could concentrate on was the seductive, sweet sway of her hips, her graceful arms rising to unfasten the hair at the top of her head.

The thick butter-colored strands tumbled down and he found he had crossed the room to catch them. Their cool, rich silk rustled through his fingers. The scent of the soap from her shower on the honey warmth of her skin rose up to greet him.

His hands cupped her face, then ran along her graceful neck to the white caps of her shoulders. He pulled off her towel with fingers already way too eager. Her deep bluebonnet eyes locked directly with his. Her cheeks were flushed, her lips parted, her nipples blushing into erect peaks.

Need clawed ravenous and raw and wanton inside him.

His body was telling him what his heart had known from the instant he saw her. She was the other part of him—the part that had been missing all these long, lonely, aching years.

He reached for her. She came with a hungry, happy sigh.

JAMIE SAT AT THE BACK of the restaurant and listened to Matt telling her about Timothy Palmer's death. He had waited until they both had a warm meal in their stomachs.

It was a good thing. Hearing the news before eating would have ruined her appetite.

She kept seeing Tony's smile as he looked at her that night so long ago. She kept hearing his voice telling her she looked pretty. Her heart—so full and happy only moments before—now sank heavy and low in her chest.

"This is all my fault."

"What are you talking about, Jamie?"

"Matt, don't pretend you don't know. My looking for him, my using your show to flash his picture. I led those murderers right to Tony!"

Matt's hand covered Jamie's, so large, so strong, so very gentle. She raised her eyes to his. It came as a shock of pure pleasure to see the warmth mixed with lust every time he looked at her now. She could gaze into this man's eyes forever. And what's more, she wanted to.

"Jamie, this is not your fault. I don't know who this Timothy Palmer, alias Tony Lagarrigue, was. But I do know that he wasn't in the witness-protection program hiding from the Mob."

"But that FBI Agent Creighton said—"

"It wasn't true."

Matt's words, his voice, his clasp on her hand—they were all combining into an emphatic assurance that Jamie felt quite forcibly.

"If you're saying this just to try to make me feel better—"

"I'm not lying to you, Jamie. Creighton isn't an FBI agent. Neither is Wilson."

"How can you know that?"

"When the FBI's safeguarding someone in the witness-protection program, they don't go running their mouths off about it. Those two are as phony as the identifications they flashed."

Jamie recognized the serious look on Matt's face. As his words sank in, so did tardy understanding. "You knew this all along, from the moment you found them in my room. That's why you acted so unfriendly and distrustful. That's why you kept me so close to your side all the time we were with them."

He withdrew his hand from hers. "Yes."

"You could've told me before this."

"Would it have made a difference, Jamie? Tony had to be the one who sent them. Just like he had to be behind the call, the note, the eighteen-wheeler trying to run us off the road. Every time before that I've tried to warn you away from him, you've refused to be warned."

"Matt, it doesn't make sense. Why would Tony warn me away if he *wasn't* in the witness-protection program?"

"I don't know."

"Okay. Let's say he had a couple of buddies pose as phony FBI agents. The story they told about his being in the witness-protection program could still be true. Could be he sent them because real agents wouldn't disclose that information."

"No, Jamie. Nothing about Creighton's story or Tony's situation fits. When the FBI puts a family in protection, they create a new identity for them, complete with new social-security numbers, birth certificates, the works. They do not borrow another family's names and history as Tony and his mama and daddy did when they lived in Sweetspring."

"If the FBI had to move Tony and his family out quickly, they may have had no choice but to temporarily use another family's ID."

"It doesn't work that way. There is nothing slipshod about the relocation of these folks. The program is administered with strict attention to every detail and every safeguard. Several years back the bureau lost a couple of witnesses in protection because things were too loose. Everything was restructured. Now only those few select agents involved in witness protection even know who is being hidden and where."

Jamie was beginning to get an odd feeling about Matt's explanation—a real odd feeling. "How do you know so much about the FBI?"

Matt sipped his after-dinner coffee quietly for a moment before responding. "I used to rub elbows with them when I was in military intelligence."

That odd feeling that Jamie had wasn't satisfied at all by that explanation. "Matt, who is Keele?"

He looked over at her. For the first time in hours, Jamie noticed Matt's eyes were guarded. Her pulse jumped.

"Keele's a...good friend," he said.

"A good friend who appeared in the middle of nowhere with a helicopter, an M-16 and a team of paramedics to rescue us. If they had been military, there would have been some insignia or identification on them or the craft. There wasn't. They were all FBI undercover agents, weren't they?"

"Jamie, let it go."

"Matt, I have to know the truth."

"Look, Jamie, even if Keele and the others are what you think—and I'm not saying they are—you have to understand it would be inappropriate for me to say."

"And if *you* were, would it also be inappropriate for you to say?"

She had to admire how quickly and smoothly the mask slipped over the features of his face. "Say again?"

"I've been wondering all afternoon how you got your gun through security at the airport. That was the only time you weren't at my side since we left San Antonio. Matt, I may be slow to catching on to things, but I'm not that slow."

"Jamie—"

"All those computer databases you accessed so easily in your office. The cellophane bags and tweezers you just happen to tote around. That 'private investigators are trained for this sort of thing' bull you've been handing me. Those aren't tricks in the P.I. trade. Those are evidence-gathering techniques taught to a federal agent."

"There's a perfectly logical explanation for everything you've—"

"Yes, and I bet you have that perfectly logical explanation right on the tip of your tongue, too. A good FBI undercover agent would have to, wouldn't he? Particularly if he was one of those special agents part of witness protection.''

Matt stared into the blackness of his coffee cup. Jamie felt his silence profoundly. As certain as she had been, his lack of denial still came as a small shock to her system. The new knowledge fizzed through her thoughts, bubbling through all her past impressions and assumptions. Her voice rose excitedly.

''Your P.I. firm. Even your 'Finder of Lost Loves' TV program. They're all a front for what you truly do. You relocate folks, give them new identities, hide them, watch over them. And you've been doing it all the time!''

# Chapter Thirteen

Matt said nothing in response to Jamie's words, just sipped his coffee calmly.

But Jamie was anything but calm. Her insides were jumping with the excitement of the news. "Liz can't know. Nor Cade. Not even your mama and daddy know, do they?"

Matt's eyes rose to meet hers squarely. "Jamie, you can't ever talk about this to them, to anyone."

There was a flat, emphatic quality in Matt's voice that Jamie had never heard before. Goose bumps popped out on her skin. She understood only too clearly that she had just been given an order. The severity of the delivery sent a chill up her spine.

"Matt, if you don't know by now that I'd rather die than say or do anything that could hurt you—"

He took her hand into his, held it hard. The warm lust was so strong in his eyes that it shocked her anew.

"I know, Jamie."

"Does Sarita have something to do with witness protection?"

"No, Jamie. She's just a little girl looking for the impossible."

"Impossible? Uh-oh. You found her mama, didn't you?"

"And she never wants to see Sarita."

"Sweet Lord, how do you tell a child something like that?"

Matt withdrew his hand from Jamie's and sat back with a long exhale of breath. "I don't even know how to tell her daddy."

"What's he like?"

"Like a man who's been kicked by a mule."

"Don't tell them about Sarita's mama, Matt."

"I can't leave 'em dangling."

"They need something else to take their minds off looking for her. Now, as I recall, Sarita's daddy's right tall and handsome and serious looking. Sort of reminds me of the kind of man whom Liz's been known to take a liking to."

Matt's face took on a look caught between angst and awe. "Jamie, you can't be fixin' on my playing matchmaker here?"

"I don't see what introducing them would hurt. They both got a lot of inside mending to do. Could be easier for them to get it done if they do it together. And you know Liz would just love Sarita. Always thought she'd make a mighty fine mama."

Matt chuckled. "Could be I should've included a woman on the makeup of my team."

Jamie smiled. "No 'could be' about it. Running a private-investigation firm as a front to keeping an eye on things makes some sense. But I confess I don't see how the TV show fits in when it comes to protecting the folks who are hiding."

"It doesn't fit in, Jamie. It was the brainchild of a boss who 'don't know nothing and has that all tangled up.'"

"Your boss?"

Matt nodded. "He thinks if some mobster wants to locate someone in our protection, he's actually going to come knocking on my door pretending to be looking for a lost love."

Jamie laughed, then caught herself on the serious edge of Matt's expression. "I'm sorry. I know it's not funny. It's just so ludicrous it struck my funny bone."

"I wish it could find mine."

"I guess this isn't just a job to you, is it?"

"Jamie, a woman's a life giver. Something else can be just a job to her. But a man's proof of potency is his work. If he's not out there doing the right thing, then whatever he's out there doing is wrong."

Jamie had the strongest impression that Matt wasn't referring only to his work anymore, but to a part of himself, some deep, personal contract etched on his soul.

The impression made her heart gulp with unease although she couldn't understand why.

But she did understand something else. She hadn't thought words necessary between them because she had believed the boundless passion she had felt in his arms. And the message in his eyes when he looked so lovingly and joyfully into her face afterward.

Now she wasn't so sure. Because now there was this new emotion there.

Slowly, deliberately, Jamie forced herself to take a deep breath and let it out.

"Matt, we need to talk about our...lovemaking."

The continuing look in his eyes caused the shadows of her unease to circle in closer.

"Jamie, I can offer you neither an explanation nor an answer."

"You're...unsure about what's happened between us?"

"I know exactly what's happened between us. I never meant to let it happen."

The shadows closed around Jamie's heart until it shivered from their cold. "You regret it."

"Regret is not the word I would use."

Jamie didn't want to hear the word he would use. She was suddenly sure it would be a lot worse. "Looks like it's time I headed back to San Antonio." She barely recognized her voice.

"Not without me, Jamie."

Matt slowly took her hand into his and one by one interlaced their fingers. Jamie's breath caught at the sensations shivering through her as she absorbed the smooth heat of his palm and the friction of his fingers.

She had never felt such eroticism from just having her hand held before. But then this man had taught her more about sensuality than she ever imagined existed.

She looked up at him. That warm, wonderful lust that filled his eyes made her pulse jump and pushed the shadows momentarily away from her heart. She wanted this. And so much more. But could he give her any more?

Matt pulled her gently to her feet.

"Where are we going?" she asked, a bit too breathless.

He brought the palm of her hand to his lips and brushed it with a kiss that sizzled down her spine.

"This business is far from over. Donald Tennisen, the driver of that eighteen-wheeler that rammed us, is Sharlyn's brother."

"The same Sharlyn we met at the cleaners?"

"The very same. She has some explaining to do. And I intend for her to do it."

MATT FIRST CHECKED AT Sharlyn's home address. She wasn't there. He headed for the cleaners. Another receptionist directed them to her office. Matt and Jamie found her there, slumped over the desk, her head in her hands.

She looked up at them, her eyes rimmed in red and swollen. She had obviously been given the news about Timothy Palmer.

"Get out of here!" she screamed.

"If you don't want your brother rotting in jail for the rest of his life, you'd better talk to us," Matt warned.

Sharlyn straightened and dabbed at her eyes with a tissue.

Her look conveyed surprise that Matt had connected her with her brother. After a nervous hesitation, she waved at the chairs on the side of her desk.

Matt and Jamie sat in the standard metal-and-vinyl seats. Matt said nothing for a long moment as he concentrated on just looking at Sharlyn, a sharp gaze that he intentionally sent her way to make her sweat.

And she was sweating, as well as shredding the tissue in her hands.

"Donald's lawyer says he's going to get him off," she tried with a faint bluster.

"You believe in the Easter bunny, too, Sharlyn?" Matt asked.

"Why are you out to get him?"

"Let's just say it was a mite unfriendly of him to take it upon himself to come after me," Matt said in an even, matter-of-fact tone.

"He wasn't after you. He was just trying to scare *her*. You could have killed him, shooting at him like that."

"If I had wanted him dead, he'd be dead," Matt said evenly.

Sharlyn blinked several times, rapidly. She obviously believed it. "What do you want from me?"

"Answers. Why did Palmer send Donald to scare Jamie?"

"Timmy send Donald? Ha! That's a laugh. Timmy wouldn't even pick up the damn phone to call and warn her off. I had to do it. I had to do everything!"

"*You* called me at the station?" Jamie said. "You sent me the card filled with soot?"

Sharlyn turned to Jamie, her lip curling, her voice trembling with anger.

"I'm only sorry it wasn't filled with acid, you witch! You led them right to Timmy! You're responsible for his death!"

"Who are 'they,' Sharlyn?" Jamie asked.

Matt was impressed by the way Jamie kept her cool, refusing to react to Sharlyn's angry name-calling.

"Who? You imbecile. The Mafia, of course! They've been after him and his family for years. And for years he's eluded them as part of the witness-protection program. Until you came along. Until you had to shove his face and yours on that damn TV program!"

"No, you're wrong," Jamie said. "Timothy wasn't—"

"Entirely truthful with you," Matt cut in before Jamie could say any more. "Palmer wanted to see Jamie. Matter of fact he was real eager to rekindle their old flame."

Sharlyn switched to Matt in an angry, jerky movement.

"You're lying. Last thing in the world Timmy wanted was for her to find him. He was afraid from the first that she'd lead those assassins to him."

"You forgetting their intimate past together?" Matt said.

"Intimate? That's a laugh. They were both just kids when they met. She meant nothing to him."

"Do the names Creighton and Wilson ring a bell?"

"What is this, 'Jeopardy'?"

"No, that's what Donald's in."

Sharlyn got the message. "Oh, okay, okay. They're two of Timmy's buddies over at the Hilton. So?"

"Palmer sent them to see Jamie and set up her meeting with him. He invited her to his home."

Sharlyn shot forward in her chair. "It's not true! Timmy loved me. He'd never let her set a foot into his house."

"You need Jamie to describe Palmer's brick fireplace and mirrored bedroom for you, Sharlyn?"

Matt watched his words sink into Sharlyn. Her mouth still twisted, her eyes still burned red. Only this time neither had anything to do with grief. She jumped to her feet, grabbed the picture of Timothy off the desk and threw it across the room. It smashed against the opposite wall.

"The two-timing bastard! And after all I did for him!"

Sharlyn reached for a stuffed bunny perched on the edge of her desk. She dropped it on the floor and stomped it as if it were a bug. She was reaching for a paperweight when Matt rose to take Jamie's arm, leading her out the door.

They left Sharlyn cussing up a storm and grabbing anything that reminded her of Timothy to smash against the wall or grind beneath her shoe.

"What will happen to her?" Jamie asked when they were back in the rental car.

"On the legal horizon, she's looking at a charge of conspiracy to commit assault. On a personal basis, I'd say she'll be getting over Palmer real soon.''

''Wasn't it cruel to lie to her about him and me?''

''Cruel? Jamie, don't be forgetting that woman threatened you and almost killed you when she sent her brother after you in that eighteen-wheeler. Besides, she didn't strike me as being in any frame of mind conducive to answering direct questions. I wanted to know exactly what their relationship had been. I also wanted her to tell me about Creighton and Wilson.''

''How did you know about the mirrored bedroom?''

''Keele got the fire department's report.''

''I thought he was the one you've been calling. Where are we going now?''

''To see Creighton and Wilson. Got a bone to pick with those two boys.''


A LADY DEALER AT ONE OF the twenty-one tables at the Fla-mingo Hilton responded to Matt's Texas charm and twenty-dollar tip by telling him that Wilson was a security guard who'd gone off duty.

She pointed Matt toward Creighton's office in the back. Nameplate on the door said he was an assistant manager.

When Matt barged through without knocking, Creighton nearly fell off his chair. Matt had circled Creighton's desk and pulled him to his feet by the scruff of his shirt before he could even think about pressing the button for security.

Creighton's face flushed crimson. ''You can't come in here! I'll have the law on you!''

''Now, I'm real pleased you've brought up the law, Mr. Creighton,'' Matt said. ''I just happen to know the office number of the local FBI. Shall I dial it and let them explain to you about the penalties for impersonating a federal offi-cer?''

All the wind blew out of Creighton's angry bluster. ''Oh, hell.''

Matt released his hold on Creighton's shirt and the man

fell back into his chair. He looked up at Matt with small, dark eyes that seemed to be shrinking more into his head by the second.

"I can explain."

"Come in and close the door, Jamie," Matt said. "Mr. Creighton wants to explain."

Jamie smiled as she complied, taking one of the chairs in front of Creighton's desk.

"Little different from the last time we met, Mr. Creighton," she said. "I didn't realize then that you were such a gambler with the truth."

Creighton swallowed. "Look, it was just a joke. Harmless."

"This is your explanation?" Matt said. "It's all right to pretend to be an FBI agent because it was just a harmless joke?"

"You don't understand. Timmy said Mrs. Bonner here was looking for him. He just wanted me and Wilson to discourage her."

"Was it your idea to use the witness-protection scam?"

"No, that was Timmy's. I swear to God. Well, you can ask him. He'll tell you how it worked."

"How it worked?" Matt repeated. "You saying he's used it before?"

"It's just that...he just has this thing against getting married, okay? So when a babe he's been dating for a while starts talking about tying the knot, he tells them this story about how he's on the run from the Mob, and if they catch up with him, they've sworn to kill him and any wife and kids he has. He tells them he won't marry them and endanger their lives."

"And this works?" Matt asked.

"Oh, yeah. Babes either quit bugging him about marriage or run like hell."

"And then he gets another...babe," Matt said, his tone full of disdain.

"What can I say? It's a town full of beautiful showgirls.

But don't get me wrong. He only pulls the scam because he has a soft heart. He doesn't like hurting them."

"Because the truth is they're expendable."

"No, it's not that way with Timmy. He cares for them. He just has this marriage-phobia thing."

"Was Sharlyn a showgirl before she hooked up with Palmer?"

"Yeah. But, she's a regular whiz with a calculator, too. That's why Timmy brought her into his business and let her loose on his books."

"Why did Timothy agree to see me?" Jamie asked.

"Didn't he tell you?" Creighton asked.

"Timothy Palmer won't be telling anyone anything, Mr. Creighton," Matt said. "He was blown up in his house this morning."

Creighton's face visibly paled. He came forward in his chair. "What?"

"He's dead."

Creighton shook his head. "No. I can't believe it."

"It'll sink in. Now, when did you talk to him last and what did he say?"

"I...I don't have to tell you anything."

"No, you can talk to the FBI instead," Matt said, picking up the phone.

Creighton gulped. "No, no. Look, okay. I called him from the coffee shop right after you and Mrs. Bonner left so I could tell him what you said."

Matt put down the phone. "Where was he?"

"At one of the other casinos, talking about a special job the manager wanted. I told him Mrs. Bonner wouldn't tell us about what was in the locket."

"Finding what was in the locket was the reason he sent you, wasn't it?"

"It was the main reason, yes."

"Go on," Matt said.

"Timmy was disappointed we hadn't found out. He was

on his way home. He told me to send you around to the house, and he'd take care of it himself."

"How did he say he was going to take care of it?"

"He didn't think it would be a problem to sweet-talk Mrs. Bonner into handing it over to him. He remembered her as a nice kid. He was also concerned about how you had found him. He thought if he asked her right, she'd tell him. Most women tell Timmy what he wants them to. I mean what he wanted them to. Damn. I still can't believe he's dead."

"Since you obviously knew his witness-protection program scenario was a scam, how did he explain away the fact that he was using another name when he was down in Texas fifteen years ago?"

"He said the babe—uh, I mean, Mrs. Bonner—had just remembered his name wrong was all."

"And you believed that?"

"Hey, man. It was fifteen years ago. Who remembers a name right after that long a time?"

"How long did you know Palmer?" Matt asked.

"Close to thirteen years. We got to be drinking buddies right after he came to Reno."

"But thirteen years ago he was only seventeen," Jamie protested.

"No, he was older than that, Mrs. Bonner. Had to be. Not that he looked it, I grant you. Still, that youthful face of his rather appealed to the babes."

"Tell us how you met him," Matt said.

"At a bar. We had a drink together, got to talking. He had some money he wanted to invest."

"Where did he get the money?"

"A lucky streak at the roulette wheel."

"Was he a heavy gambler?"

"No. He just took an occasional chance on something. Gut reaction kind of player." Creighton paused to look at Jamie. "You have to be twenty-one to gamble here, Mrs. Bonner, so I knew right away he was at least that. Nevada casinos don't make the mistake of letting anyone underage near the tables. They always check ID on someone like Timmy who didn't look his age."

"So what happened with this money he had to invest?" Matt asked.

"I told him about the problem of getting a good, reliable cleaning company at the casinos. He heard opportunity knocking and got to the door first."

"He have any other drinking buddies?"

"None consistent like he and I were. I was his closest friend. I told him things. He told me things."

"Like the scam he pulled on women?"

"Yeah. He asked me to work it for him once before when a weekend romance got sticky. Lady was from out of town and married. She didn't tell Timmy about the married part until she announced she was leaving her husband for him. When Reg and I got through with her, she was running back to that old man of hers in the South Dakota hills."

"What about this sidekick in these impersonations, Reg Wilson? What was his relationship with Palmer?"

"Barely knew him. Wilson works for me. He's a security guard here at the casino. I just brought him along for show. He's dumb but willing."

"Did Palmer ever talk to you about where he'd been before he came to Reno?"

"He was always kind of vague about his background. I didn't pry. Matter of fact, I didn't even know he'd been to Texas until he asked me to do the FBI thing with Mrs. Bonner here."

"Was he a Nevada native?"

"No, I don't think so. Not that he ever said specifically one way or another. Just an impression I got."

"Did he ever mention mama, daddy, brothers, sisters?"

Creighton shook his head.

"What about hobbies?"

"Gambling a little, whiskey a little."

"Did he favor any particular team when it came to sports?"

"He liked any team that won when he bet on them."

"Peculiarities, phobias?"

"Other than getting married, Timmy didn't fear a thing."

"You said he drank. Did he smoke?"

"No, didn't like his babes to, either. Sharlyn had to quit before he'd even go out with her. Hey, wait a minute."

"You remembered something?" Matt asked.

"Yeah, there was something else Timmy was afraid of. Ash."

"Cigarette?"

"No, volcanic ash. He'd seen a TV special on the Discovery Channel about it. How all these dinosaurs died because they breathed in volcanic ash from an eruption a thousand miles away. It was an excruciating death. The jagged edges of the tiny particles ripped apart their lungs. Really freaked Timmy out."

"Why would that TV special have such an effect on him?"

"Because he was in a little town about forty miles south of Mount Saint Helens in Washington State when that baby blew. He said he was afraid he had some of that crap in his lungs. Got a chest X ray every year to make sure his lungs were clear. Real fanatical about it."

"NOW WE KNOW TONY was near Mount Saint Helens in 1980," Jamie said once they were back on the road.

"I was trying to remember when the volcano blew."

"I'll never forget," Jamie said. "It was May. The next few days all the teachers talked about were volcanoes and the destruction they brought. I found them fascinating."

"Why fascinating?" Matt asked.

"Up until then I bought the idea that humans were number one in the hierarchy on this old earth. Then I realized the truth. One real big cough out of Mother Nature and even the most powerful of human beings could be wiped off the planet."

"You liked finding that out. Why?"

"It was a real comforting thought, knowing that those who

beat me could be beaten. I stopped looking at them as all powerful. Once I understood that their place in geologic time—any human being's place—was an insignificant unit, my perspective on a lot of things expanded.''

"Is that why you went into biogeology? This early fascination with the destructive forces of Mother Nature?"

"Destructive, yes. But not malicious. Take a volcano. As the hot molten rock erupts from inside the earth, it segregates water from rock and forms the atmosphere. Truth is, no matter how immediately traumatic or violent the process, a volcanic eruption is an essential source of life-sustaining conditions on Earth. Rocks have always been much easier for me to read than human beings.''

"You seemed to read Tony quite well. All along, you said he wasn't the one who'd been threatening you. And all along, you were right."

"I couldn't see how cruelty could come from someone who had been so kind. Still, I never knew him. He wasn't even fifteen when he was in Sweetspring. I should have tumbled to the truth when that computer-aged version of him was so far off. If he had been fifteen in Sweetspring, he should have changed over the years. And not just in his facial features. He should have become taller, broader, a boy growing into a man. He didn't. That can only mean one thing. He had already reached his full physical maturity when I first met him.''

"And possessed that Michael J. Fox quality of youthful appearance," Matt said. "Yes, I've a feeling you're right. Which opens up some real interesting possibilities.''

"Like what?''

"Like the fact that when Tony and the man and woman who said they were his folks were in Sweetspring, they were three adults using assumed names, not two adults and a teenager.''

"I see. What were they doing there?" Jamie asked, not expecting an answer, just finding herself downright curious about that question for the first time.

"I'd sure like to find out. Does it take the sting off his death some to know he purposely misled you?"

"No, Matt. I'll always mourn his loss. Whatever his real name or age or reason for being in Sweetspring, Tony was still the only one there who saw me as myself and treated me with respect. What he did for me during that time isn't going to change, no matter who he turns out to be."

"You ready to do some more traveling, Jamie?"

"Where to this time?"

"Washington State. Let's see if we can find out if Tony was from a little town near Mount Saint Helens, or if he was just passing through in May of 1980. We'll— What the—?"

The Jeep came out of nowhere, cutting across the path of Matt's rental car. Matt spun the steering wheel hard, trying his best to avoid a collision. The rental car careened across the sidewalk, headed for the glass of a storefront.

# Chapter Fourteen

Matt stomped on the brakes, just managing to stop the car shy of the storefront window. He immediately turned to Jamie.

"Are you all right?"

"I'm okay. Who was that?"

Matt looked over to see that the Jeep had pulled over to the curb. "Stay here," he said. His initial anger was turning into alarm as he recognized the man who was jumping out of the Jeep to meet him.

Perry waited for Matt at the back of the Jeep. His hands immediately came up in a gesture of surrender.

"I'm sorry, Matt. This was the only way I could get your attention and get it fast. I've been trying to track you down for nearly a whole day."

"I was set to make my daily call to Charlene to let her know where I was in just a couple of minutes. Couldn't you have waited?"

"The phones are bugged, Matt. Including Charlene's. Don't go calling her—or anyone—unless you want Nevelt listening in."

"What the hell has happened?"

"The moment you left for Reno, Randy was on the phone to Nevelt telling him about the break-in at the studio. He's convinced Nevelt it was instigated by the Mob. Nevelt's instructed us to go into a full-security alert."

"He can't do that unless there was something from the break-in to confirm such an action. What did forensics find?"

"Nothing conclusive, except that they knew how to disengage the alarm system and they wore gloves."

"That doesn't begin to substantiate an order to—"

"It's the damn charge codes, Matt," Perry said interrupting. "When you told me Ms. Bonner was to be handled as one of those cases, I assigned one of the special codes. I didn't know it automatically spewed out a computer report. Randy latched onto it and faxed it to Nevelt."

Understanding began to dawn on Matt. "So Randy tells him about the break-in and he sees the charge code and thinks that Jamie is involved in an attempt to find one of our witnesses."

"And is he ever ticked off that you didn't tell him and chose this time to take some days off. He's ready to read you the riot act. We've all been given strict orders to let Nevelt know where you are just as soon as you call in. Which is why I had to come here to find you. This way, I'm not disobeying his order. Technically, you haven't called in."

"Perry, you shouldn't have taken the risk. If Randy finds out, that squealer will tell Nevelt and your days as an agent will be numbered."

"What the hell, Matt. I was never that gung ho about being an agent. I'm an entertainment-industry type, like most of us on the show. You've been good to us, all of us, and we know it."

Matt held out his hand to Perry, who took it in a solid shake.

"You're a damn fine agent in my book, Perry. Let's see how good an emcee you'll be. Go on for me this week."

"You mean it?" Perry said, excitement riding his voice. "But Randy's going to want to pick his own emcee."

"I'm still in command until Nevelt finds me and calls it otherwise. I told Randy that if I was ever unavailable, you were my stand-in. And if he tries to deny it, Charlene has my signed letter on file."

"I'm much obliged, Matt. But what are you going to do? You can't dodge Nevelt forever. He *can* wreck *your* career."

Matt looked over at Jamie where she waited in the car, a puzzled, anxious look on her face. He sent her his half smile.

"It's not exactly a transfer, but I guess it'll have to do. Go break a leg, Perry."

MATT AND JAMIE DROVE toward Woodpine, the small town about forty miles southwest of Mount Saint Helens in Washington State. According to the map, it was the only town that fit the description Tony had given to Creighton.

Jamie was still uneasy about the unorthodox way in which Perry had chosen to contact Matt in Reno. Matt told her the information Perry had passed on about the break-in at the studio. But she sensed there was more, something Matt wasn't saying.

As soon as they entered the small wooded community, Matt headed for the local law-enforcement office. The young man manning the desk wore the insignia of the Cowlitz County sheriff. He rose to greet them and introduced himself as Deputy Easley. Easley took a perfunctory glance at Matt's private-investigator identification and waved them into chairs.

"You're quite a way from Texas, Mr. Bonner. What brings you here?"

"I'm on the trail of a mystery man."

"Sounds interesting. What's his name?"

Matt pulled out the picture of Tony. "That's what I was hoping you could tell me. Do you remember this man coming to town around the time the volcano erupted?"

Easley took the picture and gave it a long, thoughtful scrutiny. "No, sorry. I've never seen him."

"You were here during the eruption?" Matt asked.

"Oh, yeah. I was eight, sitting in a Sunday Bible class."

"What was it like being so close to an erupting volcano?" Jamie asked, not able to resist satisfying her curiosity.

"The first I knew it had happened was when some of the

older kids were pointing out the window at this huge mush-room-shaped ash cloud that was filling the sky."

"You didn't hear the explosion?" Jamie asked.

"No. Just saw that cloud that quickly turned day into night. Then it started to get hot, really hot. Our Bible teacher was so spooked he was shaking. He told us to go home."

"Were you afraid?" Jamie asked.

"Yeah, a little. I remember walking down the sidewalk and hearing the sounds of trees and automobile windshields cracking from the heat. It was eerie."

"Did your family evacuate?" Matt asked.

"Did we! My parents grabbed me and my brother and sister and we headed for my aunt's place down in southern California."

"How long were you in southern California?"

"Three months. We came back to Woodpine when they started school up again in September."

"Did the whole town evacuate?" Matt asked.

"Most families left, at least for a while. The volcanic ash falling on our town was too light to be considered hazardous. Mudflows and flooding were the real problems."

"So they were what made most folks leave?" Jamie asked.

"Actually, it was that rumor that a cloud of poisonous gas was going to move into town that had everyone spooked. Only a few die-hards stayed on after that. Locked themselves in their houses."

"I don't recall hearing about a cloud of poisonous gas," Jamie said.

"That's because it was only some silly rumor. But it scared a lot of people into packing it in."

"Do you have a newspaper?" Jamie asked.

"Not a local one, just the church bulletin. Most of us sub-scribe to the paper out of Vancouver. But if you really want to know about this town and who's been in and out of it, you should talk to one of our old-timers. They have some pretty remarkable memories when it comes to the people and faces and what's gone on."

"Can you give us the name of one of these old-timers?"

"Andy Newcastle over on Second Street. Andy was one of those die-hards who battened down the hatches and stayed on through it all. He lives in the small blue Cape Cod."

Matt and Jamie thanked Easley and headed for the house on Second Street.

It was at least a hundred years old, small, boxy, and to Jamie's way of seeing, endearingly quaint.

The man who rushed to the door in response to Matt's knock did so with such an air of breathlessness that it seemed as though his shirt ends should be flying out behind him.

Jamie thought him to be a perfect complement to his home—a compact man in his sixties with a large round head, curious hazel eyes, white hair and a real down-to-earth look.

"Mr. Newcastle?" Matt asked.

"Everybody just calls me Andy. Come on in, Mr. and Mrs. Bonner. Officer Easley just called to tell me he was sending you over."

"We appreciate your seeing us on such short notice, Andy," Jamie said.

"My pleasure." He sounded as if it were. He showed them into a small, modest living room filled with well-used country furniture that looked right at home in the rustic Cape Cod.

Jamie sat next to Matt on a weathered garden chair that looked sturdy enough, despite its noticeably repaired seat.

"Young Easley said you wanted to know about the time when the volcano blew?" Andy asked, clearly eager to start.

"We're actually interested in someone whom we believe was in town about that time," Matt said. He handed the picture of Tony to Andy.

Andy set a pair of tiny glasses on his short, stubby nose. He contemplated the picture for a considerable time, rubbing his chin with his index finger. The only sound in the room was the clicking of the old, beat-up grandfather clock in the corner.

"Yeah, I've seen him, all right," Andy said, handing back the picture.

Jamie came forward in her seat. "When?"

"Right around the time of the volcanic eruption."

"Do you remember his name?"

"No, sorry, Mrs. Bonner. Too long ago I'm afraid."

"Do you remember what he was doing here?"

Newcastle rubbed his chin some more. "Not sure. Could be he was one of those newspaper reporters who kept knocking on the door and asking questions. They drifted in after Mount Saint Helens blew her stack. Wanted the residents' reactions."

"Is there anything specific you can remember about this man, Andy?" Jamie asked. "It's real important."

"I'm pretty sure I heard his name."

"Could it have been Lagarrigue?"

"No. This boy had a plain Anglo-Saxon name like mine. That much I'm positive about."

"How about Palmer? Timothy Palmer?" Jamie asked.

"No, not Palmer, although that's closer."

"You called him a boy," Matt said. "Why?"

"Because of his young face. He looks more boy than man."

"Could he have been a high-school student?" Matt asked.

"No. I would clearly remember anyone who belonged to a family here in Woodpine."

"So your best guess is that he was a reporter?" Jamie asked.

"Yeah, I think so. They invaded the town. He…no, wait, now I remember. He wasn't a reporter. He was a scientist."

"You met him?" Jamie asked, trying to keep the excitement contained in her voice.

"Yes. I first saw him in the vacant lot just behind my backyard fence. He was with a couple of other scientists. He was gathering ash. Another was consulting a gauge on some complicated gadget."

"Did you talk to them?" Matt asked.

"Not until after he knocked on Priddy's back door."

"Priddy?"

"Priddy Stowell. She lives next door. She invited them all inside. The bald one with the complicated gadgets declined. I think he was embarrassed because he didn't speak English too well. His accent was quite thick. Anyway, Priddy saw me in my backyard and invited me too. We're good friends. Priddy started to drill them almost right away. She's always been an insatiable gossip and this was a perfect opportunity for her to get the details on what they were doing."

"What do you remember of the conversation?" Jamie asked.

"Just that it revolved around testing air quality and ground vibration and such."

"What about him?" Matt said, referring to the picture of Tony.

"He asked us how familiar we were with volcanoes. He tried not to talk over our heads. It still went over mine. Priddy acted like she understood every word. He was very polite to her, but it was obvious he knew she was blowing more smoke than that volcano."

"What did the other man talk about?"

"The dark-haired one with the nervous hands was the medical doctor. He talked about how harmful the gas and ash concentrations were. He advised me and Priddy to evacuate."

"But you didn't leave?" Matt asked.

"I was born in this town, right in this house, and I'm not leaving it until I die. Although I have to tell you that doctor's words had their effect. I stopped going out of the house after that. He scared Priddy so much that she went to her daughter's for a couple of weeks."

"Can you remember anything else about the conversation?" Matt asked.

"There wasn't anything else. They both just sipped some of Priddy's iced tea, and then the doctor went outside to smoke. And here he was worried about *our* lungs."

"You still don't remember what their names were?"

"Nope. Sorry. It has been seventeen years. But you should

talk to Priddy. She can tell you a lot more about them than I could.''

"Her memory is that good?" Jamie asked.

"Phenomenal. Priddy's going on eighty-seven and she's battling a severe case of debilitating arthritis, but she's still just as mentally sharp and nosy as she's always been.''

"We'd be much obliged if you'd perform the introductions, Andy.''

"Be happy to, Mrs. Bonner. Come on. I normally go over and visit her about this time every day anyway.''

The house next door was even older than the Cape Cod. It looked less rustic because of its symmetrical lines and neat, precise alignment of windows, which marked its Georgian style.

A woman in a nurse's uniform wearing an exasperated expression answered Andy's knock. As soon as she saw Andy, she beamed and beckoned them inside with what sounded to Matt like a heartfelt sigh.

"She's a handful today, Andy. Fretful as a fruit fly. I finally got her to rest in bed five minutes ago. Please go upstairs and keep her there so I can get something done!''

"It's what we've come to do, Claudia," Andy said. "Go about your business. We'll keep her occupied for a while."

They followed Andy inside and up the stairs to Priddy's bedroom. He knocked on the door with three quick raps.

"Come on in, Andy," a surprisingly strong female voice said.

Andy opened the door. "I've brought a couple of private detectives with me. Say hello to Mr. and Mrs. Bonner.''

Jamie stepped toward the bed. Priddy was a tiny, doll-sized creature wearing a cinnamon-colored bed coat that swallowed her thin frame. She was propped up with three pillows. Her hair was sparse yellow straw and her face was creased with more lines than a well-used Texas road map.

But there was a sparkle deep within her sunken eyes that spoke of a vibrant life and curiosity that had been untouched by the severe weathering of flesh and bone. She sent Jamie a smile as she took her offered hand and sandwiched it between her two bony, gnarled ones.

"A husband-and-wife private-detective team," Priddy said, releasing Jamie's hand. "This is exciting. Are you on the trail of a criminal?"

"Could be," Jamie said, more than willing to feed Priddy's imagination.

"If you could spare the time, ma'am, we'd like to talk to you about the folks who came to town after the Mount Saint Helens eruption," Matt said.

"Be delighted to assist you, Mr. Bonner. Pull up some chairs. Oh, there are only two in here. Andy, go into the next room and get another chair."

"I'm already on my way, Priddy," Andy said as he scrambled out the door.

"I knew he'd want to stay and hear," Priddy said in a lowered voice. "Andy is so nosy. And such a gossip! Still, he has a good heart. And he's been such a dear friend ever since my Vernon died. Vernon was my husband, you see."

"Yes, ma'am," Matt said.

Priddy switched her attention to Andy as he came barreling back into the room carrying a chair.

"Now put it there," she said, pointing a gnarled finger. He followed directions. Andy was obviously used to being bossed by Priddy and took it in stride.

Matt and Jamie drew up the other two chairs and sat on the other side of Priddy. Matt produced the picture of Tony and handed it to her.

"Andy has been telling us that he remembers meeting this man seventeen years ago here in your house, ma'am. Can you tell us what you recall of him and that meeting?"

Priddy immediately raised her glasses, resting on the beaded chain around her neck. She perched them on the end of her nose and looked closely at the picture.

"Carney," she pronounced emphatically after a moment.

"That's it!" Andy said, slapping his knee for emphasis. "I told you she had a remarkable memory."

"Can you remember the names of the other two scientists?" Jamie asked.

"Let's see."

Priddy closed her eyes. She was so still for a moment that Jamie thought she might have fallen asleep. But when she opened her eyes again, a small, triumphant smile was drawing back her lips.

"Dr. Berman. The other one didn't give me his name."

"Yes, she's right again," Andy said. "Priddy, it was Berman who wanted the smoke, right?"

"That's what he said. After his dire proclamations, he kept fidgeting like he was sitting on a burr. But I don't believe getting a smoke was the only reason he wanted an excuse to go outside."

"What was the other reason?" Matt asked.

"The woman he met out on the street. I saw him go out to her the second he left the house."

"Can you describe this woman?" Matt asked.

"They were too far away. Dr. Berman was a slim, dark, good-looking man. It surprised me that he was so eager to get out to the woman. She seemed older, chunky and plain, at least from that distance."

"The woman might have been some colleague of his whom he was eager to confer with on some scientific point," Jamie offered.

"I didn't get that impression," Priddy said. "Something about the close way they were standing together told me that their relationship was a more personal one."

"Did Dr. Berman come back inside?" Jamie asked.

"No. The last I saw of him was when he was standing talking to the woman out on the sidewalk."

"Did you get the impression that Carney and Berman and this other scientist had arrived together to investigate the eruption?" Matt asked.

"No, Dr. Carney told me they were from different institutions. Didn't even know each other until they arrived. The foreign scientist was from some university in Italy. Berman was from MIT. And Carney—now where was he from?"

Priddy paused to close her eyes, no doubt consulting that phenomenal memory of hers.

"Princeton," Andy said.

Priddy opened her eyes and looked over at him in obvious surprise. "Yes, you're right. Well done, Andy."

"I knew one of them was from Princeton," he said beaming happily at the praise.

"Do you remember anything else about Dr. Carney?" Jamie asked.

"He was very young-looking to be a doctor," Priddy said. "When I said as much to him, he explained that he'd just gotten his degree and the volcano was his first field assignment."

Priddy shifted a bit in the bed as though trying to get comfortable. She was so animated and informative, Jamie had forgotten the kind of pain she must be enduring.

"Dr. Carney seemed most eager to educate me on the purpose of taking the ash samples and what he hoped to find. It was a most pleasant conversation until Dr. Berman got started on all his gloom-and-doom predictions."

"About the dangers of the gas cloud."

"I see Andy told you. What a fright that man gave me! Kept talking about how dangerous it was for Andy and me to be in town with all the gasses and such still spewing out. When I reminded him that there was no mandatory evacuation order, he said the government was being hopelessly incompetent and remiss not to have ordered one. He said that a poisonous gas cloud was on its way, and it was going to choke us to death."

"No wonder you left," Jamie said. "I would have, too."

"Yes, I left. And lived to regret it. That's when they came and robbed me."

"Robbed you?" Jamie repeated. "Who robbed you?"

"Some looters swept through town one night, breaking in

and stealing stuff from several unoccupied homes,'' Andy said.

"What kind of stuff?'' Matt asked.

"Small pieces, some valuable, some possessing only sentimental value to their owners,'' Andy continued. "The thieves were obviously amateurs.''

"Amateurs?'' Priddy said. "They took my gold-coin collection or have you forgotten?''

Andy's round head bowed contritely.

"Gold coins?'' Jamie said. "They must have been valuable.''

"Very,'' Priddy said. "And I never got them back.''

"And they weren't insured, either,'' Andy added. "It was one of the last acquisitions that Priddy's husband had made before his death. She couldn't even claim it as a loss on her income tax.''

"Andy!'' Priddy looked at him with exasperation.

"Sorry, Priddy. I just thought they should understand what a blow it was for you.''

"Why couldn't you at least claim the loss on your income tax?'' Jamie asked.

Priddy sighed hard, but she looked more tired of spirit than body to Jamie.

"My husband believed politicians were puppets of special-interest groups who were taking the money out of modest-income people's pockets and putting it into the hands of the rich. He was determined to give them as little of our money as possible.''

"He was right about the special interests,'' Andy said.

"Anyway,'' Priddy went on, "he acquired the gold-coin collection as an investment and did not report it.''

"You mean to the IRS?'' Jamie asked.

"Yes. This was nineteen years ago. At that time, the collectibles company he dealt with wasn't required to report their transactions. My husband liked doing business with them for that reason.''

"I see," Jamie said. "You couldn't claim the coins as a loss because he had never reported he owned them."

"Nor were they listed as part of his estate," Priddy said. "He did it to protect me from taxes, but as it ended up, I lost far more than we would have had to pay in taxes. He had acquired that coin collection in trade for all our other valuables. The coins appreciated substantially over the next two years. They were worth half a million dollars when they were stolen."

"That must have been a devastating loss," Jamie said.

"What was the name of the trading firm that your husband dealt with?" Matt asked.

"The Heritage Antiques and Collectibles Company."

"And the broker there?"

"Rollo Lipicky. The company is located in Florida. It's a very reputable firm. And Rollo has always been such a pleasant man to talk to over the telephone, always asking after family. My husband relied on his recommendations. They were excellent."

"Did Mr. Lipicky know your husband wasn't reporting his capital gains on his income tax?"

"Oh, no. Vernon kept that information strictly between us. Andy never even knew until I told him when the coins were stolen."

"The thieves were never apprehended?" Matt asked.

"The sheriff's office figured it was probably some low-life opportunists taking advantage of someone else's troubles," Priddy answered.

"Long as the world is spinning, there'll always be some minds that spin that way," Andy said with a shake of his head.

"How many homes were robbed?" Matt asked.

"Four," Priddy said. "All unoccupied. The thieves broke in through windows after deactivating the security alarms. Cash and a couple of watches were all the valuables taken from the other three homes. They broke the glass in the display case my coin collection was in. Alarms, locks, nothing stopped them.''

"They don't sound like amateurs," Matt said. "Did the thieves take just your coin collection from your home?"

"And the old locket I had put in the box with the coins."

Jamie felt a small jolt. "Excuse me, Priddy. Did you say old locket?"

"My daughter had given it to me one Mother's Day, Mrs. Bonner. She'd saved up her allowance. It was just cheap metal, but its sentimental value was priceless."

Jamie exchanged glances with Matt. From the lack of surprise in his eyes, she realized that the focus of his recent questions hadn't been idle curiosity.

Still, this possibility was pretty far-fetched. Wasn't it?

Jamie turned back to face the elderly woman in the bed, determined to find out. "Priddy, was there anything inside the locket?"

"Two school pictures of my daughter. I used to wear the locket around my neck, but because it was just cheap metal, it turned my neck green. That's why I placed it in the coin-collection box for safekeeping."

"That's all that was inside the locket?"

"No, it also contained the ten-thousand-dollar note my husband had given me on our twenty-fifth anniversary."

Jamie's heart was hammering as Priddy went on.

"Vernon planned to take me on a cruise, but he'd come down with a bad flu and we couldn't go. So he took this ten-thousand-dollar collector's note he'd been holding on to for years and wrote 'P.S. I love you' on it and gave it to me."

"'P.S.' stands for Priddy Stowell," Jamie said on a long exhalation of breath.

"It was Vernon's nickname for me. He ruined the collectible value of the bill when he wrote that note on it, of course. But his desire not to let our wedding anniversary go by without giving me something made that money so much more valuable to me. I tell you, Mrs. Bonner, losing that locket was a lot harder to take than losing that gold-coin collection."

Jamie reached into her handbag and pulled out the locket. She placed it in Priddy's bony, blue-veined hands.

Jamie watched as Priddy turned the locket over, fingering it as though she couldn't believe what she held.

"It's...the locket? *My* locket?"

She opened the regular portrait part first, as though she still expected to find the school pictures of her daughter inside.

"I'm sorry, Priddy," Jamie said. "The person who stole this from you must have thrown away the pictures. But he didn't find the secret compartment with the present from your husband."

Jamie watched as Priddy turned the locket over and slipped her shaking, misshapen nail beneath the hidden spring. The secret compartment sprung open. She reached inside and took out the wadded-up money, gently and lovingly unrolling it as the tears leaked out of her eyes.

"TONY WAS A THIEF," Jamie said.

Matt knew she was saying it deliberately, maybe needing to hear it herself before it could sink in. They were walking back to the rental car they'd left in front of the sheriff's office. The thick late-afternoon cloud cover that hung low in the sky like a shroud was now disgorging a dismal drizzle.

"*They* were thieves," Matt corrected. "The one who called himself Dr. Berman and the woman he went to meet on the sidewalk could have been Tony's 'folks' in Sweetspring. Just as they posed as scientists in Woodpine, they probably donned different personas to fit into the places they traveled to to rob folks."

"A robbery ring." Jamie spat out the words with disgust. "How did they determine where to go, who to rob?"

"I strongly suspect that the connection here is the Heritage Antiques and Collectibles Company."

"Because of what Priddy said about it?"

"And because when we were in Erline Lagarrigue's living room in Louisiana, I saw a letter from that same company on her expensive antique coffee table."

"Erline Lagarrigue said nothing about having been burglarized."

"It's not the fact that the Lagarrigues were burglarized, Jamie. It was the fact that someone knew them well enough so that they could be impersonated in Sweetspring. And my money's on the friendly, talkative Rollo Lipicky from the Heritage Antiques and Collectibles Company. He knew Priddy had the gold-coin collection and came for it."

"Then the other houses that were broken into in Woodpine were just a smoke screen in order to throw suspicion on random looters," Jamie said. "Could the Kleinmans have been dealing with that collectibles company, too?"

"According to the Sweetspring *Star,* the only things that were being taking from the Kleinmans' house were Kyle's rare antique guns, which he had acquired recently from a collectibles company. I'd say that pretty well establishes the link."

"Matt, are you thinking what I'm thinking?"

"That Tony and these two who were posing as his mama and daddy were the ones who attempted to rob and ended up killing Kyle Kleinman in Sweetspring? That it wasn't your foster brother, Lester, after all."

Her eyes said she was considering it. But Matt could see she was still battling her reservations. "No, I was with Tony when the robbery and murder took place."

"You weren't with that man and woman posing as his folks."

"But you heard Judd Sistern. He and his daddy got there right after the shotgun blast. It wasn't until after they found Kleinman that Oscar Lagarrigue—or the man posing as him—came running in."

"Judd Sistern's saying it doesn't make it true, Jamie. What if Oscar didn't come running as he pretended but was already in the room, hiding behind some furniture when the Sisterns came in?"

"If he had been the one to slit Kyle's throat, he would have had blood on him, Matt. And Judd would have seen it."

"Might've been the woman who killed Kleinman."

"A woman…doing that?"

"Savagery is not gender specific."

"It's not the emotional capacity I'm questioning, Matt. It's the physical difficulty. Kyle Kleinman was a big man. How could a woman have slit his throat?"

"If she came up behind him when he had his attention on Oscar, Kyle might never have realized what was happening until it was too late."

"You say Oscar was still in the room when the Sisterns came in. That would have to mean the woman posing as Erline Lagarrigue was still there, too, covered in Kleinman's blood. Why didn't Judd and his daddy see her?"

"Oscar could have rushed forward and pretended to faint in order to draw Judd outside and give Erline a chance to escape."

"But Doc Sistern was still in the room. How could Erline escape without being seen by him?"

"Sistern was working on Kyle. He wouldn't have noticed someone sneaking out."

"They found the bloodied knife near where Lester was camping."

"Since Plotnik and the rest of the town had already made up their minds that Lester did it, Tony and them probably figured they'd plant it there to help matters along."

"This is right incredible to believe, Matt. But what's even more incredible is that I'm beginning to believe it. Is there any way we can find out for sure?"

"I can call Keele and start the ball rolling. Let's get to the inn and out of this rain."

Matt asked for one room for the night and registered as Mr. and Mrs. Bonner. He'd given up pretending he was going to even try to stay away from Jamie. Now that he knew she wanted him with a passion that damn near matched his own, there was no way he could.

He loved his brother. He would always love him. That

hadn't changed. He'd willingly give up his life to save Cade's.

But he wouldn't—couldn't—give up Jamie. She was a part of him now, as essential as the breath that poured into his lungs, as the blood that pumped through his arteries. For her, he'd sacrifice his soul.

He had sacrificed his soul. His betrayal of his brother was complete. His estrangement from the rest of his family would follow. He had turned his back on everything his mama and daddy had taught him about family love and loyalty and honor.

He could not save himself.

As he dropped their bags on the floor of their room, he closed the door and locked it. He didn't think they'd been followed, but he knew better than to take chances. And now he had to make those telephone calls.

But when he turned around and saw Jamie standing near the bed, slipping out of her coat, all he could think about was that it had been nearly twenty-four hours since he'd made love to her. And that was way, way too long.

He closed the distance between them. As always, she melted into his embrace and returned his kiss with the kind of sweet hunger that sent his senses spinning.

The phone rang. He ignored it, but Jamie pulled back to pick it up. And then handed it to him. Matt kept his arm around her, holding her close, feeling her heart beating next to his.

"We've got trouble, Matt," Keele's voice said on the other end of the telephone line.

"I was just about to call you. What's up?"

"It's hit the fan. Your boss ended up with egg on his face when he went to his boss about an attempt on someone in the witness-protection program only to find out there wasn't one. He knows you've been using the system to pursue a case that doesn't qualify. He wants your tail in D.C. and he wants it there now."

"How'd you find out?"

"Some stool pigeon, name of Randy you got in your group. He must've seen me talking to you out in the parking lot behind the studio. Took my license number. Called your boss and said we were meeting clandestinely on something you weren't passing on to any of Nevelt's staff. Nevelt checked me out and called my boss."

"You in trouble, Keele?"

"Naw. My boss isn't giving me any grief. He knows I went out on a limb for an FBI buddy. But that damn no-brainer you're working for has no idea what end to wipe. He's hopping mad and he's out to get you. You realize this could be the end of your FBI service?"

"I'm past worrying about it, Keele. How did your inquiries go?"

"This is the final installment, Matt. My boss is understanding, but he's not suicidal."

"I get your drift."

"Okay, first off, Timothy Palmer was another alias. The Timothy Palmer who matches the birth date on Tony's license was killed in a private-plane crash in Florida fourteen years ago."

"A year before the Timothy Palmer who was also Tony Lagarrigue appeared in Reno," Matt said.

"Yep. I've had the fingerprints he used to get his driver's license in Nevada run through every federal and state computer trying to come up with a match. There isn't one."

"Not good news."

"And I've got more of the same. That explosion that just missed blowing up you and Jamie was no accident. Someone deliberately rigged that gas leak, first at the kitchen stove, then at the basement water heater. And number one on the Reno police's suspect list are a man and woman seen leaving in a taxi right afterward."

"Have they found the taxi driver yet?"

"They've figured out who it is, so it's just a matter of time."

"Any other bombs you got to drop?" Matt asked, not expecting an answer. He got one anyway.

"Just the coup de grace. Seems as though it wasn't the explosion that killed this mystery man you've been chasing. Medical examiner says his skull was bashed in before the gas had a chance to do its deed. Buddy, you'd better watch your back."

# Chapter Fifteen

"So his name wasn't Timothy Palmer," Jamie said. "Matt, did I lead someone to him after all? Someone with a grudge?"

"We're never going to know unless we first find out who he actually was, Jamie. And I have a feeling Rollo Lipicky is the one to ask."

Jamie willed her stomach to settle. They were currently passing over Texas and the plane was being buffeted by the strong up-currents, just as if they were sitting atop a bucking bronco.

"I'm almost afraid to find out," she said as the last violent air draft passed. "What if I was the cause of his death?"

"You were not the cause of his death. The person who smashed his skull in gets that credit."

"But—"

"No buts, Jamie. I should have confronted that man who was following us when I had a chance. Neither of us can undo what's been done. All we can concentrate on is following the trail to his killer. That's the only way we'll be able to bring him to justice."

Jamie knew Matt was right. But that didn't mean Tony's death was weighing any less on her conscience. She stared out the window. She had been angry at Tony when she realized he had been one of the thieves who had robbed Priddy. Her anger had grown considerably when she understood he might also have been a party to Kleinman's death and tried to blame Lester for it.

But she still couldn't forget what his regard had done for her all those years before. How could he be the person who had taken her to the dance and the person who had deliberately gone out to rob folks?

All her life she wanted to be seen for whom she was. And yet, when it came to men, it didn't look like she had ever really seen them for who they were. First Tony. Then Cade. Was she taken in because she looked for only what she wanted to find?

Jamie felt Matt's hand rest on hers, enveloping it in his massive bulk. Her gaze returned to his wonderfully strong, craggy face and the warm, deep lust in his eyes.

She sighed into a smile. "I have the oddest feeling that the earth is cooling all around me, Matt, and your hand is the only thing that's keeping me warm."

He touched her face with the brush of his knuckles, so gently, so briefly she barely felt anything at all. He spoke not one word of love, but his every look, his every touch spoke to Jamie of nothing else.

Sweet Lord, she hoped she wasn't seeing just what she wanted to see again!

"Is everything okay, Jamie?"

"No, Matt. It's not. You wouldn't be in any of this trouble if it weren't for me."

"Jamie, rest easy. I wouldn't trade a moment of this past week with you. I've battled the bad guys and shone off for my gal. Darlin', that's what living is all about to a Texan. Truth be told, I haven't had such a rip-roaring good time in years."

Darlin'. He'd called her darlin'.

The endearment entered her ears like music that was too fast, too sweet to catch. *Please don't let this be just a good time for him,* she prayed.

"What happens when we get to Florida?" she asked.

"I'm going to try to catch this Rollo Lipicky at his home.

His office says he's been on vacation for the past week and isn't expected back anytime soon. When we get to Sanibel Island, I want you to stay in the hotel."

"Stay in the hotel? Why?"

"Because someone killed Tony and damned near killed us. I'm not taking a chance with your life."

"You're taking a chance with yours."

"I can always call in help."

"Matt, I know that's not true. I was close enough to hear what Keele said on the other end of that telephone line. You're in trouble because you've been using FBI resources on a case that isn't FBI. Not even Keele can help you anymore."

"Doesn't matter, Jamie. I can handle myself. Remember, I'm trained for this sort of thing."

"I won't be left in some hotel room, Matt, while you go into a situation that could be dangerous. If something happened to you—"

Jamie stopped herself just in time from finishing that sentence the way she was going to. If she hoped to have a shred of pride left if it turned out he couldn't return her feelings, then she knew she had to change her words.

"If something happened to you, Matt Bonner, Lord knows I'd never hear the end of it from Liz, Cade, Charlene or your mama and daddy."

She watched the surprised recognition of her use of his earlier words swirl through the turquoise and silver in his eyes. And then, for the first time in her life, she heard him laugh. It was a wonderful laugh—deep and strong like a sudden Texas storm thundering through her heart.

THE POUNDING OF THE nearby surf against the walls of the seaside condo was deafening. Matt and Jamie climbed the three flights of stairs to the top where end unit number thirty-two looked over the rocky shore. Matt checked that his gun was within easy reach and then pressed the doorbell. There was no answer.

He pressed it twice more, each time listening intently for any sounds coming from inside as his eyes simultaneously scanned the pathway around them.

There was no sound from inside and no movement from without.

"Now what?" Jamie asked.

"Now, I see if there's another way in," Matt said.

He walked to where the sidewalk ended on the third story. He peered around the corner, squinting into the afternoon sun. About six feet beyond the edge, a balcony bowed out over the water. Matt took a quick look around and then eased his .38 out of its holster vest and handed it to Jamie.

"Hold this for me and be sure to use it should the need arise before I get back."

"Matt, that's a forty-foot drop," Jamie said, slipping the gun into her handbag as she nervously eyed the sea breaking over the jagged shore below.

"Now don't you worry none, Jamie. I'm tough."

Jamie grabbed his denim vest and planted a quick kiss on his cheek. "For luck, tough guy."

Matt picked her off her feet and crushed her to him. He kissed her hard and thoroughly, lingering to savor the softness of her lips. Then he set her back again on her feet.

"Just figured I get some more of that luck," he said, smiling into her flushed face.

He took one last quick look around before climbing on the railing at the edge of the walkway. He measured the distance to the balcony, then leapt.

He landed on top of the white wrought-iron railing circling the balcony and quickly pulled himself up and over. After one quick look around to be sure he hadn't been seen, Matt made his way to the sliding-glass door that led into the condo from the balcony.

He cupped his hand to the glass and looked inside. The balcony fed off a living room. No lights were on. No movement.

He pulled a knife out of his back pocket and jimmied the lock. Then he rolled the sliding-glass door back.

The smell of old, stale cigarettes immediately assailed Matt's nose. The place needed a good airing. Matt left the door to the balcony open behind him. He quickly checked through the one-bedroom unit, satisfying himself that it was unoccupied. Then he went to the door and beckoned Jamie inside.

"What do we look for?" she asked.

"Answers. I'll start in here. You try the bedroom."

As Jamie headed toward the bedroom, Matt's eyes surveyed the beautiful antiques before him. He couldn't help wondering how many Rollo Lipicky had stolen from his clients. He was examining a mahogany Chippendale mirror that had to be worth close to twenty thousand when he heard Jamie call out from the bedroom.

"Matt, come look."

Matt walked into the bedroom to see Jamie standing by a eighteenth-century William and Mary blanket chest, holding up a framed picture of a man and woman.

"It's Tony's daddy, or the man who pretended to be his daddy in Sweetspring," Jamie said. "He's definitely at least a decade older in this picture, but it's him."

Matt took the photo from her hand. It was a close-up shot of a couple taken with a flash and showing the background of a nightclub. The woman was plain, with short red hair, a thin face and a big, pointy nose. The man was dark-haired, slender, fortyish, familiar.

"This is the man who was following us in Reno," Matt said. "Do you recognize the redhead beside him?"

"No."

"You're sure it's not the woman who posed as Tony's mama in Sweetspring? Long hair, different makeup—"

"I'm sure, Matt. The woman in this picture has a slim, bony face. The woman who posed as Tony's mama had a much broader look to her features."

"Well, at least we've identified Rollo Lipicky as the second one of the trio of crooks. And since he was following us in Reno, he was probably the one who found and killed Tony.''

"You think it was a falling out among thieves?''

"That's what seems to be the most likely conclusion to me. We know that Tony and Rollo and probably the woman were in Woodpine in 1980, where they stole Priddy's coin collection and locket. Then two years later, they showed up in Sweetspring and made the attempt to steal from Kleinman.''

"Only Kleinman came home early and caught them,'' Jamie said. "So they ended up killing him.''

"And a year later, Tony appears in Reno as Timothy Palmer and establishes himself in the legitimate cleaning business with a bunch of cash, supposedly won gambling.''

"His split of the profits from their thefts.''

"Or maybe something more than his split,'' Matt said.

Jamie turned to him. "Yes, I see. That was the falling out. He took more than his share. Then he assumed another alias because his cohorts knew his real name, and he was hiding from them. Matt, what do we do now?''

"We search this place to see what else we can find. It doesn't look like Rollo's been back here since Reno. He and the woman might have stayed there to see if Tony's death was judged to be an acc—''

Matt stopped in the middle of his sentence as he heard the key in the front-door lock.

"Quick. Someone's coming.'' He grabbed Jamie and pulled her behind him as he stepped in back of the bedroom door.

Matt peered into the living room through the slit in the door frame. He could hear the front door open, although he could not see who was opening it. One pair of shoes scraped across the entry tile. The owner of those shoes closed the door.

A moment later the edge of a man's sleeve came into view. Matt watched as the tall nineteenth-century case clock in the living room was moved aside. The man knelt next to it and lifted up the edge of the carpet that had been exposed. He pulled something out of a hidden compartment in the floor.

And that was when Matt got a look at his profile. And a surprise. He stepped around the bedroom door and walked into the living room. He could feel Jamie following beside him.

The dark-haired man spun around, the money he had in his hands falling to the carpet, his dark eyes wide in surprise.

"Tony!" Jamie said from beside Matt.

Tony Lagarrigue, alias Timothy Palmer, looked hopefully at the door. But when he realized that Matt was between him and it, he took what looked like a resigned breath and let it out on what actually sounded like a good-natured laugh in the face of defeat. "Well, well. You two show up at the most inopportune times."

"I thought you were dead!" Jamie said.

"That was the idea, Jamie Lee," Tony said, calmly crossing his arms over his chest.

"Whose body did they find in that explosion?" Matt asked.

"I'm afraid it was Uncle Rollo who bought it back in Reno."

"Uncle?" Jamie repeated.

"It can't hurt to tell you now. It's sure to all come out anyway. You weren't the only one cursed with a bunch of disreputable relatives, Jamie Lee. My real name is Tony Lipicky. Rollo and Val raised me when my parents died. By the time I was eighteen, they had not only taught me everything about a profitable little scam they had going, they had also recruited me as part of the operation."

"Robbing the clients of Heritage Antiques and Collectibles," Matt said.

Tony's eyebrows went up in surprise. "If I ever need a private investigator, Mr. Bonner, I'm definitely hiring you."

"How old were you when you were in Sweetspring?" Jamie asked.

"Twenty-four. Of course, I've never looked my age.

Which is why I played the part of a teenager on most of our travels. I'd mow lawns. Get invited inside for a cool drink and a quick look around to see where the goodies were kept. Then I'd be keeping company with some teenage girl who could provide me with an alibi while Rollo and Val were busy with the robberies. No one ever suspected them, of course. They were always such a nice, timid couple."

"Why did you pick me to take to the dance?"

"You were Uncle Rollo's pick. He always said select the plainest girl, because if anything ever went wrong, she'd never give you any grief. Although, I have to tell you, Jamie Lee, there is nothing plain about you now. Stunning doesn't even begin to come close to saying it. If I could have seen you then as I see you now, we would never have made it to that dance."

"Tell me how you selected your victims," Matt cut in, not liking the look Tony was giving Jamie or the sudden turn his conversation had taken.

Tony glanced up at Matt's face. What he saw there wiped off the smile on his face right fast. His tone immediately sobered.

"Rollo kept track of the really valuable pieces going through his hands at Heritage. Val kept track of the recipients who weren't reporting their capital gains to the IRS."

"How?"

"Simple. Val works for the IRS."

"Handy. Go on."

"We'd go in under false names. Sometimes we'd use the identities of other Heritage clients. Sometimes we'd borrow identities Val got off the IRS computers. Rollo had already made it a point to know a lot about our target. Once in town, we'd pin down the daily habits at the house, the exact location of the items we'd come for and then wait until we could get the owner out of the way."

"Like telling Priddy Stowell a poisonous gas cloud was on the way from the Mount Saint Helens volcano," Jamie said.

"You two have been busy. Yeah, it was Rollo's brainstorm

to get old Priddy out with that one. Worked great. Then Val disengaged the alarm and—''

"So it was them who broke into my office at the studio to get Jamie's address," Matt said.

"Wouldn't be surprised," Tony said. "Val worked for an alarm-system company before getting a job at the IRS."

"You were after Priddy's gold-coin collection from the first, weren't you?" Jamie asked.

"Yeah. We broke into a couple of other homes just to make it look like looters."

"And when you found Priddy's cheap metal locket inside the box, you decided to keep it and use it on your next gullible teenage alibi," Jamie said.

"Actually, Jamie Lee, the next girl I made up to didn't want that old locket. She said it was too cheap. If you hadn't taken it, I was going to throw it away. Which reminds me. What was it you found in that secret compartment?"

"Ten-thousand dollars," Jamie said. Matt could see she enjoyed the wince on Tony's face.

"What did you do with the items you stole?" Matt asked.

"None of the owners ever reported their specific losses because technically they couldn't admit they owned the items. Rollo generally just contacted another one of his collectors and sold the items to him or her for a full profit."

"And not just a commission, which is all he ever got as a trader," Matt said.

"That's right. Then we'd split the proceeds. Val always got fifty percent, being the brains of the outfit. Rollo and I had to split the other fifty. Still, we were making some serious dough there for about six years."

"Until you went to Sweetspring and Kyle Kleinman came home too early," Matt said. "And it escalated into murder."

Tony's brow furrowed into a frown.

"What happened?" Jamie asked.

"It was so damn stupid, Jamie Lee. Kleinman missed Rollo by a mile with that shotgun. All Val had to do was whack him good over the head and dose him in some whiskey. The

Sisterns would have just thought he was drunk and put him to bed to sleep it off. By the time Kleinman came to the next morning and told his tale, we would have been long gone, with the loot and without trace. But, no. Val had to go kill him."

"Whose idea was it to blame it on Lester?" Jamie asked.

"Rollo had heard Deputy Plotnik saying it had to be Lester. So Val told Rollo to bury the bloody knife out where Lester had been camping. Then we got out of town fast. I stole the cash that still hadn't been divvied up from the last operation out of Rollo's hole in the carpet here and took off for good. I didn't want anything to do with murder."

"You murdered Rollo," Matt said, his voice cold, cutting.

"No, you don't understand. That was an accident. I came home to meet with Jamie Lee. Rollo jumped me. We struggled. Rollo fell against the stone fireplace in the bedroom and cracked his skull. I swear."

"Why did you fake your death?" Matt said.

"When I realized he was dead, I panicked. I knew if Rollo had found me, Val wouldn't be far behind. I could have reasoned with Rollo if he let me. I knew I could never reason with Val. So I put my watch on Rollo, cleaned out his pockets, rigged the gas to go and slipped out through a side window. I found his rental car on the next block. I thought Val would think Rollo had gotten the money I'd taken, killed me and run with it."

"And he did, too," the nasal voice said from the vicinity of the balcony.

"Val!" Tony screamed just as a muffled pop flew past Matt's ear. Tony fell to the carpet, clutching his leg.

Matt whirled around, unaware until now that the pounding of the surf had hidden the sounds of someone else using the balcony entrance.

A bald man faced him with angry, dark eyes and a big black automatic with a long silver silencer screwed onto its end. He was pointing the barrel at him.

"Matt, he's her, Erline!" Jamie said. "I recognize his face.

Only he was wearing a wig and women's clothes in Sweet-spring. Val is a *he!*''

Matt looked into the unflinching black eyes of the man standing before him, the man who had just cold-bloodedly shot his own nephew. Instinctively, Matt moved right, trying to shield Jamie.

Val pointed the barrel right at her. "One more step, Tex, and I shoot her. Now open that denim vest of yours very slowly and take out the gun."

Matt opened his vest to show his empty shoulder holster. "They don't allow guns on airplanes, Val."

"You could have gotten one since you got to town. Like I did. You were a fool not to. Who knows you're here?"

"Everyone," Matt said easily, waiting for the slightest relaxation of Val's guard. "The camera crew will be here any minute to shoot Tony and Jamie's reunion for the next segment of my show."

Val snickered. "Good yarn, Tex. But not good enough. Everybody thinks Tony's dead back in Reno. His resurrection from the dead must be as big a surprise to you as to me. You two have been very helpful in leading me to my nephew. Unfortunately for you, your usefulness has just run out."

"Damn it all, Val, you don't have to kill them!" Tony yelled.

"You'd better start pleading for your own life, Tony. Because if I don't get that three hundred thousand back you took, your worthless hide is getting tossed over this balcony."

"You can't get away with killing us," Jamie said.

"Of course, I can get away with it. They're looking for you in Reno for Tony's death. If your bodies are never recovered, they'll just think you fled to avoid prosecution."

Matt judged the distance between him and Val and knew it was too far. Before he'd reached him, Jamie would be dead. He had to wait for the man's eyes to leave his, for that pistol to veer even slightly from Jamie's heart.

"Val, for God's sake—"

"Shut up, Tony. I've always liked the idea of ladies first. But prudence necessitates—"

The second the pistol's muzzle moved away from Jamie on an arc toward him, Matt leapt forward. He wasn't fast enough. He knew he wouldn't be. The distance was too great.

The bullet hit him hard in the chest.

Matt landed on Val, knocking him to the floor. Shock was his ally now, the blessed kind of unfeeling shock that cut off the nerves in the brain from the body's condition.

He could still function for a few more seconds, a few more precious seconds.

He grabbed for the gun. Val pulled it away, kicking and squirming beneath the weight of Matt's body, desperate, deadly, a man fighting for his life.

There was only one thing more deadly—a man fighting for the life of the woman he loved.

Matt rolled, knocking Val off balance in an attempt to disengage the gun. Val pulled it up and out of the way at the last second, savagely slamming it against Matt's head, kicking frantically in an attempt to push Matt off him.

But Matt held on, refusing to let himself be shaken off.

Then a hot poker drove suddenly deep into his chest. The shock was wearing off. Desperately, he fought against the sluggishness of his movements, the agonizing pain that came with every breath that tried to fill his lungs, the cloying blackness threatening his vision.

He could feel Val squirming out from under him. Val's face was red and contorted in fury as he finally pulled free and pointed the automatic at Matt.

The roar of the firing gun deafened Matt's ears. Val let out a small gurgle of surprise as a bullet whipped through his throat and put a black hole through his windpipe. His head fell backward as his body collapsed. Matt knew he would not be moving again.

Matt looked behind him to see Jamie standing in the middle of the room, her blue eyes piercingly bright, his smoking .38 still poised and steady in her hands.

He smiled, closed his eyes and let the blackness overtake him.

"YOU ARE THE DAMN luckiest man I ever did meet," Keele said.

"What day is this?" Matt asked, trying to sit up against the tight wrapping of his chest and the weight of the invisible two-ton anvil that perched on it. "Nobody around this damn place will tell me a thing."

"It's the fourth night since they brought you into this white palace. You were pretty much out of it the first three. How do you feel?"

"I've been a lot better."

"I bet. Bullet tore through your lung, smashed a rib, came out your back and dispatched a sixty-thousand-dollar vase. Another half inch over and it would have dispatched you."

"And Val Lipicky?"

"Valmer Lipicky ain't going to be robbing nobody no more, no how, thanks to your Jamie gal."

"Jamie's okay, isn't she?"

"She's more than okay. She called the paramedics and kept you from bleeding to death until they got to you."

"What about Tony Lipicky?"

"He'll be limping a mite from now on, but he'll recover. He's given us the lowdown, Matt. What with his information and Jamie's creative rounding out of the story—"

"Hold on there. What do you mean, 'creative rounding out'?"

"That's right. I keep forgetting. You've been snoozing these past few days and nights away."

"You were saying about Jamie?" Matt prodded.

"Jamie told my boss that she came to you because she found a ten-thousand-dollar note in an old locket she'd been given. According to her, you suspected right off that it was stolen property and just possibly part of an interstate robbery ring. She says you took a vacation from your P.I. practice to try to secure the proper evidence so that you could turn the matter over to the FBI.''

"But your boss knows the truth.''

"What my boss knows is a great collar when he sees one. And Jamie handed this one over to us on a silver platter. This way it looks like we've been in on this from the first. My boss has already gone to yours and told him that you were just assisting us on your own time because you'd been given a lead you knew we'd be interested in. Buddy, not only has your slate been washed sparkling clean, you're getting a commendation.''

"There's still the matter of an unauthorized use of a charge code on Jamie's case.''

"Perry's already explained that away. He said he just made a mistake and keyed in the wrong one.''

"No,'' Matt said. "I can't let him take the heat for me.''

"Matt, relax. Nevelt is happy to forgive the mistake. Perry has been emceeing the 'Finder of Lost Loves' show and getting rave reviews. Nevelt is processing your transfer as we speak. And he's so ticked at Randy for making him look like even more of a jackass than he is that he's canning Randy's hide. Thanks to Jamie you're back in the saddle again, buddy, just as soon as you're ready to mount up again.''

"Where is she, Keele?''

"Right outside, along with the rest of the family.'' Keele paused to cross his arms over his chest. "Although why I'm bringing you any of this good news I don't know, you bold-faced liar.''

"Run that one by me again?''

"You heard me. These past few days and nights while I marched up and down outside, waiting to hear whether you were going to live or die, your brother and I did some serious talking. Cade and Jamie haven't been married for more than two years. She's free.''

"She's not free,'' Matt said.

Keele smiled. "No, I figured she wasn't. Truth be told, I sort of saw this was the real lay of the land first time I heard that particular sound in your voice when you told me you'd kill me if I made a move toward her."

"What sound?"

"Same one I heard just now. Same one I heard in her voice when she told our boss that you solved the case single-handedly. Like I said, Matt Bonner. You're the damn luckiest man I ever met. Now the doctor says you can have five minutes with each one of those visitors waiting outside. I'll go get her for you."

"No. Ask my brother to come in first."

Keele lost his smile. "You're not serious."

"I have to tell him about Jamie and me."

"You don't have to tell him. A blind fool could tell how she feels. She's lived at this hospital without sleep or food waiting to see if you were okay. Trust me, Cade knows."

"I did this to him behind his back, Keele. My own brother. I have to face him."

"Face him tomorrow, Matt. When you have more strength."

"No, I have to do it now. Get him for me."

Keele shook his head as he left the room. A moment later Cade came inside. He was smiling as he approached the bed.

"Damn if you don't look pretty good for a man who near died. So, how you feeling?"

Matt's chest felt even more constricted. This was hard enough to do without Cade putting on this bold, smiling front for him.

"Cade, we have to talk about Jamie."

Cade's eyes met his squarely. "Matt, I know."

"Cade, I love her. I can't give her up. Not even for you."

Cade's smile didn't falter. "Matt, stop wasting your strength. And your breath. It's okay with me, you and Jamie."

"I know you still love her, Cade."

"And I always will. But it's not the same kind of love it once was, Matt. And it was never the kind of love she feels for you. Hell, you should have seen her when the doctors told us you were going to be okay. Why she just got all lit up inside. And just now, when Keele came out and said you wanted to see me, that light dimmed something fierce.''

Matt studied his brother's face for any sign of hurt or discomfort. He could find none.

"Cade, you have to be straight with me about this. You can't be giving her up this easy.''

"Matt, I don't think Jamie was ever mine to give up. If I'm not the one to make her happy, I'm glad it's you. Now, stop wasting time with me. I'm sending her in. And I'm taking the rest of the family home. We'll see y'all tomorrow.''

And with that Cade strode out the door wearing a smile and carrying with him the burden that had weighed down Matt's heart for so long.

Jamie was inside a second later, rushing over to the bed. Her clothes had obviously been slept in. Her hair was a golden mass of tangles. There were dark circles beneath her worried blue eyes. She was untidy and tousled like he had never seen her. And he had never seen her looking more beautiful.

"Matt, they keep telling me you're all right. Are you?''

He reached for her hand and captured it within his. "At this moment, never better. I love you, Jamie Bonner. I have since the first moment I saw you and I will until the day I die.''

His words brought such pleasure to Jamie's heart, it paused with the pure amazement of it.

Matt watched as a beautiful smile drew back Jamie's lips. Gently she wrapped her arms around his neck and covered the rough stubble on his cheeks and chin with a dozen quick kisses.

They warmed him all over, washing away his previous physical discomfort as though it had been nothing.

"Jamie, darlin', am I to take it you love me, too?''

She leaned back to look into his eyes. "Of course, I love you! I've loved you since the moment you kissed me. Why did you take so long to tell me?''

Matt looked deep into the love in her eyes and never felt stronger in his life.

"I thought Cade would always be there between us. I couldn't understand how a man could love you and ever let you go. I still can't."

She sighed. "I didn't understand about Cade at first, either, Matt. But the truth is that to him, well, folks are just like his hurt animals. All he wants is to fix them."

Matt raised his hand to her cheek, stroking the soft down of her skin. "What could he possibly fix about you? You're perfect."

Jamie smiled as she brushed her lips against his fingertips. "Cade's the kind of man who possesses a sixth sense for those he deems hurt or abandoned. He gravitated toward me because he saw my lack of family as a wound that he could fix. He married me to give me that family. And he read me right, Matt. More than anything then, I wanted to be part of the wonderful Bonner family."

"So that's why you married him."

"And because I was attracted to the gentleness in his heart. I never thought he could let me down."

"You saying he did?"

"Not intentionally. Matt, I lied when I told Liz and Cade and everyone that I was an orphan brought up by a foster family. The woman who reared me was my real mama. When she died two years ago of cirrhosis of the liver, the hospital tracked me down to tell me. Cade saw the letter. I had to tell him the rest."

"The rest?"

Jamie sighed, deep and hard. "I never knew my daddy, because my mama couldn't even be sure who he was. She'd slept with so many men around the time I was conceived, she just picked one of their names to tag on to the end of mine. It was the same with Lester. He was my half brother, but he never knew who his daddy was either."

"Why didn't you tell me this before, Jamie?"

"Because of the reaction I've always gotten when I spoke

of it. Because of Cade's reaction. He looked at me with pity. That ended everything for us. I couldn't spend the rest of my life with a man who saw me as a victim. I would've become one.''

Jamie watched as the beautiful turquoise-and-silver slashes in Matt's eyes stilled with an emotion that had absolutely nothing to do with pity and everything to do with admiration.

''Will you spend the rest of your life with me, Jamie?''

''Oh, yes, Matt. With all my heart, yes.''

He pulled her to him, his mouth claiming hers with a fierce sensuality that both thrilled and surprised her.

She drew back, suddenly breathless. ''Matt, you're still in serious condition.''

He smiled. ''Yes, and it's getting more serious by the second.'' He reached for her again.

''Matt!''

When the nurse came by with a sleeping pill a few moments later, Keele was standing guard at the door. He took a quick look inside, smiled and closed the door again.

He flashed his badge at the nurse. ''FBI. Sorry, ma'am, but you can't go in.''

''But that man needs his rest!'' the nurse complained.

''He's got what he needs, ma'am.''

''But—''

''Don't you worry none. He'll be fine. He's one tough Texan.''

# HE SAID

❤

# SHE SAID

Explore the mystery of male/female communication in this extraordinary new book from two of your favorite Harlequin authors.

Jasmine Cresswell and Margaret St. George bring you the exciting story of two romantic adversaries—each from their own point of view!

DEV'S STORY. CATHY'S STORY.
As he sees it. As she sees it.
Both sides of the story!

The heat is definitely on, and these two can't stay out of the kitchen!

Don't miss **HE SAID, SHE SAID.**
Available in July wherever Harlequin books are sold.

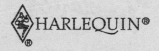

# It's hot...and it's out of control!

Beginning this spring, Temptation turns up the
*heat*. Look for these bold, provocative,
*ultra*sexy books!

**#629 OUTRAGEOUS**
by Lori Foster (April 1997)

**#639 RESTLESS NIGHTS**
by Tiffany White (June 1997)

**#649 NIGHT RHYTHMS**
by Elda Minger (Sept. 1997)

**BLAZE:** Red-hot reads—only from

HARLEQUIN®

# I N T R I G U E®

**There's a small town in New Mexico
where no one is who they seem to
be...and everyone has a secret....**

## Welcome to...

FOUR
WINDS

Join **Aimée Thurlo** as she takes you to a town of myth
and mystery and introduces you to three men who make
your pulse race....

Meet the Blackhorse brothers—
Gabriel, Joshua and Lucas—in

**#427: HER DESTINY** (JULY)
**#441: HER HERO** (NOVEMBER)
**#458: HER SHADOW** (MARCH 1998)

Come to Four Winds...the town where dreams
come true.

# HARLEQUIN®

# I N T R I G U E®

## Keep up with Caroline Burnes and FAMILIAR!

A FEAR FAMILIAR MYSTERY

You see a black cat walking across the street.
It reminds you of something familiar...of course!
Familiar, the crime-solving cat! This fabulous feline is
back for another adventure with Harlequin Intrigue in

# FAMILIAR HEART
### July 1997
#### by Caroline Burnes

# TAYLOR SMITH

**Who would you trust with your life?
Think again.**

A tranquil New England town is rocked to
its core when a young coed is linked to a
devastating crime—then goes missing.

One woman, who believes in the girl's
innocence, is determined to find her before
she's silenced—forever. Her only ally is a
man who no longer believes in anyone's
innocence. But *is* he an ally?

At a time when all loyalties are suspect, and
old friends may be foes, she has to decide—
quickly—who can be trusted. The wrong
choice could be fatal.

# THE
# BEST OF
# ENEMIES

Available at your favorite retail outlet
in June 1997.

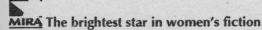

**MIRA** The brightest star in women's fiction

# And the Winner Is...
# You!

...when you pick up these great titles
from our new promotion at your
favorite retail outlet this June!

## Diana Palmer
*The Case of the Mesmerizing Boss*

## Betty Neels
*The Convenient Wife*

## Annette Broadrick
*Irresistible*

## Emma Darcy
*A Wedding to Remember*

## Rachel Lee
*Lost Warriors*

## Marie Ferrarella
*Father Goose*

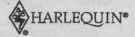

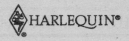

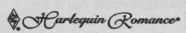

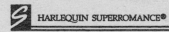